Theatre History Studies

2008 VOLUME 28

Edited by

RHONA JUSTICE-MALLOY

PUBLISHED BY THE MID-AMERICA THEATRE CONFERENCE
AND THE UNIVERSITY OF ALABAMA PRESS

Theater History Studies is an official journal of the Mid-America Theatre Conference, Inc. (MATC). The conference encompasses the states of Illinois, Indiana, Iowa, Kansas, Michigan, Minnesota, Missouri, Nebraska, North Dakota, South Dakota, and Wisconsin. Its purposes are to unite people and organizations within this region and elsewhere who have an interest in theatre and to promote the growth and development of all forms of theatre.

Theatre History Studies is devoted to research in all areas of theatre history. Manuscripts should be prepared in conformity with the guidelines established in the *Chicago Manual of Style,* submitted in duplicate, and sent to Rhona Justice-Malloy, Editor, Dept. of Theatre Arts, 110 Isom Hall, University of Mississippi, Box 1848, University, MS 38677-1848, or by e-mail to rjmalloy@olemiss.edu. Consulting editors review the manuscripts, a process that takes approximately four months. The journal does not normally accept studies of dramatic literature unless there is a focus on actual production and performance. Authors whose manuscripts are accepted must provide the editor with an electronic file, using Microsoft Word. Illustrations (preferably high-quality originals or black-and-white glossies) are welcomed. Manuscripts will be returned only if accompanied by a stamped, self-addressed envelope bearing sufficient postage.

This publication is issued annually by the Mid-America Theatre Conference and The University of Alabama Press.

Subscription rates for 2008 are $15 for individuals, $30 for institutions, and an additional $8 for foreign delivery. Back issues are $29.95 each. Subscription orders and changes of address should be directed to Allie Harper, The University of Alabama Press, Box 870380, Tuscaloosa, AL 35487 (205-348-1564 phone, 205-348-9201 fax).

Theatre History Studies is indexed in *Humanities Index, Humanities Abstracts, Book Review Index, MLA International Bibliography, International Bibliography of Theatre, Arts & Humanities Citation Index, IBZ International Bibliography of Periodical Literature,* and *IBR International Bibliography of Book Reviews,* the database of *International Index to the Performing Arts.* Full texts of essays appear in the databases of both *Humanities Abstracts Full Text* and *SIRS.* The journal has published its own index, *The Twenty Year Index, 1981–2000.* It is available for $10 for individuals and $15 for libraries from Rhona Justice-Malloy, Editor, Dept. of Theatre Arts, Isom Hall 110, University of Mississippi, Box 1848, University, MS 38677-1848.

CONTENTS

CONTENTS

CONTENTS

CONTENTS

ILLUSTRATIONS

Keynote Speech from the Twenty-eighth Mid-America Theatre Conference, Changing Theatrical Landscapes

Mapping New Directions in History, Pedagogy, and Practice in the Twenty-first Century

—LOU BELLAMY

I'm inspired by the boldness of the challenge of this conference's theme. As I thought about it while preparing this talk, I even began to wax creative and found myself becoming excited over the possibilities. "Mapping new directions" offers the opportunity to reevaluate, to extend the reach and understanding of ourselves as well as those for whom we perform and those whom we mentor and teach; to set new frameworks through which we perceive our history, our pedagogy, our practice; to understand ourselves and our power to change our world more thoroughly. It's a mandate that has as its basic tenet opening our institutions and our curricula to populations and cultures heretofore only marginally served.

Once I began to think in these lofty terms it was only a very short time before the latent "Trekkie" in me took over and I was imagining myself standing at the helm of the *Enterprise,* facing new frontiers and "boldly go[ing] where no man has gone before."

What did I mean, "no man"? Well, I meant me. Not no man. Me. It was here that I began to feel a bit of dread. Not from fear of the unknown, but something that began to rise from within myself. I repeated the phrase "where no man has gone before." The arrogance that is presupposed in my thesis staggered me. Images of Cecil J. Rhodes, King Leopold II, General George Armstrong Custer, and too many others to count here spring to mind.

So I determined that I'd give some time to thinking about respectful ways to engage the heretofore disengaged, the ignored, the misrepresented. And that thinking is what I'd like to share with you today. I've spent a good portion of my adult life (the last thirty years) stewarding a cultural institution and interacting with the dominant culture from a marginalized position. So you'll hear me today speak of myself as sort of an inside-outsider. I hope that by sharing my own trepidation at dealing with cultural nuance, I'll awaken in you a similar feeling that asks you to interrogate what you bring to the encounter.

As we inside the academy, inside the major regional theatre movement, reach out and seek to include the cultural expression that traditionally has not been part of our offerings, in our curricula and our theatrical presentations, we face special challenges. As founder and artistic director of one of the oldest and most influential professional theatrical organizations (in the world, I'm told), whose reason for being is the exploration and distillation of the African-American experience and aesthetic, I believe my experiences may be relevant to the reordering that this conference's title would suggest.

I would caution us to be aware that the information we may be seeking to engage is most likely part of a living culture, part of the ethos of live people whose lives and culture are integral to the understanding of our study or the theatre that we seek to perform or present. I would hope that our interaction would be respectful and mindful that we run the risk of misinterpreting, misrepresenting, of morphing the very thing we seek to investigate. The applied anthropological directive comes to mind: "First, do no harm!"

From my vantage point, an honest appraisal of our past behavior leads me to again propose extreme caution. Most of our expansion, if even tacitly, has as its basic assumption that before our involvement, the examined cultures either have an unappreciated worth, are simple, unadorned, messy, and/or wasteful. This perspective places us in a position of participating in a "discovery" rather than participating in a meeting or an engagement. One position places us in the role of cultural arbiter. The other makes us a guest.

One polemic places the efforts of Ridgely Torrence, Paul Greene, or DuBose Hayward as honest attempts at presenting cultures they knew little about and as interpreters of those cultures, raising folk and folklore to great artistic and aesthetic heights. The other highlights their efforts as stereotypical misrepresentations, egregious, hurtful, and damaging.

In recent months I've been witness to what may be a growing trend. That is productions of culturally specific plays (black plays) directed and interpreted by white females—from my perspective with at best mixed results. I don't mean to say that experience with gender discrimination doesn't provide a certain insight into cultural discrimination. I do mean to say that presenting the nuance of racial and/or cultural discrimination demands a special type of preparation and insight.

While white women may be able to relate to experiences of oppression because of their experience with misogyny or gender discrimination, their pain, real as it is, cannot be equated with the experience of racial discrimination. It might provide powerful insight to their readings of the work, but they must take care not to claim to know what they do not know, or to lessen the sharp reality and distinctions of cultural nuance by subsuming it under what is familiar to them. From my point of view, to equate the two is to lessen both.

Productions of Tanya Barfield's *Blue Door* at New York's Playwrights' Horizons, Darren Canady's *False Creeds* at Atlanta's Alliance Theatre, and—perhaps most interesting of all—Alice Childress's *Trouble in Mind* at Baltimore's Center Stage are illustrative. You may recall that, in her 1955 script, Childress interrogates lack of understanding and resulting tension using the "play within a play" motif. Conflicts arise between black actors and the white director as they rehearse the play, which concerns a lynching in the South.

I can imagine that the producers felt a certain level of pluck or uncanny irony in the placement of the white, female director in the Center Stage production as art imitates life and form marries content. It seems to me, however, that the complicated nuances inherent in culturally specific references in today's art and society demand a very careful treatment. I would caution anyone to be rigorous about locating his or her own perspective in the art. One must take care to critically engage one's own living, one's own history, and how that is capable of informing, coloring, changing the art. The place from which one speaks determines perspective, and perspective must be considered, because in these cases it is brought to bear on black art and representations of black life.

When he was asked by Gwen Ifill, moderator and managing editor of *Washington Week,* to comment on his dream of having a black director for the making of the film of his play *Fences,* August Wilson replied: "I think it's important that you have a black director because 'Schindler's List' had a Jewish director, because 'The Godfather' had an Italian director, you know. I think when you have a work of art that deals with a culture that's so seminal as black American culture, that you just simply have black sensibility behind the artistic development of that project."[1]

He means, of course, to point out the thorny nature of bringing cultural nuance to film or to the stage. And so, when I saw the title of this conference, "Mapping New Directions," Anne McClintock's introduction to *Imperial Leather: Race, Gender, and Sexuality in the Colonial Contest* sprang to mind.[2] Her work is worth citing here, because she is an expert in dissecting how perception influences our encounters (or discovery).

You may recall that McClintock presents us with a map from H. Rider Haggard's best-selling novel *King Solomon's Mines*, which follows the journey of a group of white explorers as they travel through the interior of unexplored, darkest Africa.[3] Africa threatens to swallow them up. It is an expanse of the unknown, a "blank darkness," as Christopher L. Miller aptly names it in his *Blank Darkness: Africanist Discourse in French*. "From earliest time," Miller explains, "Black Africa was experienced as the literal end of European knowledge: on the maps of *Ptolemy's Geography,* 'Libia Interior' and 'Ethiopia Interior' are the last namable places before the map is cut off with the label 'Terra Incognita.'"[4]

It is, of course, the mind that we are mapping here. The colonial European mind went to Africa, to the ends of knowledge, precisely because it was imagined as being devoid of anything real, anything at all. *So the project becomes projection.* As Toni Morrison writes in her wonderful *Playing in the Dark: Whiteness and the Literary Imagination,* "the fabrication of an Africanist persona is *reflexive;* an extraordinary meditation on the self; a powerful exploration of the fears and desires that reside in the writerly conscious."[5]

So in Haggard's novel, the white men must enter a treacherous mine. The men, in a symbolic birthing ritual, must climb out of the deep recesses of the cave. It is the map of the cave, and really by extension the mind of the writer, to which Anne McClintock applies a brilliant Freudian analysis. This space, this terra incognita, is imagined as a woman, a woman who can be penetrated, mapped, and known. To McClintock, Haggard's map of the route to the treasure reveals a paradox. On the one hand, it is a rough sketch of the ground the white men must cross in order to secure the riches of the diamond mine. If inverted, however, it reveals at once the diagram of the spread-eagled female body. If one aligns oneself with the male authority of the printed page and the points of the colonial compass, the map can be read and the treasure reached, but the colonial woman will be stood on her head. If, on the other hand, one turns the male book upside down and sets the female body to rights, the male colonial venture as a whole becomes incoherent.

And so I think that the intent of your considerations around your conference theme is a lofty one. I believe that it is a good thing to open the academy to everyone, to explore and facilitate our diversity by considering new and changing theatrical landscapes. We must be mindful, however, that as Christopher

Miller writes, "The gesture of reaching out to the most unknown part of the world and bringing it back as language"—*the process you now propose in mapping new pathways for pedagogy*—"ultimately brings Europe face to face with nothing but itself, with the problems its own discourse imposes."[6]

Have we exhausted our knowledge, come to the end of it? Or is the world knocking at the doors of our ivory towers? Is it coming across our borders, making indecipherable the lines and boundaries that define who we are and what we purport to know is true? What happens when the very discourse we use to reach out ends up being violent? What damage do we do when we look to another culture not to see them—their living, their knowledge, their experience—but ourselves? We are charged not with mapping what is already in the world, already alive and vibrant, but with creating layers, new spaces from, through, and around which we can find the space to read the blending of systems of knowledge, of cultural specificity, of nuanced experience.

As educators and as artists, our responsibility is not to just engender new ways of thinking but to be constantly critical of ourselves, vigilant in our implementation of the systems and the tools we use to pin down moving cultural life. To stage it, to page it, requires that we know it. But we must know it without endeavoring to change it. Rather, let it change us, the seekers. We seek to make room, to engage dialogue, not to speak for, to name, or to reinvent systems that are already viable, vital, and thriving without us. We go to them because they are rich, because we are seeking something to add to our lives. Let us not dishonor the worth of what already exists by colonizing it with applications of our own theory, experience, or knowledge as precedent, normal, or "right." We must get away from notions of "discovery" and strive instead to create space for "moments of encounter."

We come with respect, with awe, with curiosity, with need. We come with our own baggage, strengths, desires, and opinions. The idea of the frontier is one of encounter. It is well scripted into American history.

We cannot come with our pomp and flair bearing flags to drive down into the earth. We must tread lightly, ask for invitation, demonstrate our intentions clearly, prove ourselves worthy by speaking honestly about who we are, where we've been, and what *that* has allowed us to know.

Notes

1. Interview with August Wilson by Gwen Ifill, *PBS Online NewsHour,* April 6, 2001, http://www.pbs.org/newshour/bb/entertainment/jan-june01/usashakespeare_04-06.html.

2. Anne McClintock, *Imperial Leather: Race, Gender, and Sexuality in the Colonial Contest* (London: Routledge, 1995), 1–17.

3. H. Rider Haggard, *King Solomon's Mines,* ed. Dennis Butts (1989; reprint, Oxford: Oxford University Press, 1998).

4. Christopher L. Miller, *Blank Darkness: Africanist Discourse in French* (Chicago: University of Chicago Press, 1985), 22–23.

5. Toni Morrison, *Playing in the Dark: Whiteness and the Literary Imagination* (Cambridge: Harvard University Press, 1992), 17; emphasis added.

6. Miller, *Blank Darkness,* 5.

Between the Lines

Editing the Notebooks of Tennessee Williams

—MARGARET BRADHAM THORNTON

In 1997, John Eastman, the executor of the Tennessee Williams Estate, asked me if I would be willing to look at the notebooks of Tennessee Williams and give him my thoughts as to whether or not they should be published. Two weeks later a box arrived containing photocopies of the twenty-three known notebooks (during the course of the project I discovered seven more). I was slightly surprised to see how ordinary the notebooks were—the vast majority being the inexpensive kind purchased at drugstores with names such as WriteRight Composition Book and Du-O-Ring with covers of unremarkable browns, blues, and blacks. The notebooks were handwritten, and many entries were either not dated or only partially dated. It took me some time to decipher and order what I had in front of me. I discovered that Williams would frequently write in a journal, misplace it, write in another, find the original journal, and then pick up where he left off. Before long, however, I realized that I had a moving emotional record of one of the twentieth century's greatest playwrights. A decade later, these entries, along with a selection of illuminating manuscripts, letters, photographs, and commentary, would emerge as *Notebooks*.

Williams began his first entry on March 6, 1936. Almost twenty-five years old, he was living at home and taking night classes to gain enough credits to begin his final year of college. His voice is innocent, earnest, and at times melodramatic. He wrote his last entry in the spring of 1981, almost two years before his death. There is a gap of twenty years from 1959 to 1979 when Williams, debilitated by an addiction to drugs and alcohol and discouraged by his inability to create with the perfection he had done in the past, stopped keeping a journal.

Because Williams wrote to himself about himself, the journals are an exceptionally personal chronicle, unique in the information they transmit, as they are a record of his voice and his thoughts without any compression or smoothing over of a memoir or interpretation by a biographer. Williams spoke to himself in a form of shorthand. He refers to people either by their first name or their initials, and he often does not identify manuscripts by name, especially in the early years. In order to give as much meaning as possible to the notebooks, I set about trying to situate and give clarity to Williams's comments. I began by trying to contact as many people as I could find who really knew Williams. Among others, Donald Windham, William Jay Smith, Gore Vidal, Joe Hazan, Paul Bowles, and the widow of Fritz Bultman were helpful in identifying people.

One issue that constantly pulled at me as I worked on this project was Williams's sanity. Too often I had read opinions that stated Williams, like his sister, Rose, teetered on the edge of insanity. When I traveled to Tangier to see Paul Bowles, in addition to asking him about people Williams mentioned when he was in Morocco, I asked about Williams's mental stability. He was one of the sanest people he knew, Bowles told me. Given his prolific body of work, he had to be.

On occasion the journey to find people ended in unexpected ways. I visited a friend of Williams's who was severely debilitated by Alzheimer's disease. The interview yielded nothing, and as I was leaving an assistant came running down the stairs and told me he had something I would be interested in—a notebook of Williams's. He instructed me to meet him on a street corner the next day with an envelope of cash. Twenty-four hours later, and not without reservation, I found myself waiting on a desolate street on the Lower East Side of New York City with an envelope full of cash. The assistant appeared carrying a manila envelope. The moment I pulled the small brown exercise book out of the envelope and opened the pages and read Williams's first journal entry, I knew it was authentic. It began with a description of Williams's first trip to Europe, in January 1948. He was alone on a train that was on its way from Nice to Rome. "Train now pulling out for the Italian border—I am on my way to Rome. The *sun*—glorious sun—is on my face, in my eyes, and I love it." There was no question that the handwriting and voice were his.

In a desperate effort to track down the only woman Williams had a love affair with, I contacted the head of a detective agency whose firm did routine background checks for a Wall Street bank for which I had once worked. I explained to him what searches I had done and asked his advice on what more I should do. He said he would get back to me. I assumed it was his polite way of getting rid of me. Within twenty-four hours I received a call from one of his colleagues, who told me that his mother had been enrolled in the theatre department with Williams at the University of Iowa and had been asked by Williams to deliver a poem, "Remember Me as One of Your Lovers." I found the unpublished poem in one of the university archives, and there is little doubt that the poem, with the refrain "Remember me as one of your lovers, / not the greatest of these, not the least, / but in some small way distinguished from all of the others," was not strong enough to win her back.

On another occasion I learned of the existence of Williams's death mask. A few years later, after a fair amount of persistence, I gained access to the death mask and found myself carrying a box down Fifth Avenue in New York City to the studio of a photographer whose specialty is photographing African masks. I distinctly remember unpacking the carefully wrapped cast and being struck by how absent Williams seemed to be from this artifact. We spent several hours photographing it from different angles. I was aware that a person's face in death fails to resemble who he or she was in life, but I hope that the image produced reveals Williams with a certain dignity and peace. I included this image at the end of *Notebooks*.

In order to deepen readers' understanding of the notebooks, to illuminate what was written privately and sometimes obliquely, I felt it was necessary to annotate them not only with actual pages of his journals, manuscripts, and letters but also with photographs of many unknown people as well as vintage photographs of places Williams stayed. For example, he spent the summer of 1942 in Macon, Georgia, the home of his friend Jordan Massee. A deeper understanding of Macon's private worlds strongly suggests that Williams's experience in this small southern town influenced his writing not only of *Cat on a Hot Tin Roof* but also of *A Streetcar Named Desire*. Williams was part of a private world of young gay men who lived an existence secret from their families. Several of these young men went on to marry. In both plays, Williams creates men who have had unusually close relationships with other men, who marry, and who then have conflicts over the two relationships. Williams also found, in Jordan Massee's father, the model for Big Daddy.

What I came to understand from the honesty of the emotional record was that a number of commonly held beliefs about Williams are false. In the notebooks it becomes clear how free Williams was, how he did exactly what he wanted to do. His wretched whining was just a form of indulgence. For example, in the notebooks we see that Williams's dramatic statements, especially in the early years, should be understood not as expressions of inner self but as his indulgence in melodrama. In the summer of 1936 he wrote: "My situation now seems so hopeless that this afternoon it seemed there were only two possible ways out—death or suicide—however that was a bit melodramatic and I shall probably go on living and if I saw death coming God knows I'd run the other way as fast as my two legs could carry me." Williams inhabited moods and dispositions to better understand their range. For him, suicide was a romantic notion, and in more than twenty works he wrote about suicide by starvation, poisoning with gas, poisoning with Lysol, smoking opium, overdosing on pills, slitting wrists, hanging, drowning, jumping off a building, running in front of a train, and shooting with a gun.

Williams also liked to indulge in the belief that he had a bad heart, and he often gave characters afflictions he either had or imagined himself to have. It was a practice he began in his early years and continued throughout his writing career. Characters with heart conditions include Alma in *Summer and Smoke,* Kilroy in *Camino Real,* and Sebastian in *Suddenly Last Summer,* just to name a few. But as the notebooks reveal, despite Williams's fears and anxieties about his heart, his doctors could find nothing seriously wrong.

Even Williams's confessional writing in his notebooks, however, is not immune from his sense of romance. Williams mentions in a 1979 journal entry that he wishes to be buried "at sea (a day north of Havana)," where his idol Hart Crane found refuge in the vast "mother of life." He also stated such a desire in *Memoirs.* Williams, in fact, never signed the alleged codicil to his will, but he did give these lines to several characters. In *A Streetcar Named Desire,* Blanche says, "And I'll be buried at sea sewn up in a clean white sack and dropped overboard—at noon—in the blaze of summer—and into an ocean as blue as my first lover's eyes!" Williams had written almost the same lines in an earlier, unpublished play, "The Spinning Song." His character Maxine Faulk, in *The Night of the Iguana,* describes her husband's sea burial: "My husband, Fred Faulk, was the greatest game fisherman on the West Coast of Mexico . . . and on his deathbed . . . he requested to be dropped in the sea . . . not even sewed up in canvas, just in his fisherman outfit."

The notebooks reveal Williams's early interest in the visual arts. As a student at the University of Iowa, Williams looked at Grant Wood's painting *American Gothic* and wrote a one-act play of the same title about the expressionless couple, imagining them to be the parents of a Clyde Barrow–type figure. While in California in 1939 with Jim Parrott, he took painting lessons from Parrott's aunt. That same year he traveled to the San Francisco Art Fair and, inspired by a painting of Pierre Bonnard, *Salle à manger à la campagne,* wrote the poem "Garden Scene," which describes the painting. He often invoked paintings and painters in describing scenes of plays. For example, in *The Glass Menagerie* he invoked El Greco; in *Summer and Smoke,* De Chirico; in *A Streetcar Named De-*

sire, van Gogh; in *Sweet Bird of Youth*, O'Keeffe; and in *The Night of the Iguana*, Rubens, to name a few. Included in *Notebooks* are paintings and drawings that Williams produced at various stages of his life, including several self-portraits. In the last decade of his life, as he failed more and more as a writer, he turned to painting.

As one might expect, Williams often mentions manuscripts he was working on but fails to identify them by name. Pages are peppered with comments such as "4 manuscripts in the mail" or "wrote a pretty good story today." In order to identify the manuscripts Williams refers to, I compiled a database of what turned out to be more than three thousand manuscripts, both complete and fragmented, titled and untitled. Sometimes clues appeared in letters, other manuscripts, or the timing of contemporary events. One easy demarcation was Williams's 1938–39 change in signature, at the age of twenty-eight, from Thomas Lanier Williams to Tennessee Williams—a change he made to obscure his age after he had entered the Group Theatre play-writing contest for writers under the age of twenty-five.

As I began to identify the unnamed manuscripts I began to realize that the notebooks, especially from the early years, provide a record of Williams's creative journey. After one of his stories is harshly criticized in class ("Only one girl liked it and she didn't get the point"), Williams encourages himself to write "something really fine," "something strong and undefeated." He reads Saroyan's story "The Daring Young Man on the Flying Trapeze" and writes "This Spring," a story in the stream-of-consciousness style about a woman dying of tuberculosis. Touched by the fate of Bruno Hauptmann, the man convicted of kidnapping and killing Charles Lindbergh's son, Williams writes both a poem and a eulogy about him. He writes the play *Stairs to the Roof*, a fantasy about a young office worker, which was a dramatization of an earlier short story that incorporates parts of at least three other earlier stories.

In the notebooks we gain glimpses into what Williams chose from his life and fitted with twists and turns into his fiction. Sometimes the distance between an experience or contact and its appropriation spanned decades. As a student at the University of Iowa, in 1938, Williams described feeling "alienated" from the theatre crowd when a pocketbook was stolen from one of the girls. "I became quite embarrassed . . . —was afraid they might think me guilty—*for absolutely no reason*!!!" In his story "Two on a Party," begun in 1951, "Billy had the uncomfortable feeling that [Cora] suspected him of stealing the diamond ear-clip." Many of the people Williams mentions in his journal appear either as characters or as names in his work.

In his journals, Williams writes of his influences. Some are well known, but others were surprising to me. In the early years of his journal Williams commented on poets and writers he admired: Crane—"the biggest of them all"; Chekhov—"above all the prose writers"; Lawrence—"I read from his letters and conceived a strong impulse to write a play about him"; Strindberg—"his unfailing fire to strike out profiles of life"; Faulkner—"by distortion, by outrageous exaggeration he seems to get an effect closer to reality"; Wolfe—*You Can't Go Home Again* has the "stamp of genius on it"; and Dickinson—"love her." Later Williams commented on Joyce—"a lyric talent which is controlled by intellect, the rarest of happy accidents in the world of letters"—and, perhaps most surprisingly, Hemingway, whose "great quality, aside from his prose style, is this fearless expression of brute nature."

Williams makes various comments on the craft of writing. One of the most important entries occurs in the spring of 1939, after he has received an award from the Group Theatre for a group of one-acts, *American Blues,* and can be interpreted as marking the end of his apprenticeship. Williams writes: "My next play will be simple, direct and terrible—a picture of my own heart—there will be no artifice in it—I will seek truth as I see it—distort as I see distortion—be wild as I am wild—tender as I am tender—mad as I am mad—passionate as I am passionate—It will be myself without concealment or evasion and with a fearless unashamed frontal assault upon life that will leave no room for trepidation." Such confessional writing would demand a courage Williams would soon find. Along the way he offers advice to himself, such as this entry from 1941: "I believe that the way to write a good play is to convince yourself that it is *easy* to do—then go ahead and do it with *ease.* Don't maul, don't suffer, don't groan—till the first draft is finished." Within a few years, Williams had begun to work intensely on the manuscript that would evolve into *The Glass Menagerie,* his important play about his sister.

In fact, as the notebooks reveal, Williams had begun writing about his sister as early as 1938. A year earlier, Rose, age eighteen, had been diagnosed with dementia praecox, an early name for schizophrenia. About her condition Williams had written, "We have had no deaths in our family but slowly by degrees something was happening much uglier and more terrible than death." Thoughts about her appear randomly in his journals: "Rose, my dear little sister—I think of you, dear, and wish, oh so much that I could help!" Unable to save her, Williams turned to his writing. On May 30, 1938, he notes, "have written a rather nice short story—'The 4-leaf Clover'—about a girl going mad—memories of Rose." More than three and a half years later, he records in his notebook that he had "just finished writing 'The Spinning Song' a play suggested by my sister's tragedy." Interestingly, fragments of "The Spinning Song" reveal material that relates both to *The Glass Menagerie* and to *A Streetcar Named Desire.* For example, in one fragment a woman named Blanche lives on a plantation with her two children and is estranged from her husband.

Three months after his sister underwent a prefrontal lobotomy in January 1943, Williams began the play "The Gentleman Caller." He drew on his short story "Portrait of a Girl in Glass," begun in February 1941, and borrowed parts of more recent works, "A Daughter of the American Revolution," "Blue Roses and the Polar Star," and, most importantly, "The Spinning Song." The process of shifting scenes, borrowing bits from one piece for another, and returning to the short story as the basis for a play was representative of the nonlinear way in which he created. Williams continued working on this play during the summer and early autumn of 1943. He experimented with form, including a film treatment, as well as with endings, including a comedy in one act that ended happily with Jim and Laura kissing and then metaphorically walking off into the sunset.

Williams's notebooks offer insight into the possibilities Williams allowed himself, how he played with texts for years to arrive at an extraordinary conclusion. For example, in December 1946 he wrote: "I worked on 'Poker Night' and find it surprisingly close to completion. . . . The ending is not yet right." Williams considered several endings for *A Streetcar Named Desire,* including Blanche throwing herself under a train and Blanche being forcibly removed from the stage, before deciding on the final one, which was physically quieter. The line "I have always depended on the kindness of strangers" was borrowed from his 1933 letter to Harriet Monroe of *Poetry:* "Will you do a total stranger the kindness of reading his verse?"

In December 1948 Williams notes that he is trying to write a political play, a play he would describe as being drawn mostly from Huey Long: "So far I have not written anything—except certain scenes in *You Touched Me!*—that did not come out of my heart. . . . [Politics] is a big and important theme that doesn't really interest me very much: gets too far away from my own experience."

Williams borrowed heavily from his personal life no more than with his sister, who was, beside the model for Laura in *The Glass Menagerie,* the model for over fifteen characters, and Williams would give her name to many others. While the most important, Rose was not the only person Williams appropriated from life for his work. For example, stopping in El Paso in 1939 on his way to the West Coast, Williams noted in his journal that he met an "odd rather dear little person" named Trinket. More than two decades later he would borrow her name for the pitiful, maimed woman in *The Mutilated.* Other people who appear first in his journals and then later as characters or names in his works include Warren Hatcher, Marian Gallaway, Hazel Kramer and her grandfather Mr. Kramer, Carl Butts, Jim Connor, Harold Mitchell, and Emily Jelkes. In wondering if his lover Frank Merlo will leave him, Williams concludes: "If he left me, and perhaps he will, I would go on living and enduring and I suppose turn him into a poem as I've done with others." On another occasion he protests too loudly: "First draft of a story today about the place where I had lunch, 3 Easter egg villas between here and Amalfi but the hero is *not* Gordon [Sager] and the lady is sort of a composite of various vampires I have known but *not* Peggy [Guggenheim] & *not* Libby [Holman]."

The notebooks were Williams's companion on his solitary journey—both emotional and physical. There is no better example than the small flip-top notepad in which he records a hitchhiking journey from New Orleans to St. Petersburg in the autumn of 1941. He gives himself a pep talk: "Most of the cars are headed west. Well here comes another—Look bright, son!" In 1943 he says to his journal, "I haven't talked to you these past 4 nights." And shortly later, "Thought you were lost Mr. Blue Book. Searched high and low till I found you between some newspapers."

In 1979 Williams looked back over the past decades and wondered, "Did I die by my own hand or was I destroyed slowly and brutally by a conspiratorial group? . . . Perhaps I was never meant to exist at all, but if I hadn't, a number of my created beings would have been denied their passionate existence. . . . The best I can say for myself is that I worked like hell." This heartbreaking entry reveals that *Notebooks* is at its core a record of a journey of courage. Between 1959 and 1979 Williams wrote fifteen new plays, revised and expanded three earlier ones, and published a novel, a volume of poetry, and a collection of short stories. Only one work from this period, *The Night of the Iguana,* a play based loosely on the 1946 short story of the same title, received positive reviews. Even the response to this play, which Williams described as being about "how to live beyond despair and still live," was mixed. Williams followed *The Night of the Iguana* with *The Milk Train Doesn't Stop Here Anymore,* derived from the 1953 short story "Man Bring This Up Road." Largely damned by the critics, the play closed after two months. From this point onward it was rare that a play by Williams ran for more than a few months, and many closed after only a few weeks or even days. Perhaps he had run out of subject matter, or perhaps he was trying to adapt his work to suit a public he no longer understood.

By the end of the journals, Williams, who had made "a positive religion of the simple act of endurance," was tired, discouraged, and morose. His final entry, written in an almost illegible scrawl, records a paranoid fear about an agent and a lost manuscript. Williams asks, "Where do I [go] from here?" Very few individuals could have withstood the sustained and at times gratuitously mean-spirited critical reaction Williams faced over such a long period. The end of his life should not be interpreted so much as a failure but as an extraordinary example of resilience, the type of resilience that randomly appears throughout his journal. "Openings come quickly, sometimes, like a blue space in running clouds. . . . A complete overcast: then a blaze of light: and there is heaven again. And I am in it."

Research and Performance

A Roundtable on the Future of the Archive

—KENNETH SCHLESINGER

The American Society for Theatre Research's Fiftieth-Anniversary Conference in Chicago in November 2006 chose as its theme "'America,' 'Society,' 'Theatre,' and 'Research.'" For the plenary on research, conference chair Shannon Jackson proposed a special roundtable on the state of the archive, which would be jointly organized by ASTR and the Theatre Library Association (TLA). She envisioned an interactive dialogue between theatre history scholars and archivists exploring shared and conflicting issues. Performance studies scholar Tavia Nyong'o of New York University and I were enlisted to organize the panel.

Our call for papers—initially titled "Performing History/Historicizing Performance: The Archive as Negotiator or Co-Conspirator?"—solicited contributions investigating archival challenges in theatre research as well as performative aspects of the archive. As a stimulus for discussion, we posed the following questions:

- What is the difference between performance history and performative history?
- What is the relationship between performance history and theatre history?
- What does it mean conceptually and professionally to think of the archive as static? as dynamic? or performative?
- How does serious engagement with performance and performativity change archival research and protocols? Correspondingly, how does engagement with archival research and protocols affect theories of performance and performativity?

· How should the archive transform its methods of collection, description, and access to respond to new strategies of performance scholarship?

Further, as a performing arts archivist, I was interested in considering some ethical and philosophical issues of personal interest during more than two decades in the profession. While archives are ostensibly designed to preserve access to the historical record, are archival organizations essentially hierarchical and elitist in their construct? In other words, do they exist institutionally to uphold and reinforce the dominant culture? Are archivists stewards of this storehouse of knowledge, gatekeepers in their unavoidably subjective interpretation of records, unintentionally misleading in their organizational schemes and finding aids? Moreover, this leads to larger questions about the construct of "history": Who gets to tell it? How do we determine the big picture based on the minutiae of selected documents? What about the interstices, the gaps—the *silences*? Finally, how do new technologies simultaneously extend access yet possibly misrepresent the original context of historical documents?

We received some fascinating submissions, including two that aren't included in this volume: Odai Johnson's "Theatre Research and Reconstruction of America's Oldest Theatre," which employs archaeological evidence and creatively assesses quotidian historical records to guide reconstruction of an original playhouse in Colonial Williamsburg; and Mary Keelan's "Archival Definition as Barrier: The Case of the New York State Archives Film Script Files," an analysis of inconsistent subject headings and probable censorship impeding access to records documenting classic Russian film screenings in the United States from the 1920s to the 1940s.

In terms of structure, we asked participants to present a ten-minute snapshot of their research, which could be a jumping-off point to further discussion among panelists and the nearly one hundred audience members who attended. Predictably, this roundtable ended up raising more questions than it resolved, but attendees appreciated the high level of provocative and entertaining discourse. Since archives are primarily concerned with issues of documentation, it seemed appropriate that *Theatre History Studies* asked me to edit these papers for publication.

Elin Diamond's "Performance in the Archives" opens with a discussion of New York City mayor Rudolph Giuliani's controversial and contested decision in 2001 to privatize his administrative papers by transferring them to an independent foundation rather than depositing them in the municipal archives. Widely and effectively protested by the Society of American Archivists, this peremptory move clearly violated the principle of the transparency of government records as well as the public's right to know. Professor Diamond also traces the resonances of this action to the Bush administration's conduct of secrecy, imposing access limits on historical archival records that had already been declassified, all in the name of national security—while simultaneously violating the public's privacy and trust by engaging in illegal wiretapping.

Diamond then shifts gears by wittily relating a recent visit to the Fales Library and Special Collections at New York University. She describes the processes of registration, submitting call slips, and—with feverish anticipation—receiving the transfer of records from the archival assistant as a formalized, performative ritual, as she is imbued with the solemnity of this transfer of knowledge. She is at once amused and awestruck by her sober role as interpreter of history.

Francesca Marini's "Performing Arts Archives: Dynamic Entities Complementing and Supporting Scholarship and Creativity" investigates the unique contributions of performing arts archives in the United States and Italy. Part of what distinguishes them is that the archivists are usually current or former artistic practitioners, which gives them intimate knowledge of the art form and enhances their ability to provide both practical and theoretical reference support. Further, given these institutions' primary role in documenting the performance process, they definitely behave like dynamic, symbiotic entities capturing the artistic evolution and serving as a potential future wellspring of creativity.

The remaining two essays examine current technologies and their impact on traditional scholarship and the reconstruction of historical events. Margaret M. Knapp's "eBay, Wikipedia, and the Future of the Footnote" considers the uncertain future of scholarly citation within the shifting sands of the digital universe. With Web sites proliferating and disappearing daily as well as the richness yet vagaries of online collaborative software, how will we be able to consistently document academic evidence? Framed by Kevin Kelly's controversial *New York Times Magazine* article "Scan This Book!"—in which Kelly modestly posits digitizing all of civilization's cultural artifacts—Knapp is willing to embrace this perhaps inevitable challenge, but she wonders what will happen when we abandon our time-honored tools of academic inquiry by the wayside.

Tavia Nyong'o's "Period Rush: Affective Transfers in Recent Queer Art and Performance," which was not part of the original discussion, critically evaluates the capacity of new technologies to migrate and integrate historical performance into the present day. Examined through the lens of contemporary queer performances—the participatory reenactments *The Muster* and *The Battle of Orgreave,* the films *Ghost World* and *Homotopia,* and the play *Red Tide Blooming*—the tendency toward nostalgia and smoothing over historical reconstructions can be disrupted by a subversive outsider with the ability to interrogate, recontextualize, and make visible the uncomfortable contradictions embedded within a superimposed narrative. Although historical evidence is shaped and spun by the dominant culture, it can be represented as an artificial construct or as one multifaceted interpretation among many. It's only a matter of whose hand is on the remote.

In order to promote accessibility and transparency of their collections, archives are involved in major initiatives to migrate finding aids to their Web sites—as well as to offer a virtual presence through increased digitization. Dialogues such as these between theatre scholars and archivists are important contributions to understanding research needs and corresponding services. By developing a sophisticated comprehension of our users' behavior, archivists will be better equipped to respond appropriately, enhancing the quality of the scholarly record.

Performance in the Archives

—ELIN DIAMOND

On Christmas Eve in 2001, New York City's outgoing mayor, Rudolph Giuliani, signed an agreement with city authorities that allowed him unprecedented control over his public records. Giuliani convinced the commissioner of Records and Information Services to allow him to box up his mayoral papers and transfer them to "The Fortress," a high-security storage facility in Queens. He then incorporated a private consulting firm to manage the archives with the aim of depositing them in a new site, to be called the Giuliani Center for Public Affairs.[1]

Among those who protested the mayor's action was the Society of American Archivists, the oldest and largest professional organization of archivists in North America. On February 20, 2002, at a conference convened to register the society's outrage at the mayor's maneuver, archivist Thomas Connors said: "By transferring his documentary record as a public servant to a private entity . . . Mr. Giuliani effectively removes his actions as mayor from the scrutiny of members of the public who wish to learn how, why, and when certain decisions were made in order to assess specific Giuliani-era policies. . . . What particularly concerns the Society of American Archivists is that Mr. Giuliani's action is taking place against a national backdrop wherein other government officials, namely President Bush, are attempting to create barriers to access to public information."[2]

Giuliani's flaunting of civic protocol was so flagrant, so egregious as to recall the legendary antics of Tammany Hall. His actions nicely illustrated Jacques Derrida's notion of the archive as both an exterior site that houses truth in the form of original documents *and* as a site of power and authority. Clearly, Giuliani understood the link between public memory, power, and the archive. He hijacked his own archive because he knew that such documents might reinforce or drastically revise public memory. In Derrida's words, "There is no political power without control of the archive ... democratization can always be measured by this essential criterion: the participation and access to the archive, its constitution and its interpretation." By sequestering the raw data of his mayoral administration, data that were waiting for evidentiary interpretation and critique, Giuliani gave municipal archivists, political historians, and future plaintiffs a nasty case of "archive fever"—Derrida's term for the hunger for evidence, the desire for full knowledge, and the delusional belief that definitive origins are recoverable and redemption attainable by delving into the archive's inner sanctum.[3]

What I have just recounted might be the initial foray for an essay in Antoinette Burton's wonderful new anthology *Archive Stories: Facts, Fictions, and the Writing of History.* Historian Burton goes beyond the historian's typical "boot-camp narrative ... the drama" of getting to an archive, living in terrible digs (inevitably too hot or too cold) while working at the archive, and surviving the gatekeeping caprices of the guardians *of* the archive. The boot-camp narrative usually has a self-congratulatory happy ending when the long-suffering scholar hits pay dirt by finding "it"—the proof needed for his or her tome on the domestic handicrafts of Brabant in the Middle Ages.

Instead, Burton wants to go "backstage" in order to "historiciz[e] the emergence of state and local archives, interrogat[ing] how archive logics work, what subjects they produce, and which they silence in specific historical and cultural contexts; enumerating the ways in which archival work is embodied experience, one shaped as much by national identity, gender, race, and class as by professional training or credentials, pressing the limits of disciplinary boundaries to consider what kind of archive work different genres ... do, for what audiences and to what ends."[4] "Embodied experience"? "Pressing the limit of disciplinary boundaries"? As I hear this admirable list I would say Burton has been reading Joseph Roach or Shannon Jackson or Diana Taylor or Mike Pearson.

While our performance studies scholarship has annexed the archive to the hegemonic written record of history, and has aligned performance to the deep continuities of social memory or the embodied repertoire, certain historians have decisively crossed and intertwined these vortices and taken performance to the archive. Tavia Nyong'o and Kenneth Schlesinger, our conveners at the 2006 American Society for Theatre Research plenary session, asked us to consider the following question: To what degree should performance studies scholarship seek to make visible the silences, tensions, and/or contradictions of the archival record? To a large degree, professional historians are borrowing our tools and doing just that. But I am not offering another useless disciplinary binary.

Theatre historians and scholars who use the archive often take performance to the archive. But it is interesting that, at this theory-dead moment, when performance and literature scholars—professors and graduate students alike—know that work in the archives hikes the value of their research, the historians, who as a group have long claimed the archive as their badge of legitimation, their proudly worn letter "A," now view their beloved cobwebby archives as a vexing force field or, as Carolyn Steedman writes, an "oneiric space . . . that is to do with longing and appropriation."[5] Is it possible that under the historians' A-for-Archive badges are the even more ornate letters "PS" for Performance Studies?—to be revealed only in dark bars far from academic conferences? We in theatre and performance studies surely have something to say about this.

The archive sits in its silent vault, but when you and I take hold of it, it becomes a performance site, a materialization of an implied narrative already spatialized and arranged. Like performance, the archive is a site of transformation, its "material substrate" transformed by touch and interpretation into knowledge. Like performance, the archive solicits and interacts with a reader/spectator who, drawn by texts, objects, or perhaps something unlooked for, is seduced into desirous identification with writers, figures, and events. (Steedman notes that Jules Michelet, upon reading the work of Vico in 1824, wrote in his diary, "I was seized with a frenzy caught from Vico, an incredible intoxication with his great historical principle.")[6] Like performance, the archive conceals its backstories, like the one I've told you about the former mayor of New York City. Like performance, activity in the archive often departs from the script: How many times do we approach the archive with one question only to have it deflected into another? Apparently dormant until the labor of interpretation begins, the archive soon takes on its own voice: it reads us as much as we read it. And like performance, the archive has secrets, "ghosts," as Derrida puts it, that promise an untold story. If I analogize the archive to performance it is not to be fanciful. Jon McKenzie reminded us years ago that to speak of performance is to invoke hidden systems of meaning and power, from the molecular to the spectacular. And, writing of the legal implications of social performance, Joseph Roach notes that there are no trivial rituals.

No, indeed. However casually I may have seemed walking into the Fales Collection at New York University's Bobst Library in January 2006, I was not casual. It is not a normal place. I was not, as I usually am, daydreaming; and I was fairly nicely dressed. With firm intentions I approached the desk, the gateway to the inner sanctum.

You know the drill. "Welcome to the Fales Library. In order for you to use the collections, proper identification and registration are required." (That is, only the elect may approach and touch.) "Coats, hats, purses, bags, briefcases, and other personal property must be stored in the lockers next to the entrance of the Reading Room." (The body must be stripped clean of impure detritus.) "If some personal books are critical to your research, please present them when you enter. You will be issued a 'Personal Book' flag that must be kept with your books." (What is tainted or not of the archive must be marked as such.) And so on. I show my credentials. I sign in three places that I will not violate the Elizabeth Robins papers that I came to inspect. I fill out the slips and the suspense mounts. I am excited, even though I already have a headache and can feel my neck muscles knotting in anticipation of the work ahead. The contracts for Robins's play *Votes for Women* lie in a folder twenty-seven inches long. The archive assistant slides the outsized envelope of loose papers and places it flat on his arms and, as though holding a priestly stole, slowly walks to me. I rise at his approach. To take the envelope from him I have to extend my arms and bend at the knee, an inadvertent curtsy. Carolyn Steedman reminds us that the modern European public archive came into being in order to solidify and memorialize first monarchal and then state power, all of which is remembered in my awkward curtsy as the file passes from king to subject, from magistrate to citizen, from the Fales Collection librarian to me.[7]

These rituals of the archive *in the archive* repeat and reaffirm the archive's very being: it holds, through legal arrangement, material that is the basis for the truths a seeker feels compelled to tell. For Steedman, "Archive is a name for the many places in which the past (which does not now exist but which did actually happen, which cannot be retrieved but which can be represented) has deposited some traces and fragments, usually in written form."[8] To Burton, "Archives are traces of the past collected whether intentionally or haphazardly as evidence."[9]

In the spirit of "traces and fragments," Steedman, who admits to her own archive fever throughout *Dust,* notes that "though the bundles in my case boxes may be mountainous, there isn't in fact very much there. Compared with the great brown strandless slow-moving river of Everything, your archive is just a tiny flotsam that's ended up in the record office you are at work in."[10] Burton chimes in: "The history of the archive is the history of loss."[11] But Burton's definition, while acknowledging the haphazard as well as the intentionality behind the archive, adds a crucial term: evidence. "Evidence" suggest the legal boundaries of the archive, the legal decrees that establish it and the laws, scholarly or juridical, that turn mere objects or writings into the basis (evidence) for this or that truth. The archive reeks of legality and ceremony. It's where you curtsy even when you don't intend to. It's where you mark the difference between this place and every other place.

I would suggest that in theatre and performance studies we seek evidence too, but the truths we propose will stay close to the messy places they come from: I'm proposing an archive scholarship derived from the contents of the long folders *and* from their performative resemblance to a sacred mantle draped over the arms of an acolyte; scholarship that sorts and re-sorts those contents with the researcher's "archive fever," laid bare and analyzed. Performance in the archives necessarily confronts the archives' implication in regimes of power. I am referring to the "gotcha" moment described at the beginning—in which Rudolph Giuliani was publicly shamed for sequestering his administration's archive by Thomas Connors and the Society of American Archivists. Giuliani's mayoral archives were naturally subject to the privileges of state power, but all archives are embedded in what Derrida, in *Archive Fever,* calls "archontic power," derived from the first *archons,* or guardians of the archive. As Steedman writes, archive fever is not about power's "inaugural moments," traceable through the "quietly folded and filed documents" of the archives, but about "Power itself."[12] Yet, as in performance, power in the archive "speaks" as much through a researcher's embodied response as through official proclamations.

Consider Michel Foucault's account of his experience reading the following passage at the Bibliotheque Nationale: "Mathurian Milan, placed in the hospital for the insane at Charenton, 31 August 1707: 'His madness was to hide from his family, to lead an obscure life in the country, to have actions at laws, to lend usuriously and without security, to lead his feeble mind down unknown paths, and to believe himself capable of the greatest employments.'" Foucault describes a moment of archive fever: "It would be hard to say exactly what I felt when I read these fragments. These stories, suddenly emerging from two and a half centuries of silence, stirred more fibers within me than what is ordinarily called literature, without my being able to say even now if I was more moved by the beauty of that Classical style, draped in a few sentences around a character that was plainly wretched, or by the excesses, the blend of dark stubbornness and rascality, of this life whose disarray and relentless energy one senses beneath the stone-smooth words."[13] Having a form of archive fever does not mean understanding its cause: Was it the classical style of the prose that condemned the "madman" or the visceral sensation (that "stirred . . . fibers within me") of Mathurian Milan, whose "rascality . . . and relentless energy" were frozen into submission by the "stone-smooth words" of civic authority?

Like Foucault's case of archive fever, mine was also unbidden but no less a response to the power that circulates in every archive, whether digital or material. Holding pride of place in the Elizabeth Robins archive are immaculate studio photographs, taken at the Vaudeville Theatre in April and May 1891, of Robins in her memorable role as the first Hedda Gabler on the English stage. There she is with her big Victorian hair, her confident actressy gestures in a role that almost single-handedly made the theatre truly modern. In the back pages of the album is another series of photos: a sheet of passport photos, faded duplicates taken in the late 1930s when Robins was in her seventies. She lived to almost ninety, and there is vigor in the seventy-year-old face. Posing not for fans of Ibsen but for the bureaucrat's camera, Robins, wearing a large, utterly unfashionable Victorian hat, is unsmiling. Though any archive will serve linear history, the story of time passing from youth to age is not what "stirred . . . fibers within me." It was rather the inchoate but palpable sense of the archive's deep connection to record keeping, to the vast civic bureaucracy of statistic gathering and classification that grew exponentially in Robins's long lifetime and, as Marx observed, was the secret power within the nation state.[14] With its glossy stills, the archive enshrines Robins's singular role in producing dramatic modernism, but her faded passport photos and my unwonted curtsy are performative witnesses to the archive's role in the power of bureaucratic modernity. This pleasurable oscillation between photos and embodiment, between library protocols and systems of civic power, is an archive story that we in theatre and performance studies are best positioned to tell.

Notes

1. For a full account of this episode see Nancy Cricco and Peter Wosh, "The Past, Present, and Uncertain Future of Presidential Records," http://www.ala.org/ala/acrl/acrlpubs/rbm/backissuesvol3no2/cricco.pdf, 88–89.

2. Thomas Connors's "Statement before NY City Council's Committee on Government Operations on the Matter of Rudolph Giuliani's Mayoral Records" can be found at the Web site of the Society of American Archivists, http://www.ala.org/ala/acrl/acrlpubs/rbm/backissuesvol3no2/cricco.pdf, 88–89.

3. Jacques Derrida, *Archive Fever: A Freudian Impression,* trans. Eric Prenowitz (Chicago: University of Chicago Press, 1996), 4 n. 1. The French title of *Archive Fever* (*Mal d'archive: Une impression freudienne*) brings into prominence more than the feverishness of archival engagement, although Derrida does discuss the physical symptoms of muddled vision, of burning with passion in those who are "en mal d'archive"—that is, "in need of archives" (91). In reading Yosef Hayim Yerushalmi's meditation on Freud's *Moses and Monotheism,* Derrida revisits psychoanalysis itself as a field obsessed with the past and with "searching for the archive right where it slips away. . . . It is to have a compul-

sive, repetitive, and nostalgic desire to return to the origin . . . to the most archaic place of absolute commencement" (91). But *mal* in French can mean trouble, misfortune, hurt, sickness, pain, wrong, sin, badness, malice, or evil. Carolyn Steedman writes in *Dust: The Archive and Cultural History* (New Brunswick, N.J.: Rutgers University Press, 2002): "[Derrida] emphasises . . . the institution of archives as the expression of state power. . . . [He] will deal not only with a feverish—sick—search for origins, not only with archives of evil, but with *le mal radical,* with evil itself. The two intertwined threads of argument to follow in the main body of the text, about psychoanalysis and Yerushalmi's questioning of Freud's Jewishness, underpin a history of the twentieth century that is indeed a history of horror" (8–9).

4. Antoinette Burton, *Archive Stories: Facts, Fictions, and the Writing of History* (Durham: Duke University Press, 2005), 8.
5. Steedman, *Dust,* 80–81.
6. Ibid., 69.
7. Ibid.
8. Ibid.
9. Burton, *Archive Stories,* 3.
10. Steedman, *Dust,* 18.
11. Antoinette Burton, "Thinking beyond the Boundaries: Empire, Feminism, and the Domains of History," *Social History* 26, no. 1 (2001): 66, quoted in Steedman, *Dust,* 5.
12. Steedman, *Dust,* 6.
13. Michel Foucault, "Lives of Infamous Men," in *The Essential Foucault: Selections from Essential Works of Foucault, 1954–1984* (New York: The New Press, 2003), 279–80.
14. Derek Sayer, *Capitalism and Modernity: An Excursus on Marx and Weber* (London: Routledge, 1991), 79–80.

Performing Arts Archives

Dynamic Entities Complementing and Supporting
Scholarship and Creativity

—FRANCESCA MARINI

The Role of Archives in Democratic Societies

In the course of history, whenever political and social oppression take place, many records that document the past and the rights of countries or individuals are destroyed in order to make essential evidence unavailable to anyone who may try to counteract the oppressors' actions. Existing memory is erased. The task of democratic archives is exactly the opposite: to preserve memory and the records "created and received in the course of individual or institutional activity and set aside (preserved) as evidence of that activity,"[1] as well as "for action or reference."[2] By keeping the records safe from malicious tampering and destruction, archives in democratic societies hold individuals and institutions accountable for their actions, making it possible for citizens to access the records and exercise their rights. Many types of archives house the records of government, business, institutions of all kinds, and individuals, to name just a few examples. All of them, including those that house performing arts materials, participate in preserving democracy as well as cultural and artistic heritage. It is therefore important to make a clear distinction between those who create the records and the archivists who preserve these records for future reference and use. The archival profession supports and fights for service and accountability to the public. Therefore, archivists frequently oppose the actions of an administration or individual when these actions are anti-democratic. Recently, for example, the Society of American Archivists has been very vocal in objecting to the government's attempts to restrict access to public records.[3] From an archivist's perspective, archives are a means to democracy, and working for an institution or individual should never imply supporting wrongdoing. In a democratic society, everyone who uses archives needs to remember that without the work of archivists, many records would not survive and could not be used.

The archival community fully participates in international intellectual and political discourse. Archival theory and practice have changed over the years, embracing new ideas and challenges. Archivists such as South African Verne Harris have been active in reshaping archives and archival practice in ways that support and reflect progressive political and cultural changes in South Africa and other countries.[4] Much of archival literature and practice focus on the debate on archives as power;[5] this debate also takes place in other communities and disciplines, such as theatre and performance studies. The thinking of philosopher Jacques Derrida[6] and the postmodernist approach have played an important role in current archival discourse.[7] But even before these approaches emerged, those in the archival community were engaged in self-reflection and change.[8]

Performing Arts Archives and Sources

Archivists are active on many fronts and engage with different communities; their work is complex, and not all of its aspects are directly visible to users. For this reason, some users tend to have an oversimplified view of what archivists do, and the role of the archival community is not always properly recognized. Archivists' work is highly interdisciplinary, relies on strong theoretical and practical knowledge, and is carried out in a variety of settings and contexts. Performing arts archives are part of this variety. Archivists are players in the discussion that surrounds the documentation of live performance, which is a highly controversial topic in artistic, archival, and scholarly communities. The selection and preservation in archives of materials that are directly or indirectly related to performance may be seen as an imposition of power[9] and is often condemned as contrary to the spirit of live theatre and performance.[10] In many instances there is a lack of communication and understanding among artists, scholars, and archivists.

In reality, our goals are the same. We all love theatre and performance for its live quality and its cultural, political, and social meaning. No one is interested in turning theatre into a fixed, immutable entity. Performing arts archives make it possible to preserve the memory of artists, movements, and performances.

Archivists want this memory to stay alive and be used for new creations. One Italian archivist who works in the archives of an active theatre, and whom I interviewed for one of my studies, remarked: "The archive has to be alive; it has to be an entity active for everybody. To the set designers whom . . . I have the pleasure to know, I say: 'This archive is waiting for your work. You know it is here.' . . . Because it [an archive] has to be alive. If its existence is not known, if it does not coexist with the city, the people, the scholars . . . it is a dead archive. And theatre cannot be a dead issue: on the contrary, it has to make people understand everything that is out there, convey the possibility to do and discover things."[11]

Other performing arts archivists and scholars with whom I have been in contact through my studies and experience share this opinion. It is also recognized that the materials held in archives—for example, photographs, videos, promptbooks, programs, posters, sketches, plans, and stage models—are only one part of what is needed to study and understand theatre and performance. People and places are among the many sources used by scholars and artists. In dance, for example, the dancer's body is seen as an archive. "Dancers are the living archives of dance history," writes American dance critic and historian Martha Ullman West. "Long after they leave the stage, in their minds and muscles they hold the memory of form, rhythm, mood, and intent, constituting an irreplaceable resource for performers, historians, and frequently the choreographers themselves."[12] The dancers' bodies are a source of information and insight for others as well as for the dancers themselves; an American scholar and tap dancer whom I interviewed pointed out that she discovers connections as she dances.[13] Performance knowledge can be transmitted in many modes, as performance studies scholar Diana Taylor discusses in *The Archive and the Repertoire*.[14] Archivists do not only work with materials in archives; they also act as liaisons among communities and make users aware of all other types of sources available elsewhere.

Some Characteristics of the Work of Performing Arts Archivists

Much of what I discuss in this article is drawn from results of a study of mine that provided an overview of methodological approaches to theatre research and scholarly uses of sources and of the interaction among theatre scholars, archivists, and librarians.[15] Carried out over the course of three years (2002–5), the study gave me the opportunity to broadly survey theatre research and the practices of performing arts archives and libraries in Italy and the United States and, to a lesser degree, in France and Belgium. I conducted more than forty interviews, including twenty-two with theatre scholars and nineteen with archivists and librarians in major university departments and performing arts archives and libraries. Except for two independent scholars, those interviewed are faculty teaching in leading performing arts programs in public and private universities. The archivists and librarians manage the performing arts archives and special collections, as well as some circulating collections, of active theatres, opera houses, and theatre festivals; leading libraries and research institutes; museums; public and private universities; a major national society; and private impresarios.

These archives and libraries have a variety of users. University students in several fields and disciplines—for example, performing arts, the arts, architecture, and fashion design—working on theses and dissertations compose one large group. Large numbers of established scholars use the most specialized archives and libraries. Other significant groups of users are performing arts practitioners and critics. Internal users are predominant in in-house archives of active theatres. Other users are members of the general public, especially in circulating collections but also in archives and special collections.[16]

Theatre is as complex as life itself. At the creative, intellectual, and practical levels, issues merge and cannot be separated. Performances are dynamic, interactive, situated in space and time, set in many intertwining contexts, and based on creativity, collaboration, and research.[17] Performing arts materials and scholars' and archivists' work mirror these characteristics. Some overarching categories that cut across the data and encompass the specific issues addressed by scholars and archivists emerged from my study. These categories are context, time, creativity, engagement, and interdisciplinarity. Since I have discussed them in detail elsewhere,[18] here I will briefly summarize only some aspects of my findings. I will focus on the archivists' involvement in and understanding of performing arts practice, understanding of context, and understanding of dynamic sources.

Involvement in and Understanding of Practice

Direct involvement in and understanding of practice is a key element in the study of theatre and performance and in the management of its sources held in archives. Performing arts archivists are always in close contact with theatre practice and are often directly part of it. The group I interviewed included actors, dancers, singers, and musicians. Similarly, performing arts scholars are in touch with practice through collaboration with artists or through direct involvement as actors, directors, dramaturges, playwrights, composers, and designers.[19] This involvement with practice informs the work of archivists and scholars; one cannot conduct research, elaborate theories, generate new knowledge, support new generations of artists, or manage sources unless one fully understands theatre and performance. As theatre historian David Mayer points out, archivists can help scholars only if they "understand how theatre scholars work on 'the event' as well as on 'the production' and 'the performance,' and . . . are receptive to evidence which helps to increase understanding of the event."[20]

For archivists, close contact with practice also requires knowing what is happening in the performing arts and therefore where to acquire materials. It is also essential in order to communicate with artists, who often fear that archives may turn their work into a static entity. By showing they are part of the performing arts world and know the process of performance, archivists may start fruitful collaborations with artists. Some artists and companies simply do not think about documenting their work or do not have enough time or funding to organize and preserve their materials; in these cases, artists usually appreciate help from archivists. Other artists and companies are already engaged in documentation and may or may not be interested in donating their materials to archives. Some artists thoroughly document their work. Robert Wilson maintains his own archive; he has also donated videotapes of his performances to the Theatre on Film and Tape Archive of The New York Public Library for the Performing Arts, and part of his papers to Columbia University's Rare Book and Manuscripts Library.[21] Wilson wants to preserve his vision for future audiences, as is shown in the documentary *Absolute Wilson*, which provides useful examples of his interest in documentation.[22] Some artists, however, do not wish to document their work. "I don't like it being there forever," remarked an Eastern European professor and costume designer based in the United States. "I like the fact that it's gone."[23] When artists do not want to preserve their work, archivists simply have to respect this desire.[24] Archives are as much about remembering as they are about forgetting, as Harris discusses.[25]

Understanding Context

Theatre practice takes place in specific contexts at first, and later on it is reinterpreted according to other contexts. Scholars and archivists must thoroughly understand the different contexts (cultural, artistic, political, and social) in which materials were created. When working with performing arts materials, archivists and scholars also need to be aware of and openly acknowledge their own professional and intellectual standpoints at the time. For archivists, understanding the context of creation is crucial in order to correctly arrange, describe, and make available materials. Archivists work with specific collections and conduct as much research as scholars do. Some archivists publish their research independently, but even when they have no interest or time to do so they are as qualified as researchers as scholars are.

Understanding context is also crucial because archivists often have to explain the materials to users, especially when it comes to technical records such as stage plans. They also need to show users the relationships with other materials existing inside and outside their archive. "Sometimes I am lost and I cannot find the solution to a problem," an Italian professor and director told me, but "I know archivists that can get me out of trouble and tell me where the sources that I am looking for are. It is like being a detective who has his informant friends."[26] The context of the archival profession and the context of the institution in which archivists work also play important roles. Since performing arts materials differ from other archival materials, traditional archival principles often need to be adapted. The different environments of archivists' work are relevant. Archivists who work in in-house archives within active theatres at times have less control over materials than do archivists who work in research institutions. Sometimes, active theatres do not see their archives as a priority and do not assign proper funding or decisional power to them.

Being Proactive, Understanding
Dynamic Sources, and Promoting Use

Performances are instantaneously past, so you cannot wait for performing arts sources to come to you—you have to go out and gather everything available, as well as actively document what is going on and create sources when appropriate. The close contact with practice and understanding of performance enable archivists to identify where existing sources are. Many sources are ephemeral and may easily disappear after initial use. Materials created in relation to a production are dynamic entities, and some never become fixed; for example, scripts get annotated and reused. Some materials never reach the archives, and those that do have generally acquired a specific form. Even then, they still get creatively reused. Archives have to accommodate this vitality. Archives at times have to deal with sources that never stop evolving—this happens, for example, within the digital environment. Archives play an active role in the creation of new documentation; among other activities, archivists may be involved in conducting oral histories or promoting the recording of performances and events. In more traditional archival theory and practice, archivists are usually not actively engaged in documentation efforts.

One school of thought promotes the "documentation strategy."[27] According to Richard Pearce-Moses, "Documentation strategies are typically undertaken by collaborating records creators, archives, and users. A key element is the analysis of the subject to be documented" in order to assess "how that subject is documented in existing records" and to identify what "information about the subject . . . is lacking in those records." The outcome of this analysis is "the development of a plan to capture adequate documentation of that subject, including the creation of records, if necessary."[28] More-traditional archivists consider this stance controversial, but in the performing arts a proactive approach seems to be necessary owing to the temporal and dynamic characteristics of theatre and performance.

Besides being proactive, performing arts archivists are engaged in promoting the use of the materials they manage; "the archive has to be alive," as the Italian archivist said. Other interviewees said there is no point in keeping materials unless they are used, and they discussed ways to promote use. One American special collections librarian promoted a research initiative that led to a theatre performance using sources from the repository.[29] An archive in Italy involved scholars in research projects based on its sources and promoted related seminars and publications.[30]

Conclusion

Performing arts archivists and scholars are dynamic and passionate groups interested in a vast range of topics and projects, closely engaged with performing arts theory and practice, and deeply concerned with artistic, social, and political issues. Archivists have strong research skills and a thorough understanding of performance and context. They manage dynamic sources, are proactive in their role, and strongly promote use of materials. This article has highlighted some characteristics of performing arts archives and archivists' work. While I continue to address these issues in more detail in other venues, I hope this discussion may further strengthen the dialogue among archivists, scholars, and artists.

Notes

1. Richard Pearce-Moses, *A Glossary of Archival and Records Terminology* (Chicago: Society of American Archivists, 2005), s.v. "record."

2. The InterPARES 2 Project, *Terminology Database-Glossary* (current as of April 26, 2007), s.v. "record," http://www.interpares.org/ip2/ip2_terminology_db.cfm.

3. See the Society of American Archivists, "Guantanamo Detainee Records May Be in Jeopardy; SAA and Others Seek Clarification," April 20, 2007, http://www.archivists.org/news/Guantanamo.asp.

4. See Carolyn Hamilton et al., eds., *Refiguring the Archive* (Cape Town, South Africa: David Philip, 2002).

5. See, e.g., Randall C. Jimerson, "Embracing the Power of Archives," *American Archivist* 69, no. 1 (2006): 19–32.

6. See, e.g., Jacques Derrida, *Archive Fever: A Freudian Impression,* trans. Eric Prenowitz (Chicago: University of Chicago Press, 1996); and Verne Harris, "A Shaft of Darkness: Derrida in the Archives," in Hamilton et al., *Refiguring the Archive,* 61–81.

7. Among many postmodern archival writings, see Terry Cook and Joan M. Schwartz, "Archives, Records, and Power: From (Postmodern) Theory to (Archival) Performance," *Archival Science* 2, nos. 3–4 (2002): 171–85; and Tom Nesmith, "Seeing Archives: Postmodernism and the Changing Intellectual Place of Archives," *American Archivist* 65, no. 1 (2002): 24–41.

8. As an example, see Jimerson, "Embracing the Power of Archives."

9. See, e.g., Matthew Reason, *Documentation, Disappearance, and the Representation of Live Performance* (New York: Palgrave Macmillan, 2006).

10. Ibid. Among many writings that address performance documentation, see, e.g., Kenneth Schlesinger, Pamela Bloom, and Ann Ferguson, eds., *Performance Documentation and Preservation in an Online Environment* (New York: Theatre Library Association, 2004); Denise Varney and Rachel Fensham, "More-and-Less-Than: Liveness, Video Recording, and the Future of Performance," *New Theatre Quarterly* 16, no. 1 (2000): 88–96; Peggy Phelan, *Unmarked: The Politics of Performance* (London: Routledge, 1993); Diana Taylor, *The Archive and the Repertoire: Performing Cultural Memory in the Americas* (Durham: Duke University Press, 2003; reprint, 2005); and Reason, *Documentation.*

11. "L'archivio deve vivere, deve essere un nucleo attivo con tutti quanti. Agli scenografi che … ho il piacere di conoscere, dico 'Questo qui è un archivio che aspetta le vostre opere. Sapete che c'è.' … Perché [l'archivio] deve vivere. Se non è conosciuto, se non convive con la città, con le persone, con gli studiosi … è un archivio morto. E il teatro non deve assolutamente essere un discorso morto, anzi deve far capire agli altri tutto quello che c'è, la possibilità proprio di fare, di scoprire." Francesca Marini, "Sources and Methodology of Theater Research in the View of Scholars and Information Professionals" (Ph.D. diss., University of California, Los Angeles, 2005), 174–75 (interview 3). In the discussion, I am withholding the names of the interviewees and of their institutions. This is an established practice in qualitative research and is required by the regulations enforced by the Office for Protection of Research Subjects of the University of California, Los Angeles, with which I was affiliated at the time of the study. The English translation of the quotes is mine. Since literal translation is not always possible, I have included the original quotes in the notes to allow for comparison.

12. Martha Ullman West, "Dancers as Living Archives," *Chronicle of Higher Education,* April 7, 2006, B14.

13. Marini, "Sources and Methodology," 107 (interview 28).

14. Taylor, *The Archive and the Repertoire.*

15. Marini, "Sources and Methodology"; see also Marini, "Archivists, Librarians, and Theatre Research," *Archivaria* 63 (Spring 2007): 7–33.

16. See Marini, "Sources and Methodology," 148–50. Research on the uses of performing arts archives is currently under way at the Theatre Museum in London, conducted by Bonnie Hewson. Bonnie Hewson, e-mail to author, April 17, 2007.

17. See Richard Schechner, *Performance Theory,* rev. ed. (New York: Routledge, 1994); Marvin Carlson, *Performance: A Critical Introduction,* 2nd ed. (London: Routledge, 1999).

18. Marini, "Sources and Methodology" and "Archivists, Librarians, and Theatre Research."

19. Ibid.

20. David Mayer, e-mail to author, January 26, 2002.

21. "The Robert Wilson Archive," http://www.robertwilson.com/archive/overview.php.

22. *Absolute Wilson,* directed by Katharina Otto-Bernstein (USA/Germany: Film Manufactures, 2006).

23. Marini, "Sources and Methodology," 99 (interview 31).

24. I am currently investigating the ethical aspects of documenting performance in my research project "Future Memory and the Performing Arts: Ethical and Artistic Considerations in Documenting and Preserving Performances."

25. Harris, "A Shaft of Darkness," 81.

26. "Certe volte non riesco a cavarmela su certi problemi . . . mentre invece conosco degli archivisti che mi tirano fuori d'impiccio e mi dicono dov'è [quello che cerco]. È un po' come un detective che ha qualche amico informatore in un angolo." Marini, "Sources and Methodology," 164 (interview 16).

27. On the documentation strategy process see Helen W. Samuels, "Who Controls the Past?" *American Archivist* 49, no. 2 (1986): 109–24; and Helen W. Samuels, *Varsity Letters: Documenting Modern Colleges and Universities* (Lanham, Md., and London: Society of American Archivists and Scarecrow Press, 1998). See also Richard J. Cox, "The Documentation Strategy and Archival Appraisal Principles: A Different Perspective," *Archivaria* 38 (Fall 1994): 11–36; and Richard J. Cox, *American Archival Analysis* (Metuchen, N.J.: Scarecrow Press, 1990), especially chapter 13 (291–303). See also Pearce-Moses, *Glossary,* s.v. "documentation strategy."

28. Pearce-Moses, *Glossary,* s.v. "documentation strategy."

29. Marini, "Sources and Methodology," 173–74 (interview 41).

30. Ibid., 173 (interview 17).

eBay, Wikipedia, and
the Future of the Footnote

—MARGARET M. KNAPP

This essay began as an attempt to explore the disconnect I perceived between the theoretical innovations in historiography that have occurred in theatre scholarship over the past few decades and the traditional scholarly structures in which most of us still deliver that thinking in print or through electronic media. Although most of us have abandoned positivist approaches to researching and writing history in favor of more situated, partial, and contingent strategies, we still employ footnotes and citations, positivist vestiges of an attempt to superimpose on humanistic inquiry the traditional scientific requirements of accuracy and reproducibility. But as I began to think about that conflict between theory and practice in our scholarship, I found I could not ignore the huge impact that the Internet has had, and will increasingly have, on our scholarly research and communication, and so I decided to trouble the issue of scholarly citation further by beginning an investigation of how the Internet can render traditional scholarly usage obsolete. I will briefly survey some of these digital transformations as a means to begin a disciplinary conversation about footnotes and citations in the digital world we now inhabit.

First to the macrocosm in which our scholarship will increasingly reside. The May 14, 2006, issue of *New York Times Magazine* contained an article titled "Scan This Book!" by Kevin Kelly of *Wired* magazine.[1] Kelly writes of current efforts by Google and others to scan all existing books into a digital format. Because of the reduced cost of scanning books, especially when outsourced to China and India, Kelly believes that in the future every book; every article in a newspaper, magazine, or journal; every film; every TV or radio broadcast; every painting, photograph, or piece of music; and every one of the billions of dead

Web pages and blogs will be available on the Web. The obvious result is that billions of people worldwide who do not live in proximity to physical libraries can research in a universal, totally searchable library (assuming, of course, that they have access to computers). A further-reaching result, in Kelly's estimation, will be that, once scanned, each word in a digitized source can be "cross-linked, clustered, cited, extracted, indexed, analyzed, annotated, remixed, reassembled, and woven deeper into the culture than ever before." Kelly points out that the reader of a digitized book will be able to turn to the book's bibliography and click on a link that will lead to the entire book or article being cited, and then can click on the sources listed in that second book's bibliography, and so on through all of the links that seem useful. The reader can then assemble his or her own bibliography or virtual bookshelf of sources on the subject.

That capability may seem like Nirvana to scholars, and especially to students who can, for example, quickly discover the more important sources on a subject by using links to determine which authorities are most often cited.[2] But the ability to access a seemingly infinite number of sources brings with it another tool with more fundamental consequences for scholarship: as Kelly puts it, "Once text is digital, books seep out of their bindings and weave themselves together." Readers can take digitized snippets from books and remix them with other materials to create collections of reordered books, which can also exist on the Web and, in turn, be accessed and searched by other readers. When no two of these virtual copies are alike, the sources of information for a scholarly project will no longer be the physical library of stand-alone copies that we are used to dealing with but rather a universal library with seemingly infinite variations on a seemingly infinite range of materials. Every reader will be his or her own scrapbooker-archivist.

When will this world of interrelated texts come fully into being? That depends largely on whether Congress and the courts are willing to take on the inconsistencies and oppressions of the present copyright laws, which have already stifled our traditional scholarly research and publication and now threaten to deny scholars the exponentially advanced capabilities of linking and communicating their research on the Internet.

These new capabilities challenge scholars in two ways. On the one hand, the new possibilities offered to us by the Internet invite us to sample, link, argue with, "cut and paste," or otherwise make new uses of source material, much of it previously unavailable. The process of scholarship on the Internet thus brilliantly demonstrates our own historiographical beliefs about the instability and situatedness of knowledge. In fact, one could argue that without the evolution in historiographical thinking, maximum use of the Internet's capabilities as a research tool would not be possible. On the other hand, observing the canons of fair use (an extremely hazy concept in legal circles) and being careful about citations are absolutely essential in avoiding litigation over the use of copyrighted material, especially because, according to current copyright laws, almost everything written in the last eighty to one hundred years is still under copyright protection.[3] We thus are stuck with traditional footnoting and citation systems, not because they serve either our evolving historiographical assumptions or available digital research methods, but because they (may) save us from a lawsuit we cannot afford.

The conflict between copyright law and Internet creativity is a complex legal tangle that I do not pretend to understand completely, but it does seem important for scholars to be aware of both the promises and the pitfalls of digital research and scholarly production, and I hope that our field and others will find ways to participate in the public debate about these subjects. In the meantime, I'd like to add some more microcosmic developments to the mix, developments that are already here and already disrupting the traditional ways of identifying evidence and citing sources.

My first example is the identification and citation of sources purchased on eBay, the online auction site. While I have found eBay to be a gold mine for discovering—and in some cases purchasing—early-twentieth-century editions of Shakespeare for my own research, I have learned that in most instances the sellers on eBay have little understanding of what they're offering. Some think an edition of a Shakespeare play that predates 1970 is "rare" or "vintage"; others seem to have no idea how to discover a book's copyright date. While the latter is a minor problem that can usually be solved by a visit to the *National Union Catalogue,* a more serious difficulty arises with unpublished materials. For example, I bid on and won one of the *New York Times*'s special supplements on Shakespeare that was published in the spring of 1916. Along with it came lithographic reproductions of engravings of characters from Shakespeare's plays. These pictures are pasted on heavy paper and labeled "Shakespeare" or "Shakespeare's plays" in lovely copperplate handwriting. Perhaps they had been part of a school's or library's picture collection. Some appear to have come from one of the many editions of Charles and Mary Lamb's *Tales from Shakespeare,* while others have no provenance whatsoever. Given enough time and resources I could probably uncover the identity of the publishers and possibly the artists, but would that information get me any closer to answers to the questions raised in my mind by the way the pictures are mounted? Did these pictures hang in a classroom, library, or Shakespeare Club? Who were their intended viewers? What did viewers think about Shakespeare and his plays as a result of seeing them? That information seems lost forever. While I could cite these in a footnote or bibliography as coming from the "Author's Collection," or even as "purchased on eBay," or from a printed source I was lucky enough to track down, the engravings' rich history as cultural artifacts would be lost to future scholars.

My second example is the online encyclopedia Wikipedia. As you no doubt know, a wiki is a Web site or database whose entries are created, not by a single authority, but by the efforts of dozens, even thousands, of anonymous contributors who provide data, refine existing entries, or debate controversies within a topic. The idea is that from the sheer number of participants the entries will eventually become far more accurate and exhaustive than would be possible with a single author or small handful of authors. Wikipedia is, of course, controversial among academics at all levels of education as well as among the publishers of traditional, hard-copy encyclopedias.[4] My point about Wikipedia in the context of this essay is that its entries are constantly changing. To use a Wikipedia entry as a citation in an article or book that may take several months or even years to appear in print is to refer to something that may already be nonexistent, at least in the form in which the researcher originally found it. The traditional concept that a bibliography in a humanities work should enable the reader to reproduce the author's research process, much as a scientist can reproduce another's experiment, thus becomes meaningless. And, of course, there are myriad other Web sources that have the same or a greater degree of transience than Wikipedia and present the same problems regarding citation. Will scholars need to print out in hard copy every Web source that they may wish to use someday in order to document the source as it looked on the day it was accessed? What if the source is later changed or has information added to it? Will scholars have to keep accessing sources and then continue to update their work accordingly?

A third, more material challenge to the traditional citation system is the increasing reluctance of publishers to devote space in their books to extensive notes and bibliographies.[5] The footnote has already virtually disappeared, to be replaced by the notes gathered at the end of the book, where the reader has to memorize the note number and page number in order to find it among the dozens squeezed together there. For the same financial reasons, publishers are also reluctant to include extensive bibliographies, preferring shorter bibliographic essays or eliminating bibliographies entirely, leaving the reader to extract the sources from the notes. Some publishers have suggested that authors initiate Web sites where interested readers can find the bibliographic information, but the creation and maintenance of such sites would be left to the author or to the author's institution. If books were published entirely on the Internet there would be no problem in including extensive documentation, but thus far the e-book has not caught on to any great degree. Perhaps Google's scanning project, by bringing so many older works into wider availability on the Internet, will make the prospect of publishing new work on the Web more enticing.

So, while our family of disciplines—theatre history, theory, performance studies, and so forth—has successfully negotiated the leap from old to new approaches to scholarship, we, like others in the humanities, have not stopped to look at the consequences of that leap for the forms in which we deliver that work to our readers. As the *Chicago Manual of Style* and the *MLA Handbook* struggle to keep up with the rapidly evolving world of cyber sources, the notion that it is still possible to include meaningful citations in our scholarship has been left unchallenged. We accept the instability of knowledge as a foundational assumption in the content of our work, yet we ignore it in our scholarly apparatus.

Are there solutions to this dilemma that make sense for both the present and the not-so-distant future? The most feasible ones seem to require a thorough reformation of the U.S. copyright law. One suggestion I'd like to put forward is the virtual bookshelf that Kelly mentions in his article. Perhaps we should look upon bibliographies as journeys that have largely virtual destinations. Since sources are increasingly likely to change or disappear entirely, it may be necessary to judge a work's scholarship by the collection amassed electronically on the author's virtual bookshelf. This might include Web sources as they appeared at the particular time when the scholar accessed them; links to scanned books in their entirety; snippets of books, articles, and other items that were of interest to the researcher; annotations and comments found in other scholars' copies; redactions of resource material; and ideas, comments, and questions recorded by the researcher at each point in the research process. This virtual bookshelf could be submitted by doctoral students along with the dissertation itself in whatever form that may take. For scholars seeking to publish their work, the bookshelf could be a Web link provided along with a book or article, or, as we move more extensively into electronic publication, an appendage to the digitized book itself. And perhaps someday we will view the scholar's virtual bookshelf as having its own value as both an indicator of scholarly rigor and a historical document in its own right.

Notes

1. Kevin Kelly, "Scan This Book!" *New York Times Magazine*, May 14, 2006, 42–49, 65, 71. I am grateful to my Arizona State University colleague Tamara Underiner for alerting me to this article.

2. For a brief analysis of the pros and cons of digitization of books, see Katie Hafner, "History, Digitized (and Abridged)," *New York Times*, March 10, 2007, sec. 3:1.

3. For an eloquent analysis of the current copyright situation and its stifling effect on creativity, see Lawrence Lessig, *Free Culture: How Big Media Uses Technology and the Law to Lock Down Culture and Control Creativity* (New York: Penguin, 2004).

4. A brief summary of the controversy may be found in Eric Rauchway's article "Source Wars," *TNR Online*, March 21, 2007, http://www.tnr.com/doc.mhtml?i=w070319&s=rauchway032107.

5. For a fuller treatment of the decline of the footnote, see Chuck Zerby, *The Devil's Details: A History of Footnotes* (New York: Touchstone/Simon and Schuster, 2002); and Anthony Grafton, *The Footnote: A Curious History* (Cambridge: Harvard University Press, 1997). Both authors are primarily concerned with the future of the "content" footnote, in which an author makes a point not directly germane to the main argument or gives additional information or additional sources for the subject of the main text.

Period Rush

Affective Transfers in Recent Queer
Art and Performance

—TAVIA NYONG'O

In Terry Zwigoff's 2001 film, *Ghost World,* the malcontent Enid Coleslaw is firmly ensconced in the post-adolescent malaise her best friend, Rebecca, wants to grow out of. Tension erupts when Rebecca suggests they "pretend" to be yuppies. Enid acts out by dyeing her hair green and sporting a leather jacket. This response provokes Rebecca's outrage, and a smirk from Enid's nemesis, John Ellis, who sneers: "Oh my God, didn't they tell you? Punk rock is over. If you really want to fuck up the system, go to business school. That's what I'm gonna do. Get a job at some big corporation, like fuck things up from the inside." Enid's response to John is memorable for what it captures of the emotional alchemy through which queer and minoritized subjects negotiate subcultural histories: "God! Fuck you. . . . You know, its not like I'm some modern punk, dickhead. It's obviously like a 1977 original punk rock look. But I guess Johnny Fuckface is too stupid to realize it!"[1]

In distinguishing her respectful approach to punk from mere trendiness, Enid bids for insider status despite her age, gender, and suburban location. Scoffing at such a claim to authenticity would miss its spirit. In marking off her homage from derivative 1980s hardcore, Enid displays the ideological hairsplitting that is the genius and insolence of youth. Yet such stringent logic permits her to avoid the cynicism that her peers display toward subcultural histories. Enid and John float in the same cultural effluvia of suburban America, where the past is blandly recycled as kitsch, but Enid's sensibility stands out amidst such simulacra. She longs to maintain contact with a ghost world unlike her own, a world where it is she, not John, who truly understands that punk is dead.

What I will call the "affective transfer" Enid performs between past and present illuminates recent debates regarding the archive in performance. Where some scholars emphasize the autonomous transmission of embodied histories through performance,[2] I argue that Enid's subversive genealogy reflects less the difference *between* archive and repertoire than the difference *within both.* Her critique hinges upon the difference between reenactments that recycle the past as kitsch and those that renew the impact of historical emotion. Such affective transfers still occur in our post-historical times, fiercely attached to untimely feelings. They are postmodern, along the lines outlined by Lev Manovich, Fredric Jameson, and Sue-Ellen Case, but they do not succumb to the "end of history."[3]

Rather than simply end, history has transformed under conditions guided by new media and "the virtual." Case speaks of our living in the era of "The Great Upload" and argues that "previous practices of gender, sexuality, materiality, community, and corporeality have been uploaded into various new technological zones."[4] Manovich calls this the "spatialization" of historical time, which has "replaced sequential storage with random-access storage; hierarchical organization of information with flattened hypertext" and the "psychological movement of narrative in novels and cinema with physical movement through space." "In short," he concludes, "time became a flat image or a landscape, something to look at or navigate through."[5] Conceptual transfers from one media to another harbor this transformation.

Emphasizing affect pushes "the virtual" beyond new media, as Case's genealogy of the virtual in both theatre and science suggests. Affect calls attention to the synesthesia of past and present, as the flattened landscape of historical time becomes not only a space of interactivity but a zone of affective noise and distortion. Technological *effects* have correlative *affects.* As a form of temporal feedback, affective transfers resist the disorientation that sometimes accompanies conceptual transfer. Brian Massumi defines affects as "*virtual synesthetic perspectives* anchored in (functionally limited by) the actually existing, particular things that embody them."[6] Affective transfers are "anchored" in the unmooring of historical time itself; they perform our disorientation. They seek repoliticized perspectives amidst the virtual.

Queer theatre and performance depends upon affective transfers to sustain a particular slant on temporality and continuity.[7] Taylor Mac's play *Red Tide Blooming,* performed at PS122 in New York City in 2006, sought to rescue affective fragments of a queer past in a manner comparable to Enid's. In a kind of theatrical reverse gentrification, Mac plotted the apocalyptic end of Coney Island and of all the gender freaks and sexual outlaws who thrive in it. The play sprang from a commission to honor drag legend Ethyl Eichelberger, and while *Red Tide Blooming* reflects her influence, it also protests a future that would quarantine her difference in nostalgia.[8] Mac's cast thus did double duty, playing their roles in the farce before stepping out of character (and into yet other characters) at the conclusion in order to reflect upon the current pace of change in New York. Generational succession, epitomized in the casting of downtown icon Ruby Lynn Reyner, played a ghost note throughout Mac's madcap play. But historical fidelity only heightened the imperative to speak to present concerns. Even the surrogates for the past in the play reflected this interdependency. One older character mock-apologetically told the crowd that, although her generation didn't manage to change the world, they did at least invent glitter.

This vision of a virtual history still in the process of becoming contrasts with the traditional conception of history as "the past as it really was." Indeed, it exposes this traditional conception as a fetish. It seems to me that the conceptual transfers of post-historical time enable such encounters but do not of themselves politicize the past. "Navigating" through time is inherently ambivalent. It is not intrinsically queer, but it can be queered.

We encounter such queerings in recent art that engages the process reenactors employ to reconstruct the habitus of past wars.[9] They adopt the costumes, weapons, tactics, and sometimes even the foodstuffs, diseases, and names of past soldiers. Their hyperattentiveness to verisimilitude—expressed in hostility toward "deviations" such as modern eyewear or female soldiers—contrasts with the exhilarating abandon they feel in navigating the past as present. The Holy Grail of historical reenactment, reports artist Allison Smith, is what reenactors term "period rush": a powerful feeling of excitement, danger, or even fear when one has successfully downloaded into one's chosen historical moment. Period rush names a potentiality contained in a literally *regimented* framework. But even at its most literal-minded, a glimmer of the virtual can be discerned in this rush.

That reenactment, because of its regimentation, should be associated with political and cultural conservatism is less unusual than the fact that, nevertheless, progressive and queer artists remain drawn toward its possibilities. Jeremy Deller created *The Battle of Orgreave* (2001), a large-scale reenactment of a famous labor struggle from the 1980s. Like *Red Tide Blooming*, *Orgreave* commemorated a traumatic defeat. In a public forum about the event, Deller discussed the participation of politically conservative reenactors, recruited from various reenactment societies, who ostensibly supported the victors in this struggle.[10] Aware of the artist's politics, many still participated. The period rush of reenactment overcame other concerns, and focusing on historical fidelity helped them avoid the thorny questions the performance raised. Even for its participants, then, *Orgreave* remained ambivalent. But if reenactment risks reifying the past as it was, the transmission of affect permits us to reimagine as well as to repeat, inserting new subjectivities and new desires into familiar landscapes.

An embrace of the potentialities of the period rush characterizes two recent projects in queer art and performance: Allison Smith's participatory performance *The Muster* (2005) and Chris Vargas and Eric Stanley's film *Homotopia* (2006). Both projects approach the past through affective transfers that release the virtual element of an ostensibly settled historical record. Both do so by way of deviations that purist reenactors and traditional historians might scoff at. Participating in the spatialization of historical time, they resist its debilitating political effects, in part by highlighting the artifice of reenactment itself. Both draw from sources that are themselves reenactments, constructing a moebius strip in which the pursuit of the real forever turns back out on the side of the virtual.

The Muster gathered artists, intellectuals, and enthusiasts in the spring of 2005 for a two-day encampment on Governor's Island in New York City. Inspired by Civil War reenactors but demurring from their devotion to the politically confining details of the past, Smith issued a call to muster that asked each potential participant: "What are you fighting for?" Placing the onus upon the individual or small collective, reenactment changed from a pursuit of authentic detail to an active consideration of what the past meant to us, and how. Smith's call to arms invited recruits to "Conjure your insurgent grandparents, bra-burning aunts, funny uncles, and the trans-revolutionaries who have paved the way for your life's work. Summon your historical peers and chosen family throughout time, and the Causes for which they fought and bled."[11] As a participant observer I was struck by the intensity of homage to pasts real and imagined: a Civil War uniform entirely in hues of pink; an old-fashioned mail carrier delivering one of the few handwritten letters I have received in years. Insisting upon incongruity, *The Muster* challenged the reality effect of traditional reenactment.

The optimism of Smith's call ought not obviate what Jameson terms "the negative purpose" of any utopia.[12] A collective named Core[13] flew a sign quoting New Orleans's Sister Gertrude Morgan: "I No We Can Reign Here." An apocalyptic evangelical might seem an unlikely inspiration for a genderqueer and transfeminist collective, but the appropriateness of the slogan in its new context bespeaks the bleed of affect across identitarian and ideological boundaries. The substitution of "No" for "Know" reflected a spirit of negation secured to the utopian spirit. Much has been made recently of queer negativity,[14] but Core's homage suggests the compatibility between utopia and negation, based in the shared impulse to refuse a present context.

Plumbing even deeper into the affect of revolt, *Homotopia* also imagined a political utopianism for our dystopian present. Here reenactment was less as an organizational principle than a strip of behavior spliced into filmic structure. Also opening with a call to arms, *Homotopia* took a playful but politically disgusted stance toward the current normalization of lesbian and gay politics in the United States. The film's refusal was accomplished in part through an affective transfer of the spirit of rebelliousness. The most relevant example of this was the citations of Gillo Pontecorvo's Italian neorealist masterpiece, *The Battle of Algiers* (1966). Based on the Algerian War of Independence from France (1954–62), *The Battle of Algiers* was a fictional film shot in documentary style using mostly amateur actors.[15] As with Sister Gertrude Morgan, *The Battle of Algiers* makes an unlikely historical influence for contemporary queer art. And yet Vargas and Stanley successfully reinvented key moments in the original film, such as a harrowing sequence in which several Algerian women cut their hair, apply makeup, and transform their appearance into a "modern" look in order to infiltrate the French Quarter undetected and deliver their payload of explosive devices. Reminiscent of Enid's chameleonic shifts in *Ghost World,* Vargas and Stanley ingeniously adapted this scene into one where a band of gender outlaws assimilates their appearance to the norms of the deserving queer subject, all the better to disrupt an upcoming gay nuptial with their particular brand of chaos. Both Jasbir Puar and José Muñoz have written about the affinities between queer and terrorist bodies.[16] *Homotopia* playfully but seriously delves into the historical resonances of this affinity, signaling both the desperation and hope of the gender outlaw destined, like the insurrectionary citizens of Algiers, to lose the battle but perhaps not, ultimately, the war.

In these examples, to conclude, we encounter an affective engagement with the past that cannot be reduced to conservation or nostalgia. Enid does not want to become a 1970s punk, Smith a Civil War soldier (or reenactor), Vargas and Stanley subjects of French colonization. Rather, reenactment seeks a *presencing* of the past, locating it squarely in the virtual. We tend to associate the virtual with the future and the futuristic, but Case helps us see how it illuminates theatre and performance history as well. The demise of linear historical narrative, traditional and hierarchical archives, and a fidelity to the fact as objective and unalterable datum of the past has been much lamented.[17] What the politics of the period rush suggest, however, is that we are not in the position to opt out of the Great Upload. Our political imaginations must find their orientation not beyond but within its dynamic, guarding against any nostalgia for the historical foundations. History marches on, but glitter sticks in its floorboards.

Notes

1. My queer reading of the film is supported by the lesbian undercurrent in the Enid/Rebecca relationship that is made explicit in the graphic novel on which the film is based, and also by the transgender identification implied in Enid Coleslaw's very name, which is an anagram of the name of her male creator. Daniel Clowes, *Ghost World* (Seattle: Fantagraphics, 1998).

2. Paul Connerton, *How Societies Remember* (Cambridge: Cambridge University Press, 1989).

3. Lev Manovich, *The Language of New Media* (Cambridge: MIT Press, 2001); Fredric Jameson, *Postmodernism, or, the Cultural Logic of Late Capitalism* (Durham: Duke University Press, 1991); Sue-Ellen Case, *Performing Science and the Virtual* (New York: Routledge, 2006).

4. Case, *Performing Science,* 5.

5. Manovich, *Language of New Media,* 47, 78.

6. Brian Massumi, *Parables for the Virtual: Movement, Affect, Sensation (Post-Contemporary Interventions)* (Durham: Duke University Press, 2002), 35.

7. See also Judith Halberstam, *In a Queer Time and Place: Transgender Bodies, Subcultural Lives* (New York: New York University Press, 2005).

8. Joe Jeffreys, "An Outré Entrée into the Para-Ridiculous Histrionics of Drag Diva Ethyl Eichelberger: A True Story," *Theatre History Studies* 14 (1994): 23–41.

9. On historical reenactment in living museums see Scott Magelssen, "Performance Practices of [Living] Open-Air Museums (and a New Look at 'Skansen' in American Living Museum Discourse," *Theatre History Studies* 24 (2004): 125–49.

10. *Clark Symposium: A Historic Occasion: The Uses of History in Contemporary Art,* Sterling and Francine Clark Art Institute, Williamstown, Massachusetts, February 23–24, 2007.

11. Allison Smith, *The Muster: A Project of the Public Art Fund* (New York: Public Art Fund, 2007), 47.

12. Fredric Jameson, *Archaeologies of the Future: The Desire Called Utopia and Other Science Fictions* (New York: Verso, 2005), 7. I am grateful to Tianna Kennedy for leading me to this source.

13. Core consisted of Ginger Brooks Takahashi, Math Bass, Leidy Churchman, Ryder Cooley, Bruce Mingles, Edie Fake, Megan Palaima, Pony, and James Tsang.

14. Lee Edelman, *No Future: Queer Theory and the Death Drive* (Durham: Duke University Press, 2004).

15. *The Battle of Algiers* became a touchstone for the left and even has its admirers in the

military-industrial complex, who screen it as a cautionary document of urban insurrection. Like *Orgreave, The Battle of Algiers* is unquestionably on the side of the rebels, but its vivid and imaginative accuracy does not lead to a single propagandistic message.

16. Jasbir Puar, "Monster, Terrorist, Fag: The War on Terrorism and the Production of Docile Patriots," *Social Text* 72 (2002): 117–48; José Esteban Muñoz, *Disidentifications: Queers of Color and the Performance of Politics* (Minneapolis: University of Minnesota Press, 1999).

17. See the debate reprised in Keith Jenkins, ed., *The Postmodern History Reader* (London: Routledge, 1997).

Goon, Warrior, Communitarian, and Mythos

The Lincoln Legend of Dramatic Literature
and Live Performance

—SCOTT R. IRELAN

Roy Basler offers a noteworthy if not comprehensive distinction between historicized Lincoln biographical narratives and the Lincoln Legend, postulating that the former "is a catalogue of detached facts, which have no other connection than time, place, circumstance, and cause, and effect," while the latter is the "creation of actions according to the unchangeable forms of human nature, as existing in the mind of the creator, which is itself the image of all other minds."[1] To be sure, the image of Lincoln that resides in the hearts and minds of many today is not significantly influenced by biographers present or past, because "Abraham Lincoln" is largely a mythic construction that plays fast and loose with specific historicized lived experiences while ignoring others.

To better illustrate how the Lincoln Legend reveals itself within dramatic literature and live performance, this survey delineates four points of reference: Lincoln the Yankee Goon, Lincoln the Warrior, Lincoln the Communitarian, and Lincoln the Mythos. Before continuing, I should note three conditions that frame my work. First, I limit my discussion to play texts appearing in print and/ or performance between 1861 and 1962 within the portion of North America known as the United States. I stop with 1962 because of the new directions politics, critical thought, and theatre take up in the form of the Cuban Missile Crisis and the CIA's escalating involvement in Vietnam, Thomas Kuhn's "paradigm shift," and the budding underground movement in New York City.[2] Second, Lincoln must appear in a scene at least once over the course of the play text. Third, I freely borrow both language and concepts from existing Lincoln studies scholarship, tempering them with that of theatre and American studies so as to chart a course through an interdisciplinary landscape rarely traversed.[3]

Lincoln the Yankee Goon

The Yankee Goon plays are derisive satires penned between 1861 and 1863 by either Southerners or Copperheads who are wary not only of Lincoln's prairie ingenuity but also of his political motives. Similar to Royall Tyler's Jonathan, a "true born Yankee American son of liberty," the Yankee Goon possesses a simple wit and otherwise mirrors a rube-like frontier worldview as head of state.[4] Distinct from the naively optimistic Jonathan, the Yankee Goon appears to be a dour dunce put in place by much savvier constituents of the Republican Party who set him up as their "fall man" for ineffectual policies. Sometimes he is prone to heavy drinking and womanizing, while at other times he is spineless and looking out only for the welfare of himself and his immediate family. Regardless, the Yankee Goon is out of his element as commander in chief. As the comically embellished core of "Northern values," his homespun cunning is innately second-rate when put side by side with the affectations of those from the Confederate States of America. It is the manipulation of Lincoln by those around him that gives the Yankee Goon a piteous quality. This gangster of ghastly grandiosity delights Southerners and Copperheads alike, who find in his lesser traits that which will lead to the ultimate demise of Northern antagonism.

Though it seems that the Yankee Goon first appears as a guilt-ridden, suicidal fool in Stephen Miller's 1861 closet drama *Ahab Lincoln: A Tragedy of the Potomac,*[5] it is not until John Hewitt's 1863 *King Linkum the First* that a Yankee Goon play clearly meant for live theatrical performance emerges.[6] Set in Washington, D.C., the burletta seeks not only to account for the rise of the Royal Linkums but also to project an imminent fall from grace. In usual burletta form, the piece has three acts, farcically deals with both legend and historicized details, and has (depending on your point of view, of course) the requisite happy ending. With Confederate victories at Secessionville (South Carolina), Harper's Ferry (Virginia), and Chickasaw Bayou (Mississippi) prior to the live performance event in Augusta, Georgia, Hewitt's rendering is certainly not surprising.

At rise King Linkum takes his morning coffee in a drawing room of the

Figure 1. "Tricks v. Honours," *Fun,* July 18, 1863. A Confederate soldier with the names of the battles the South has won on his uniform tells a cowering Lincoln to try something new. Courtesy of the Indiana Historical Society Jack Smith Lincoln Graphics Collection.

Executive Mansion. He is nostalgic for Illinois, saying: "Enough I have had of lofty sitting / Oh for the days of fence-rail splitting!"[7] Shortly thereafter, Queen Mother enters with Prince Bob. The prince is a spoiled brat who drinks and gambles, spending most of his father's money on women. Queen Mother, always in control of King Linkum, reminds him that Bob is a special boy who is entitled to a life of elite encounters. So, says she, "Fork over Abe,—boys must have money."[8] Abe, as always, capitulates. Before exiting, Prince Bob sings of his forays, fancies, and foppery in the Northern kingdom. For the rest of the play, the Royal Linkums drink, sing, and demean their lessers. Eventually, the king, after a dream visit from Black Ghost and Ghost of Credit, elects to take his family and flee the Executive Mansion. Strains of "Dixie" are heard. They are spotted by Confederate forces, and a cannonball "passes over the stage and knocks the King down."[9] The tyrant Linkum and his entourage are killed. Miraculously, though, they all come back to life, singing: "Yankee Doodle, you're no go / Racked by feuds and cabels; / Tho' you rant and sputter so / You can't put down the rebels!"[10] As with all Yankee Goon plays, the candor of *King Linkum* is far from subtle and reflects Confederate wartime fervor. As expectations of swift victory by the Confederate States of America precipitously slip away shortly after the fall of Vicksburg in 1863, and as Lincoln "the man" proved to be anything but an ill-bred lout, Yankee Goon depictions were no longer viable. Other examples include William Russell Smith's acerbic *The Royal Ape*[11] and Steven Carpenter's *The Irrepressible Conflict,* released as a serial in the *Wisconsin Patriot*[12] just prior to the Emancipation Proclamation's becoming law.[13]

Lincoln the Warrior

After his death on Holy Saturday 1865, it took two years for the apotheosis of Lincoln to find its way into dramatic literature in the form of Lincoln the Warrior. These depictions can be subdivided into Lincoln the Warrior-Savior of the Union and Lincoln the Warrior-Emancipator of Enslaved Peoples; the division is determined by textual allusions to either the importance of saving the Union at whatever cost or accepting whatever cost to free enslaved peoples. This difference, while quite subtle, is grounded in an ongoing dialogue in Lincoln studies.[14] Whether Warrior-Savior or Warrior-Emancipator, Lincoln the Warrior is a self-made intellectual who wins the hearts and minds of friends and foes alike with wit. He is a great conversationalist who uses personal anecdotes to get his point across. While he does not take up weapons per se, he always fights for the best interest of the country as prescribed by the Constitution. Lincoln the Warrior is often a deeply religious Christian who is keenly aware of U.S. history, regularly quoting the Bible to support his decisions. A wise humanitarian, he is slow to anger and always prizes the lives of others over his own. Often, his brief time as captain during the Black Hawk Indian War(s) is referenced to invoke a "traditional" warrior spirit. In the end, Lincoln the Warrior dramas are most involved in exploring the confluence of prophecy and martyrdom.

All indications are that Stephen Downey's 1867 *The Play of Destiny as Played by the Actors from the Kingdom of the Dead in the Theatre of the Universe* is the

Figure 2. "In Memory of Abraham Lincoln. The Reward of the Just." Creator, D. T. Weist, 1865. Publisher, William Smith, Philadelphia. In this lithograph Lincoln is surrounded by angels, Columbia, an American Indian, and an eagle with a shield. Courtesy of the Indiana Historical Society Jack Smith Lincoln Graphics Collection.

earliest Warrior characterization as well as the initial Lincoln Legend play to appear after assassination.[15] Performed in five acts, it is meant to "perpetuate and keep green the memory of Abraham Lincoln in the hearts of the American people."[16] Given this, the action encompasses Lincoln's inauguration, Southern secession, the Emancipation Proclamation, and the end of the war, Lincoln's assassination, and the capture of John Wilkes Booth. A narrator introduces each act in prose, while all characters—including the ghosts of George Washington, John Brown, and Joan of Arc—speak in verse. This melodrama clearly implicates Jefferson Davis, John Wilkes Booth, and General Breckenridge in the plot against Lincoln and his cabinet. Near the play's end, just before *Our American Cousin* begins in Ford's Theatre, Lincoln conveys his gratitude to all who fought so hard for the restoration of national harmony.[17] He is then shot. As with successive nineteenth-century Warrior plays, Downey's Lincoln is a sacrificial victim for the ages. Others include Hiram Torrie's *The Tragedy of Abraham Lincoln*,[18] Cyrenus Osborne Ward's *The Great Rebellion*,[19] J. W. Rogers's *Madame Surratt*,[20] and William A. Luby's *John Wilkes Booth; or The National Tragedy*.[21] These are sensational, heroic melodramas, sated with spies, conspiracy theories, and Christ-centered ethics.

It appears that Lincoln the Warrior did not make its way into live theatrical performance until 1915, when Ethel Theodora Rockwell's *The Freeport Pageant of the Black Hawk Country* presented Senate candidate Lincoln professing, "I'm in this campaign to save this country of ours" because "she's sick."[22] Another early-twentieth-century Warrior play of note is Thomas Dixon's *A Man of the People*,[23] which focuses on the "great spirit" (God) that binds together a "great people" (whites) while overlooking the fact that some among the population (non-whites) are in great suffering.[24] Given Dixon's *Birth of a Nation* proclivities, *A Man of the People* seems to give Lincoln the position of keeper of whiteness through his self-identification as a proud citizen from Southern bloodlines.[25] Nearly twenty years later, Paul Horgan's *Yours, A. Lincoln*[26] featured a diffident servant who is "trying to make peace under any circumstances" in order to stop needless carnage.[27] Told mostly in flashback, Mark Van Doren's *The Last Days of Lincoln* offers much the same.[28] Norman Corwin's *The Rivalry* features Lincoln extolling the virtues of emancipation because of "the monstrous injustice of slavery."[29] The play makes it clear that emancipation from all forms of servitude is fundamental to U.S. democratic liberty. In the end, the overwhelming obsession with conspiracy and assassination distinguishes nineteenth-century Warrior plays from those of the twentieth century, which are more concerned with broader looks at Lincoln Legend material.

Lincoln the Communitarian

This rendering of Lincoln Legend material heightens several factors innate to Warrior portrayals. However, Lincoln the Communitarian is rarely, if ever, exclusively focused on saving the Union or freeing enslaved peoples. Rather, he is wrapped up in using his actions and thoughts within the world of the play to not only influence humankind but also to protect animals, children, and anyone he perceives to be less fortunate than himself. Whether as a teenager or as president, the Communitarian has no need for affluence or authority. He is, in general, a voracious reader of history and religion. Like the Warrior, he values others' lives over his own and clearly discriminates between right and wrong, his moral compass based largely on a frontier ethic learned while growing up in Kentucky and southern Indiana. No one and no thing is too insignificant for Lincoln the Communitarian. His is a way of life that young and old should emulate.

Appearing in 1912, Constance D'Arcy Mackay's *Abraham Lincoln: Rail Splitter* is one of the earliest examples of Lincoln the Communitarian.[30] The play, which begins when Abe is just fourteen, presents a charitable, hardworking, empathetic young man motivated by learning. Two years later, Mary Hazelton Wade's *Abraham Lincoln,* which shows an eleven-year-old Lincoln, offers much the same. In this case, though, young Lincoln senses that he will be a great man.[31] Both plays express several Warrior sentiments, but the Communitarian can be seen in the way the young, pre-political Lincoln interacts with those around him. In 1923, W. W. Davies's *Transfusion* shows a mature Communitarian whose distinct spirituality comes from blending ancestral voices found within U.S. history books with his devotion to a Christian God. *Transfusion,* like *A Man of the People,* suggests that superior bloodlines allow the Communitarian to rise to national prominence. Unlike *A Man of the People,* however, *Transfusion* places greater emphasis on the transference of status and abilities from President Washington to Lincoln. Admittedly, *Transfusion* reads like a Warrior play until the closing scene, "The Might-Have-Been," which imagines the final days of a second-term Lincoln who remains "inspired with the spirit" he "gave out everywhere."[32] In this case, Lincoln is guided by his love of the Constitution, his esteem for President Washington, and the morals bestowed upon him in his youth.

With Harold Winsor Gammans's *Spirit of Ann Rutledge* (1927) we see an adult Communitarian deriving a sense of strength and reserve from his eternal connection to his first love, Ann Rutledge. Arriving in spirit form at play's end to help Lincoln cross over, Ann assures him that his legacy "shall live forever and ever."[33] Henry Thomas's 1939 monologue play *Lincoln's Last Soliloquy* offers much the same, only it is Mary Todd and not Ann who helps this Communitarian rise above his frontier beginnings.[34] Four years later, Robert Knipe's *And There Were Voices* presents a Communitarian who wanders the prairie alone for weeks until he comes to terms with the need to use God-given talents to address the well-being of the struggling nation.[35] Kermit Hunter celebrates the Communitarian's importance to New Salem, Illinois, in *Forever This Land* (1951),[36] and roughly a decade later, Richard Berstein and John Allen's *Young Abe Lincoln* uses the strength derived from Ann and their life together in New Salem in order to launch into his national public life.[37] Regardless of style, form, or decade, Lincoln the Communitarian "recognizes the fundamental nature of America's experiment in self-government, its inherent opportunities through which he was able to fulfill himself, and his willingness to participate in his community to maintain his political heritage for others."[38]

Lincoln the Mythos

Lincoln the Mythos personifies the fundamental nature of the American experience and, as such, has the ability to rise above limitations of gender, sex, ethnic, and racial stereotypes in order to speak directly to our social consciousness as "a symbol of democracy and freedom."[39] While at times acting as both Warrior and Communitarian, Lincoln the Mythos is tied more to the values, feelings, and faith that comprise prevailing notions of U.S. democratic morality than to anything else. As a result, Lincoln the Mythos is free to question and even harshly critique an existing state of affairs. In effect, what makes Lincoln the Mythos so compelling is the way in which historicized Lincoln-like ideals appeal to broader concerns and not just to those of the characters living within the world of the play. Often pushing Lincoln Legend material into a fully allegorical function, Lincoln the Mythos routinely works in some way to salve wounds, calm anxieties, or impart a sense of hope for the future.

Martin Bunge's 1911 *Abraham Lincoln* initiates Mythos depictions. Set before thoughts of the presidency and empowered by the love of Ann, Lincoln pledges himself "to do justice and love to all, malice to none."[40] Subtitled *A Historical Drama in Four Acts,* plot points and character elements match those of the Communitarian. However, subtle clues imbedded within discussions of labor relations and fair wages reveal Lincoln the Mythos attending to the pains of a quickly mechanizing twentieth century. Toward the end of World War I, Lincoln and Washington are brought together in William Chauncey Langdon's *The Masque of the Titans of Freedom.*[41] Performed under the auspices of University of Illinois War Committee on May 30, 1918, the play establishes Lincoln as the omniscient spirit of the United States, a revered guide of democratic rights, and the protector of all soldiers dutifully fighting to defend these principles both abroad and at home. This Mythos drama is also unique in that it is the first to present a wholly supernatural force not tied to historicized, earthbound settings of all previous depictions.

Figure 3. "Washington and Lincoln (Apotheosis)." Carte de visite of Lincoln being embraced by President Washington. Entered according to Act of Congress in the year 1865, by J. A. Arthur, in the Clerk's Office of the District Court for the Eastern District of Pennsylvania. S. J. Ferris, Pinxt. Photo and Pub. by Phil. Pho. Co., 730 Chestnut Street. Courtesy of the author.

Wide ranging in style and content, Mythos dramas of the 1930s reflect a "pressing need to find answers to the riddles" of the day.[42] Clarence Gallup's 1931 *Abraham Lincoln* gives us a self-effacing servant of democracy beheld by many as "the martyr whose blood, as so many articulate words, pleads for fidelity, for law, for liberty."[43] Henry Bailey Stevens's *Lincoln Reckons Up* (1934) features Lincoln the Mythos as a soul trapped in "The Hall of Fame in the Hereafter" and concludes that even in death he cannot rest, because Reconstruction was never fully realized.[44] Edgar Caper's 1931 marionette play "Lincoln and the Pig" also handles remnants of failed Reconstruction.[45] So great is the misery in the Hoover era that Arthur Goodman wonders what might have happened in *If Booth Had Missed* (1932). Subtitled *A Drama for the Reconstruction Period,* the Broadway play is more about indicting the failures of a corrupt, out-of-touch federal government for the Depression than anything else.[46] The radical nature of Goodman's Lincoln previews those to come during Franklin Delano Roosevelt's second presidential term. These include Howard Koch's *The Lonely Man* (1937), in which Lincoln is reincarnated as a professor in southeastern Kentucky during the "Bloody Harlan" coal strikes; E. P. Conkle's *Prologue to Glory* (1938), which speaks to New Deal masculinity; and Robert E. Sherwood's *Abe Lincoln in Illinois* (1939), which has Lincoln articulating the doctrine of New Deal democracy in a way that helps crystallize Roosevelt as the Lincoln Democrat he so often claimed to be in the media.[47] At no other time before or since does the Lincoln Legend of dramatic literature and live performance serve such an essential function, tied both to cultural production and national identity negotiation in what Alfred Kazin identifies as a "passionate addiction to Lincoln."[48] Though numerous Communitarian and Warrior dramas were written between Roosevelt's 1940 election and the bombing of Pearl Harbor, after *Abe Lincoln in Illinois* closed its national tour, nearly twenty years pass before another newly conceived Mythos depiction appears.

Closing Thoughts

So, why should we concern ourselves with the study of the Lincoln Legend of dramatic literature and live performance? Do we really need to add one more stage character to the likes of the Yankee, Indian, Negro, Frontiersman, and so forth? Certainly these conceptions cannot attend to our daily lived experiences. Nevertheless, each of the types discussed here grew out of interconnected regional, national, and sometimes international concerns during a time of great uncertainty not unlike our own. Couple this with our ever-expanding conceptions of "liveness," "theatre," and "performance," and the Lincoln Legend of dramatic literature and live performance indeed persists as an ideal site of exploration. In fact, in the nearly five years it has taken me to get to this point in my exploration, our geopolitical landscape has shifted considerably. President Bush landed on the USS *Abraham Lincoln,* declaring the mission in Iraq accomplished; Donald Rumsfeld likened the discord in Iraq to that of the 1860s friction between North and South; and Barack Obama, whose parallels with Lincoln have been well noted, announced his presidential candidacy on the steps of the Old Statehouse in Springfield, Illinois. Beyond these cultural performances of Lincoln the Mythos, dramatic texts such as Suzan-Lori Parks's *The America Play* and *Topdog/Underdog* continue to experiment with the interrelationship between "the recycling of specific narratives and the recycling of specific characters," especially those central to both Lincoln Legend material and U.S. national identity.[49] As Terry Eagleton notes, "whenever we are confronted with a sign, object or event, something else must already have happened for this to be possible."[50] If our current cultural moment continuously marks its need for the Lincoln Legend in such discernible and detectable ways, then a sustained spirit of inquiry ought to accompany it.

Notes

1. Roy P. Basler, *The Lincoln Legend: A Study in Changing Conceptions* (Boston: Houghton Mifflin, 1935), 306.
2. Lawrence Freedman, *Kennedy's Wars: Berlin, Cuba, Laos, and Vietnam* (New York: Oxford University Press, 2000); Thomas Kuhn, *The Structure of Scientific Revolutions* (Chicago: University of Chicago Press, 1962); Stephen J. Bottoms, *Playing Underground: A Critical History of the 1960s Off-Off Broadway Movement* (Ann Arbor: University of Michigan Press, 2004).
3. I would be remiss if I did not mention Bruce Nary's "The Study of Major Lincoln Dramas in Relationship to Selected Lincoln Biographies" (Ph.D. diss., University of Michigan, 1956) and Ruis Woertendyke's "The Character of Abraham Lincoln as He Has Been Portrayed in the American Theatre from 1861 to 1987" (Ph.D. diss., New York University, 1991), which have been of great assistance in my journey thus far. While they are related inasmuch as they look at Lincoln and dramatic literature, my work transcends theirs through its explicit use of Lincoln studies language and concepts and the reliance on tenets of both New Historicism and cultural materialism in making distinctions between these four character types.
4. Royall Tyler, "The Contrast," in *American Drama: Colonies to Contemporary,* ed. Stephen Watt and Gary Richardson (New York: Harcourt College Publishers, 1995), 38.
5. Stephen Franks Miller, *Ahab Lincoln: A Tragedy of the Potomac* (1861; reprint, Chicago: The Civil War Round Table, 1958). The play is one extended scene between President Ahab Lincoln, Secretary of State Seward, Lt. General Scott, Jefferson Davis, Confederate Vice President Stephens, and Confederate Brigadier General Beauregard. Something of a courtroom drama, it takes place in a public room in Alexandria. The play opens with Lincoln revealing that he was "smuggled by officious and misguided friends" into the "Presidential canvass as champion / Of the black man's rights" (7). He is a man who is scared, full of melancholy, and longing to return to his frontier life: "I find myself a prisoner, doomed and helpless. / My scepter holds none but broken sway, / And rank rebellion hath defied my power" (10). Ahab Lincoln is a befuddled, self-loathing weakling who regrets the death and destruction incurred since not accepting the initial Confederate compromise. So distraught is he that he "stabs himself and dies" (16). Having wit-

nessed Lincoln's suicide and his office "cast on Hamlin, / With negro blood is said to be defiled" (16), General Scott begs for mercy on his soul before driving his sword through his heart. With the two lifeless bodies on the floor, President Davis and Vice President Stephens leave as General Beauregard "remains standing with folded arms, reverently gazing on the face of Gen. Scott" (21).

6. John Hill Hewitt, *King Linkum the First: As Performed at the Concert Hall, Augusta, Georgia, February 23, 1863*, ed. Richard Barksdale Hewitt (Atlanta: Emory University Library, 1947).

7. Ibid., 13.

8. Ibid., 14.

9. Ibid., 31.

10. Ibid., 32.

11. William Russell Smith, *The Royal Ape* (Richmond: West and Johnston, 1863). Set in Washington City, this five-act drama written in heroic couplets is a vicious send-up portraying Lincoln as a crazy-eyed monarch and a rampant womanizer who drinks too much. The play often leaves Lincoln and his family to their follies while celebrating the gallantry of the Confederate States of America. As the play comes to a close, the royals are running from the Battle of Manassas when they receive news that Confederate forces will not make it all the way into Washington City. Robert, dressed in drag to hide from the enemy, runs into his father, still in his scotch cap disguise, and they make their way back to the Executive Mansion with Kate, Kitty, and Mrs. Lincoln in tow. The last line gives us the title. Robert says, "I'd play'd the girl, and Dad, he play'd the ape" (85).

12. S. D. Carpenter, *The Irrepressible Conflict* (1862; reprint, New York: Judd Stewart, 1914). Abraham the First is a "tall, and jocose Sucker Barrister" (10). After a closed-door meeting at the Wigwam in Chicago, he finds himself chosen "King" of the Republican Party by delegates because, even though dimwitted, he is a "bear" in barroom brawls. Realizing that he has ascended to the throne through the devious workings of the Cormorants, he drinks. He drinks a lot, actually. Once safely in the Federal Mecca, Abraham the First reveals his insatiability through asides, informs a group of ex-slaves who visit the royal palace that they are "much inferior to our noble race" and as such "must be slaves" (36–37), and protests signing the Emancipation Proclamation, ultimately signing it only to keep his throne. The play concludes with the cabinet in a fistfight and the now-melancholy Lincoln pleading for them to stop "strewing blood and hair about my virtuous court" (53). Carpenter's epilogue reads: "May God in the future forbid such exhibitions, / And rid the country of such politicians, / Lest they our rights and liberties destroy, / Is the ardent prayer of the Carrier Boy" (53).

13. While William Bush's *The Young Republican; or The Sixteenth President* (Washington, D.C.: Library of Congress, 1871) appears to be of this type, I am hesitant to definitively categorize it as such, because I cannot clearly tell whether my impressions are derived from the playwright's intent or poor playwriting attempting nothing more than historical drama. See also Woertendyke, "Character of Abraham Lincoln," 19–22.

14. Lincoln studies scholars, at times, still discuss Lincoln "the man" and his decision making in terms of either saving the Union or freeing enslaved Africans but not quite both simultaneously. See Basler, *The Lincoln Legend*, 202–27.

15. Steven W. Downey, *The Play of Destiny as Played by Actors from the Kingdom of the Dead in the Theatre of the Universe* (New Creek, W.V.: Steven W. Downey, 1867).

16. Ibid., 3.

17. Ibid., 60.

18. Hiram Torrie, *The Tragedy of Abraham Lincoln in Five Acts by an American Artist* (Glasgow: James Brown and Son, 1876). The pensive Lincoln places his life in God's hands, fears little in his earthbound existence, and mentions even less about preserving the Union. This Lincoln Legend drama ends post-assassination with Booth being shot and killed by Union soldiers and is most concerned with the ills of the Confederacy. Torrie's abhorrence of the South and its implicit guilt in Lincoln's death is scathing.

19. Cyrenus Osborne Ward, *The Great Rebellion: Reminiscence of the Struggle That Cost a Million Lives* (New York: C. Osborne Ward, 1881). What makes *The Great Rebellion* distinctive among all late-nineteenth-century Lincoln Legend dramas is the closing stage direction: "Play closes, with a transfiguration scene, embracing tablaux; also a magnificent stereopticon view of a panoramic ascension or apotheosis, representing Lincoln in the arms of Washington" (126).

20. J. W. Rogers, *Madame Surratt: A Drama in Five Acts, The Magazine of History* (1879; reprint, New York: William Abbatt, 1912. Extra No. 20). Act 1, scene 2 distinguishes this drama from the others. Set in Arlington Cemetery as two sentinels guard the gate, a cadre of ghosts, including George Washington, Pocahontas, Chief Powhatan, Columbus, and John Brown, grieve over the Civil War. In a grand display of Americana, the entire scene is full of singing and speeches that preview what will become known as pageant plays in the early twentieth century.

21. William A. Luby, *John Wilkes Booth; or The National Tragedy* (1880; reprint, Kalamazoo, Mich.: Kalamazoo Publishing Company, 1914). As the title suggests, Luby features the assassination conspiracy and tracks Booth's involvement in it.

22. Ethel Theodora Rockwell, *The Freeport Pageant of the Blackhawk Country* (Madison, Wisc.: Ethel Theodora Rockwell, 1915), 36.

23. Thomas Dixon, *A Man of the People* (New York: D. Appleton, 1920). The show opened at the Bijou Theatre on September 7, 1920. Best known at the time for his novel *The Clansman*, which he and D. W. Griffith adapted into *The Birth of a Nation*, Dixon keeps the blatant racism of both his book and movie in check within *A Man of the People*, but such is the perspective from which this Warrior drama is derived. At this point the term *racism* still refers to blood heritage and family/clan lineage. It is only subsequent to the Nazi appropriation of U.S. eugenics research for use as a mass-murder tool that the word is habitually equated with physical features.

24. It is never more obvious who the "great people" are than when Lincoln is talking with a delegation of freed slaves. The stage direction states, "The ebony faces with their cream white teeth showing in smiles and their wide rolling eyes make a striking contrast to the rugged face and poise of the President" (Dixon, *Man of the People*, 48). Dixon reveals earlier that "they are typical Africans" (47) who revere Lincoln as their savior-leader and "Father."

25. As Dixon writes, "While the popular conception of Lincoln as the Liberator of the Slave is true historically, there is a deeper view of his life and character. He was the savior, if not the real creator, of the American Union of free Democratic States. His proclamation of emancipation was purely an incident of war. The first policy of his administration was to save the Union. To this fact we owe a united Nation to-day. It is this truth of history which I try to make a living reality in my play" (ibid., vii).

26. Paul Horgan, *Yours, A. Lincoln* (New York: Experimental Theatre, 1942). Produced by the Experimental Theatre, directed by Robert Ross, and appearing at the Schubert, the play is based on Otto Eisenschiml's book *Why Was Lincoln Murdered?*

27. "Experimental Theatre Offers 'Yours, A. Lincoln,' With Vincent Price in the Leading Role, for a Matinee at the Shubert," *New York Times*, July 10, 1942. *Yours, A. Lincoln* closed after only two performances—one meant only for industry professionals, the other to benefit the Stage Relief and Actors Funds. This short run had more to do with the goals of the Experimental Theatre—which the Dramatists' Guild and Actors Equity founded for plays and actors that might not otherwise be heard on Broadway—than with the quality of the Legend performance event.

28. Mark Van Doren, *The Last Days of Lincoln* (New York: Hill-Wang, 1959).

29. Norman Corwin, *The Rivalry* (New York: Dramatists Play Service Inc., 1960), 17.

30. Constance D'Arcy Mackay, *Abraham Lincoln: Rail Splitter* (New York: Henry Holt, 1912).

31. Mary Hazelton Wade, *Abraham Lincoln* (Boston: Gornam Press, 1914), 59.

32. W. W. Davies, *Transfusion* (Louisville: John P. Morton, 1923), 55.

33. Harold Winsor Gammans, *Spirit of Ann Rutledge: A Drama of Abraham Lincoln in Four Acts* (New York: Samuel French, 1927), 66.

34. Henry Thomas, *Lincoln's Last Soliloquy* (Boston: Walter H. Baker, 1939).

35. Robert Knipe, *And There Were Voices* (Boston: Baker's Plays, 1943).

36. Kermit Hunter, *Forever This Land* (Petersburg, Ill.: New Salem Lincoln League, 1951).

37. Richard Berstein and John Allen, *Young Abe Lincoln,* music by Victor Ziskin, lyrics by Joan Javits, special lyrics and dialogue by Arnold Sundgaard (New York: Golden Records, 1961).

38. Frank J. Williams, *Judging Lincoln* (Carbondale: Southern Illinois University Press, 2002), 156.

39. Basler, *The Lincoln Legend,* 296.

40. Martin L. Bunge, *Abraham Lincoln: A Historical Drama in Four Acts* (Milwaukee: Milwaukee Press, 1911), 38.

41. William Chauncey Langdon, *The Masque of the Titans of Freedom: George Washington, Abe Lincoln,* music by John Lawrence Erb (Urbana: University of Illinois, 1918), 22.

42. John Dos Passos, *The Ground We Stand On: Some Examples from the History of a Political Creed* (New York: Harcourt Brace Jovanovich, 1941), 3.

43. Clarence M. Gallup, *Abraham Lincoln* (Providence: Clarence M. Gallup, 1931), 26. What distinguishes Gallup's play is the wrestling match with Buck Legree, for in Harriet Beecher Stowe's *Uncle Tom's Cabin* Legree is the given last name of the slave owner Simon. By having Lincoln pummel Legree, Gallup points to Lincoln the Mythos's ability to trounce servitude.

44. Henry Bailey Stevens, *Lincoln Reckons Up* (Boston: Walter H. Baker, 1934), 7.

45. Edgar Caper, "Lincoln and the Pig" (Detroit: Paul McPharlin, 1931).

46. Arthur Goodman, *If Booth Had Missed: A Drama of the Reconstruction Period* (New York: Samuel French, 1932).

47. Howard Koch, *The Lonely Man* (Washington, D.C.: National Service Bureau, 1937); E. P. Conkle, *Prologue to Glory: A Play in Eight Scenes Based on the New Salem Years of Abraham Lincoln* (New York: Samuel French, 1938); Robert E. Sherwood, *Abe Lincoln in Illinois* (New York: Scribner, 1939). The in-depth exploration of these three plays is the

crux of my dissertation, "Plays, Production, and Politics: The Lincoln Legend of Dramatic Literature and Performance as Staged during FDR's Second Presidential Term by the Federal Theatre and the Playwright's Producing Company" (unpublished, Southern Illinois University Carbondale, 2006). This dissertation was a finalist for the Richard and Donna Falvo Outstanding Dissertation, 2006–7.

48. Alfred Kazin, "What Have the 30s Done to Our Literature?" *New York Herald Tribune,* December 31, 1939.

49. Marvin Carlson, *The Haunted Stage: The Theatre as Memory Machine* (Ann Arbor: University of Michigan Press, 2001), 17.

50. Terry Eagleton, *Against the Grain: Essays, 1975–1985* (London: Verso, 1986), 80.

Author's Note: Both recent research and the acquisition of images for this essay were made possible by the Augustana College Fund for New Faculty Research.

Ole Olson and Companions as Others

Swedish-Dialect Characters and the
Question of Scandinavian Acculturation

—LANDIS K. MAGNUSON

Since the late 1970s, extensive research has focused on ethnic stereotypes in American popular theatre and vaudeville of the nineteenth and early twentieth centuries—especially studies on German (commonly called Dutch), Irish, Hebrew, and Negro dialect humor.[1] As a product, in part, of the ethnic revival of the 1960s and 1970s and the growing academic acceptance of popular culture studies, considerable ethnic history has been uncovered, reclaimed, and elevated. Still awaiting intensive exploration, however, are less-prominent ethnic Others. Among the groups making an important contribution to the ethnic comedy of an earlier period and deserving of more focused analysis is the Swedish immigrant.[2]

In a comprehensive overview dating from the early 1980s, theatre historian Anne-Charlotte Harvey accounts for the rise and eventual decline of play performances in the Swedish language for and by Swedish immigrants, which dates in the United States from the early 1860s.[3] In this research Harvey outlines an evolution from productions performed entirely in Swedish, to "mixed-language" productions of Swedish and broken English, to the use of only the Swedish accent by Swedish actors, to eventually the "non-Scandinavian-speaking performer who puts on a Scandinavian stage accent and assumes a Scandinavian personality."[4] This last alteration of the performance of Swedish-dialect plays became possible only when the Scandinavian immigrant "type" became immediately recognizable in American society as a caricature. With the peak of Swedish immigration occurring from 1880 to 1900,[5] a societal carica-ture of the Swede underwent formation and became fixed in the public mind-set: the golden-haired transplant who is slow in mind and body, engaged in ongoing struggles with the English language. Having once acquired stage im-portance in the 1890s, Swedish-dialect plays and the ethnic caricatures they por-trayed proved a successful box-office attraction well into the Depression era and beyond.

As historian James H. Dormon argues, ethnic caricatures were in large part created by ascribed qualities emphasized for stage purposes. Dormon asserts: "The qualities that define the type are in fact *ascribed* qualities, qualities be-lieved to exist in reality, are *presumed* to exist in reality, by outside observers and sometimes by members of the group as well. But the stereotyping process isolates these ascriptive qualities for emphasis (and thus distortion), thereby affording a form of mental shorthand that renders close personal observation and differentiation unnecessary. In brief, ascription establishes the qualities that collectively constitute the stereotype."[6]

Dormon further emphasizes, "It was the standard practice of such come-dians simply to exaggerate the primary ascriptive qualities to the point of cari-cature in order to render the stereotype more comical." Appertaining to stage caricatures, Dormon is emphatic: "invariably the racial comics rendered ethnic stereotypes *in caricature form*."[7] While addressing the closely related topic of whether or not such ascriptive qualities exist in reality (the "kernel of truth" hypothesis), Dormon stresses that the question is not necessarily relevant. This hypothesis, however, does play a part in the creation of the Swedish immigrant stereotype and should not be dismissed. The realities facing the newly arrived Swede, such as challenging language acquisition, slow adjustment to societal norms, and the cultural tradition of a rugged stoicism, all provide the basis for exaggeration leading to the level of caricature. An observation made concerning the character of Ole Olson in 1890—"for while it may be to some extent an ex-aggeration, it is to a considerable degree true to nature"[8]—recognizes the "ker-nel of truth" hypothesis in play, and the "considerable degree true to nature" sentiment also speaks to the active process of isolation and emphasis leading to stereotype.

Concerning the Swedish immigrant, history records that Scandinavians were never subjected to the intense discrimination and prejudice that befell many other groups new to these shores. Persistent thought holds that Swedes were highly assimilable and responded by rapidly becoming Americans. Fueling this belief, according to historian Robert Salisbury, is the idea that Swedes possessed the "triple advantage" of being "white, Protestant, and Northern European, which immunized them from racial prejudices."[9] Whereas a slower acculturation period for Swedish immigrants is now accepted and appreciated, the danger remains of oversimplifying the experience.[10] Immigration specialist Rudolph J. Vecoli warns us that we must view "immigrants as agents of their own destinies . . . as fullbodied social beings, capable of adapting, creating, and resisting."[11] Furthermore, concerning an immigrant's process of Americanization, Vecoli reminds us that this must be seen as "much more complex and unpredictable than an automatic and inevitable absorption by the dominant culture."[12] Above all, we must resist the simplistic dismissing of Swedish-American stage characters, in the words of one noted historian, as simply "ludicrous."[13]

It is, indeed, imperative to heed Vecoli's admonition by recognizing that conditions affecting the Swedish immigrant and the development of the Scandinavian immigrant "type" differ from the time of the origin of this performance phenomenon to the final vestiges of Swedish-dialect presentations. Prior to 1900 the majority of Swedes settled in the Midwest, having been farmers who came from rural districts of their homeland. Following the turn of the century, however, an intensification of Swedish relocation to the industrial centers of New England and the Atlantic coast unfolds. By 1910 the peak of Swedish immigration to the United States had taken place, with the last prominent wave occurring during the 1920s.[14] During the roughly fifty years that Swedish-dialect plays toured this nation, variables such as the longevity of the Swedish presence in an area, the relative percentage of Scandinavian immigrants in a locale, and even the aggregate mix of immigrant nationalities present in a region influenced the reception of Swedish-dialect performances by the general public as well as within the Swedish community. While certainly real, these fluid forces remain difficult to separate out and quantify, yet we must be cognizant of potential impact.

To date, significant research on theatre presented in the Swedish language in the United States has been completed, but performances featuring dialect characters such as Ole Olson and his companions remain largely underexplored.[15] In order to address this need and provide a catalyst for further research, this study will focus on the history of the phenomenon of Swedish-dialect performances and the perceived positive impact of such characterizations upon Swedish immigrants. Evidence reveals that although Scandinavians were not immune to negative societal stereotyping, Swedish immigrants largely embraced the comic stage portrayals of the period as a way, in part, to consider and define their own Americanized identity in response to the challenges of acculturation.

Development of the Stage Character

With upwards of 1.3 million Swedes arriving in the United States between 1850 and 1930, the potential models and audience for Swedish-dialect theatre took root, chiefly in the heartland of America.[16] Swedish-dialect companies primarily trouped through Scandinavian strongholds in Minnesota, Wisconsin, Illinois, Nebraska, and the Pacific Northwest. Supported by appreciative audiences, a unique assemblage of male and even female characters—such as Ole Olson, Yon Yonson, Sven Hanson, Yennie Yensen, and Tilly Olson—populated a wide array of plays, such as Lawrence Russell's *A Prince of Sweden* (1905), Charles A. Lindholm Sr.'s *The Man from Minnesota* (1911), and Perley Henry Ames's *Ole, the Nonpartisan Leaguer* (1921).

Over time the stage caricature of the Swedish immigrant developed and solidified. The blond, curly haired Swede is routinely viewed as innocent in nature, possessing considerable physical strength while maintaining a weak grasp on the intricacies of the English language: "slow to speak and quick to act, with more strength of arm than cleverness of tongue."[17] The image of the new immigrant "type" (clearly marked with a prominent destination tag and perched on a trunk of his worldly possessions) forms the basis of various early advertisements for Swedish-dialect plays (fig. 1). Onstage the recent emigrant often displays a slow, methodical, and somewhat awkward walk; in addition he projects a low, calm voice demonstrating a serious and unexcitable nature. A visual used in the *Minneapolis Sunday Tribune* in 1889 captures the fresh immigrant "type" newly arrived, complete with too-small clothes and pigeon-toed feet (fig. 2). The temperament of the stage caricature is deemed truehearted, honest, and brave, while equally being hardheaded, unsophisticated, and uncultivated. The *New York Daily Tribune* maintains: "He is ... kind ... and he seems to be almost a simpleton, but in emergencies he becomes shrewd and can act with decision. His strong point is an impassive countenance combined with a phlegmatic demeanor."[18] The Swedish stage figure is described by one newspaper as "full of contradictions, at times hopelessly stupid and immediately thereafter possessed of honest perception and good judgment; manly when aroused by occasion, but mostly dormant and above all stoical."[19] A frequent promotional illustration of the early years captures the projected vulnerability of the Swedish immigrant when confronted by the "philistines" of the streetwise and unscrupulous (fig. 3).

But is the description of the Swede tendered in period newspapers that of the developing stage caricature or that of the evolving image of the Swedish immigrant "type" held by society? Normally it appears that the two were

Figure 1. Publicity for Gus Heege's *Yon Yonson* in the *Kearney (Neb.) Daily Hub,* November 3, 1892, 4

not intended to be separated and quickly became one. On occasion, however, a clear distinction is made. The *Brooklyn Daily Eagle* describes in 1891 the play *Yon Yonson* as being set in Minnesota, "a state that is rapidly filling up with hard headed Swedes."[20] Concerning the developing stage caricature, the *St. Louis Post-Dispatch* lists that same year elements highlighted for performance: the "unconquering stolidity of the race, the sparing use of words, the simplicity and 'freshness,' [and] the latent sense of humor which sometimes breaks through a crust of apparent hopeless stupidity," concluding that they all "unite in forming a stage part which has at least the element of novelty in its favor."[21]

Perspectives on the developing stage caricature from actual performers of the period could be of importance, but few have survived. Cliff Ohlson, who performed in various renderings of Carl M. Dalton's *Ole Olson in Spiritland* (1902) prior to the Depression era, recalls from experience that "Ole was a mild, polite, innocent and slow-speaking person. . . . His wardrobe was neat, but just a little bit small for him which made him appear amusing but not ridiculous. . . . He apparently had some education."[22]

Figure 2. Publicity for Gus Heege's *Ole Olson* in the *Minneapolis Sunday Tribune,* November 3, 1889, 11.

Whereas the vast majority of the texts in question are based upon a male lead character, shows such as *Tilly Olson*—the title character advertised on occasion as "The Funny Swede Girl from Minnesota"—present a novelty in Scandinavian plays.[23] The action revolves around a young Swedish girl serving in the capacity of a "charity domestic" to a Minnesota farm family. The *Omaha Bee* records that *Tilly Olson* "is a melodrama that is as replete with thrill-producing dramatic climaxes as any dyed-in-the wool wild and western drama that ever held a gallery-god in thrall." Even though a stated time element is undoubtedly exaggerated, plot details reveal that "Tilly is interrupted at her prayers by the bad wicked henchman of the villain, who comes to kidnap her and throw her

In The Hands of The Philistines

Figure 3. Publicity for Gus Heege's *Yon Yonson* in the *Philadelphia Inquirer*, February 25, 1894, 11.

over the cliff to the rocks below. After a ten-minute hand-to-hand conflict between the two, Tilly prevails and throws the would-be murderer bodily out of the window."[24] Fortune does come to the fair Swedish lass, and she eventually marries the man she loved during her days of adversity.

Due to their popularity, Swedish-dialect plays were occasionally plagued by overexposure. Minnesota's *Murray County Herald* observes in 1917: "The entertainment *Ole and His Sweetheart*, which showed at the Woodgate's Hall last Saturday evening, was not greeted by a very large crowd, owing to the fact that similar plays have been here many times before. The show, however, was good and clean and those present were satisfied with the production."[25] Despite sporadic problems with having too many companies on the road, characters such as Ole and Tillie traditionally struck a resonant chord with grateful and enthusiastic audiences.

Gus J. Heege: Actor, Playwright, Originator

Of the handful of prominent Swedish-dialect comedians to take to the legiti-mate stage, arguably the earliest and the one most responsible for establish-ing this particular performance genre was Augustus "Gus" J. Heege (1862–98).[26] A German American, Heege was born in Cleveland, Ohio, in the early 1860s. The son of a prominent member of that city's police department, Heege grew to early adulthood in the area and graduated from Cleveland's Central High School. As a young man, however, he could not resist the siren call of the East Coast, and as early as 1880 he left Cleveland following commencement exer-cises to seek his fortune in New York City. Early performance credits reportedly include a production of *Peck's Bad Boy* and membership in Frederick Warde's company. But the talented Heege soon found himself penning plays as well as performing in them. His works for stage include *Wanted the Earth* (1887; made famous by John Dillon), *Criss Cross* (1888; which starred Nellie Walters), *Sky Scraper* (1888), and *Rush City* (1893).[27]

Despite these productions, Heege undoubtedly will be remembered fore-most for his trilogy of Swedish-dialect compositions, modeled, we are told, after the success of J. K. "Fritz" Emmet in German American roles.[28] Heege's initial offering was *Ole Olson* in 1889, followed late the following year by *Yon Yonson,* and finally by *A Yenuine Yentleman* in 1895. As for mounting productions of his scripts, two producers are worthy of special mention. After the completion of *Ole Olson,* Heege established a business association with James H. Shunk for the promotion of his first ethnic offering, but it ended by late 1890 when Heege posted notice of severing "all business relations" due to contractual vio-lations and a "flagrant disregard of the rights of the author and lessor."[29] Heege's Swedish-dialect productions fared better under the management of Jacob Litt, a prominent New York City–based producer of the era. By 1891, Litt, only thirty-two at the time, owned theatres in Chicago, Milwaukee, St. Paul, and Minne-apolis and boasted of having both *Yon Yonson* and *The Stowaway* on the road.[30] But reports of a significant split between Heege and Litt in early 1896 signaled serious problems and foreshadowed the eventual demise of this successful busi-ness relationship.[31] Figure 4 offers a promotional line drawing utilized by Heege in the early 1890s.

Heege's Inaugural Offering, *Ole Olson*

Federal records reveal that Gus Heege filed for copyright protection on *Ole Ol-sen* (note original, short-lived spelling) on the concluding day of 1888. By Feb-

MR. GUS HEEGE.

Figure 4. Publicity image of Gus Heege in the *Milwaukee Journal,* January 14, 1893, 12.

ruary of the following year Heege deposited the required copies of his four-act comedy with the Library of Congress, and local newspapers chronicle initial performances under way. Advertising prominently pitched the show as "The First American Comedy Drama Ever Produced with a Swedish Dialect Character as the Star."[32]

An important early performance of *Ole Olson* took place in late March 1889 in Stillwater, Minnesota. The Grand Opera House in this bustling river community served as the venue. Concerning the performance in Stillwater, the *New York Dramatic Mirror* reported only a fair house, stressing that "as this was the first time a Scandinavian dialect has been presented here where there is a large Swedish population everybody was anxious to see the play. There was general disappointment. Mr. Heege's dialect work was very defective."[33] The *Stillwater Daily Gazette* advised that "the dialect of Gus Heege, the author and star of the play is imperfect. But the view of the action makes a go of the production. It will not last, however, because it is too light."[34]

Other reviews of initial performances of *Ole Olson* are openly critical. Of an appearance in Hastings, Minnesota, we learn that "the entertainment given was not up to the usual standard."[35] A performance in Winona, Minnesota, drew similar negative response: "The play was short and without particular merit, although some of the situations were amusing. The players were mostly of an inferior stamp and had evidently had little practice in the profession."[36] Regarding this performance in Winona, we learn in unflinching terms that "the Ole Olsen company played to a thin audience at the Opera house last evening. The play was even thinner than the audience. It is possible that worse shows have imposed upon the Opera house management in the past, but a good many of last night's audience will have hard work to believe it."[37]

Route lists place *Ole Olson* almost exclusively in Minnesota for one-night stands during March and April 1889. Figures 5 and 6, two Shober and Carqueville posters of the period, do not faithfully capture a stage moment of *Ole Olson,* but they do place a premium on entertainment value and the ability to seize attention. The first poster, titled "The Comedy Novelty," uses a collection of grinning and garish ethnic and character types to frame a scrubbed and polished Ole Olson, thus highlighting the newness and freshness of the Swedish characterization while also displaying apparent approval by the types, including caricatures of the Irish and the Chinese. The second poster presents a distortion of the stage action that calls for Ole to throw Bridget O'Flannigan into a cistern. Perhaps such a distortion was thought to be more comic and eye-catching.

Despite the largely negative reception of initial appearances, the first performance of *Ole Olson* in St. Paul in the spring of 1889 garnered some qualified praise: "The Ole Olson Comedy company played last night to one of the largest houses of the week. The play is something unique in the line of farce comedy, the central figure of the play being a Scandinavian dialect character. The play is as yet crude, but has a ground work of considerable strength. From a laughing point of view it was a success."[38]

Following some three months on the road, the production began the traditional summer inactivity until the autumn of 1889. By then the offering reportedly sported more polish and experienced a triumphant weeklong stand in Minneapolis, presenting "an entirely new line of business." Performances of *Ole Olson* packed the Bijou Opera House from "pit to dome" and caused applause that was "at times tumultuous."[39] The *Minneapolis Tribune* documented a significant turnout by the Swedish population of the Twin Cities for this event: "To caricature the national points of character and make laughing stock of its dialect before hundreds of its representatives would seem audacious, but the Scandinavian portion of the audience last night was by far the most enthusiastic. At every entrance of Ole Olson's the applause was deafening, and at times

Figure 5. *Ole Olson* publicity poster, Shober and Carqueville Co.,
ca. 1890, Library of Congress, Prints and Photographs Division
[POS-TH-1890.04, no. 1 (C size)].

was only quelled by hissing. . . . The originality of the part makes it successful,
particularly in Minneapolis, where it can be so thoroughly appreciated."[40]

In the following years the script of *Ole Olson* drew its share of criticism.
As one might anticipate, negative critical response often increased as the distance from the Scandinavian strongholds of the upper Midwest increased. For
example, a critic from New Orleans felt that the piece seemed to "lack spirit,"
adding: "There is a good deal of meritorious humor in the play, and just a little
too much horse play, and the plot is entirely lost sight of except when the vil-
lains are in the scene. The plot lacks continuity, and the specialties are not
strong enough to keep up attentions during the gaps. The performance is by

Figure 6. *Ole Olson* publicity poster, Shober and Carqueville Co., ca. 1890, Library of Congress, Prints and Photographs Division [POS-TH-1890.04, no. 6 (C size)].

no means a poor one, but it fell below what a New Orleans audience demands and evidently expected in this case."[41]

The assessment of the *Arkansas Gazette*, however, was repeated in various forms across the nation: "Now, the play as a literary effort will not set the world afire, but as a vehicle to amuse it has few equals."[42] Perhaps the combination of positive audience response and ongoing poor critical reaction motivated Heege to obtain the noted James A. Herne to rewrite portions[43] of the script (especially the third act) in 1892.[44] While it remains unclear what elements of the script Herne addressed, the *Cleveland Plain Dealer* attributes to Herne a chiefly scenic and technical change in the third act when the powder mill "at the side of a stream, during the progress of a terrific storm, is struck by lightning and explodes." This account declares that Herne found his alterations successful, producing one of his "cleverest scenic effects."[45]

Heege's Popular *Yon Yonson*

Regardless of the specifics of origin, Heege's second Swedish-dialect composition (with coauthor credit to W. D. Coxey)[46] was christened *Yon Yonson*. After Heege filed for copyright protection in November 1890, an important early production took place in late December of that year in Utica, New York. We are told that only a small audience viewed this performance, the *New York Dramatic Mirror* recording that "the piece seemed to drag very much, and became quite tedious at times. The support was very good, and the scenery in the third act is attractive."[47] With two scripts now in production, Heege chose to tour in the newer, and arguably better, effort. As he performed in *Yon Yonson,* Heege kept *Ole Olson* on the road with other dialect performers in the title role.[48]

Instead of promoting or even acknowledging his multiple playwriting efforts, Heege chose to back his current touring vehicle at the expense of any and all other Swedish-dialect productions. In time he claimed to be "the original and only Swedish-American dialect comedian."[49] While the former claim stood unchallenged, the latter assertion is outright subterfuge in an attempt to control a small niche in popular entertainment. As for the general nature of the play, the *Seattle Post-Intelligencer* contends that *Yon Yonson* "gives a truer and broader idea of the Swedish character than 'Ole Olson.' The latter play in many respects was a burlesque, and emphasized only the humorous possibilities of the character."[50]

Indeed, objective evaluation reveals *Ole Olson* to be the less sophisticated of the two scripts. The play relies heavily on brash, rough-and-tumble physical action as well as an excessive amount of largely unmotivated vaudeville turns, known as specialities. A considerable amount of the humor is built upon farcical action and sight gags, such as when Ole dives off the bridge, only to return with a catfish in his arms. In *Yon Yonson,* however, one experiences an emotional depth in the title character, especially when Yon is called upon to relate the death of his father and his separation from his sister. A far greater dependence upon major scenic elements is also present, the most famous being when Yon rescues Grace (whom he later discovers to be his sibling) during the breakup of a massive logjam to end act 2.

During the 1891 theatrical season Heege toured *Yon Yonson* widely throughout the Midwest and reportedly refined the work. Although no evidence clearly identifies the specific steps taken to improve *Yon Yonson,* every indication is given that Heege (as both playwright and performer) remained a practical man of the theatre who responded, first and foremost, to the critical reaction of audiences during performances and adjusted accordingly. In addition, the influence of his producer, Jacob Litt, should not be underestimated. At one time plans for revising *Ole Olson* for an upcoming season included "cutting out much that is undesirable in the way of commonplace melo-drama" and having the "supporting company materially strengthened." According to this strategy, success in all parts of the country was to be found in the simplistic-sounding goal of "a better play and better company."[51] *Yon Yonson* undoubtedly followed a similar design for alterations. As to whether or not Heege solicited input from the Scandinavian community concerning script changes, no evidence exists that he fostered contact with Swedish immigrants or heeded critical response in Swedish-language newspapers.

Of considerable importance for any successful tour of this era was the quality of the "line of paper" used to promote the production and *Yon Yonson* received outstanding support. Figures 7 and 8 are images of colorful Strobridge lithograph posters illustrating action from the play. While the first poster offers a montage of key stage events, the second captures the climatic conclusion of act 1 when, as prescribed by the stage directions, Yon falls through the ceiling of the train depot while being chased by Mrs. Laflin and boards the train safely free from her grasp.

In addition to performing in traditional and familiar venues during 1891, Heege toured to major cities on the East Coast, including Boston, Baltimore, Philadelphia, and New York City. Records reveal that various Swedish-dialect performers appeared in and around the traditional theatre center of the United States during this general era, but the history of performing in these environs is clearly dominated by Heege. George C. D. Odell reported in his *Annals of the New York Stage:* "Gus Heege, whom we have met in the outskirts, brought to the Park, on December 28th [1891], his Scandinavian dialect, in *Yon Yonson;* to the surprise of the uninitiated public, he kept it going for four weeks, departing January 23rd."[52]

Soon after *Yon Yonson* opened at the New Park Theatre (Broadway and Thirty-fifth Street), paid advertisements boasted of "vociferous applause" and claimed that "all the critics were well pleased" with this production co-written by and starring Gus Heege.[53] Such an assessment, however, places a positive spin on the events. While it is true that the *New York Times* review begins by citing a "tribute of boisterous applause" from a large audience, considerable concerns are enumerated. This critic flatly alleges that "there is a superabundance of material in a crude state, and melodramatic sentiment and variety hall fun are hopelessly entangled in it." The critic argues further that "such a play can produce no illusion whatever upon a well-cultivated, sophisticated mind, and the object of the dramatic art is always to produce a perfect illusion of nature." The reviewer, nevertheless, acknowledges an audience seemingly well suited and eager for the production and one receiving what it desired: "Such a piece as 'Yon Yonson' exactly suits such theatregoers, and it is not altogether devoid of attractions for others. In its farcical elements it is quite abreast with these times."[54]

Figure 7. *Yon Yonson* publicity poster, Strobridge and Co., ca. 1899, Library of Congress, Prints and Photographs Division [POS-TH-1899.Y65, no. 5 (C size)].

Concerns regarding the quality of the written script, coupled with praise for the performance and entertainment value, largely became the standard critical response to *Yon Yonson*. Like the *New York Times* reviewer, the critic of the *New York Daily Tribune* focuses almost exclusively upon the construction and performance of the theatrical event minus any real acknowledgment of appreciative audiences. This reviewer establishes little doubt in criticizing *Yon Yonson*, suggesting the plot exists as "a mere thread on which to hang variety features and tableaus." Whereas criticism is centered on the text, promise is viewed in the ability of Heege, who, enacting the title role, "produces a better impression with his acting than with his pen. He was yet, indeed, in the chrysalis state—on his way from the variety stage to that of the regular drama, and not far advanced in the process of evolution—but he possessed the two fine quali-

Figure 8. *Yon Yonson* publicity poster, Strobridge and Co., ca. 1899, Library of Congress, Prints and Photographs Division [POS-TH-1899.Y65, no. 4 (C size)].

ties of repose and grace; his theory of farce was right; and his practice of it was adroit. He preserved absolute gravity of manner and, at the same time, pursued a line of comic conduct." The review concludes by suggesting that the "Swede dialect is novel, but not agreeable, and possibly this hampers the art that Mr. Heege would otherwise display."[55]

Apprehension over the quality of the script prompted various offers of advice for improvement. "It would be better all around," the *Brooklyn Daily Eagle* coldly suggests, "if the play were to pass through the hands of some man like Bronson Howard or Edgar Fawcett for expurgation and finish. There is much in it that is intended to be humorous that is as devoid of fun as Yon Yonson himself is supposed to be."[56] The *Boston Daily Globe* felt that the pronunciation substitution of "Y" for "J" went too far when Yon was required to repeat "a rigmarole of words" each beginning with the letter J and that improvement was possible through restraint.[57]

Rarely, however, did criticism of Swedish-dialect plays take on such a vitriolic nature as in a review from Buffalo, New York, in early 1891: "Let it be said with sweet softness of speech that Yon Yonson cannot too soon return to the Northwest, whence he came; and if he will immediately lose himself in the chilliest part of his native pine lands he will confer an inestimable benefit on a suffering public. The piece called 'Yon Yonson,' which was presented at the Academy last night, is utterly nondescript: farce comedy of the lowest order, queer 'specialties,' shrieking melodrama, burlesque, and genuine comedy tread on one another's heels in this play with bewildering rapidity." Yet the critic praises the character of Yon and the setting of the lumber camp, concluding: "If the character of Yon Yonson were vitalized and put in a good play, there might be recorded something new and cheerful in things theatrical, but this 'Yon Yonson' is a deplorable and lugubrious hodge-podge of musty old things that were long ago supposed to be relegated to the dramatic waste-basket."[58]

On the whole, perhaps the viewpoint of "H. B." places the question of the dramatic quality of *Yon Yonson* in a more balanced perspective: "At least the whole spirit of 'Yon Yonson' is pure and healthful and stimulating. It may be over-rollicking, but it is not morbid or pessimistic or cynical, and that, in these days of Zola and Oscar Wilde, is perhaps all we can ask. Still, we must wonder, what might not Mr. Heege do with a play as good as 'Rip Van Winkle'?"[59]

Heege's Finale, *A Yenuine Yentleman*

A Yenuine Yentleman dates from 1895 and is the final offering in Heege's trilogy of dialect plays. As no copy of the play is extant, we must glean knowledge of this stage offering from promotional and review materials. Various plot elements in *A Yenuine Yentleman* do sound a familiar refrain: traveling to America to seek one's fortune, acts of heroism, feats of strength and endurance, solving of complications, discovery of a long-lost brother, and development of a love interest. Such a list notwithstanding, publicity instructs us that a distinct difference is found in the character of Sven Hanson, an ambitious young Swede who has been educated at Sweden's Uppsala University and has traveled to America with the hopes of becoming a success in mine engineering.

Due in part, one must believe, to the widespread negative response to his previous Swedish-dialect scripts, we are told that Heege "has been more anxious to achieve literary as well as financial success" with this stage offering.[60]

Even so, critical response to *A Yenuine Yentleman* often mirrors the reactions received by its predecessors. For example, the *Chicago Tribune* alleges that it is "a variety 'turn' elaborated into a melodrama. Gus Heege . . . is the chief figure in the performance, and all the other characters are merely, so to speak, ball bearings, as the story is merely the axle for his wheel." Yet, despite previous criticisms being leveled again, a subtle softening in reactions is found concerning *A Yenuine Yentleman.* In the eyes of the *Chicago Tribune* critic, Sven is "a striking sketch of character, rough in outline, crude and glaring in color, bearing about the same resemblance to the reality as the stage Irishman bears to the Irish immigrant; but still striking if viewed at the proper distance. It is a portrait done by a scene painter and not intended to be inspected through a handglass. But seen from the gallery of the theater it must appear admirable, for the applause in that quarter was deafening and frequent."[61]

The begrudging acknowledgment of the value and power of these theatrical events once they are placed into proper perspective—often downplayed or missing in the past—seems newly evident. Of additional significance is the discovery that the reporting of attributes of the Swedish stage character trends conspicuously toward the positive at this time, as in this *Boston Herald* listing concerning Sven: "He is awkward, phlegmatic, imperturbable, slow to anger, rarely excitable, but he thinks right, is clearheaded, shrewd, amiable, honest, straightforward and frank and open as the blue eyes which gaze at you so innocently."[62]

Critical response concerning Heege's work seems to have turned a corner. But to what can we attribute this change? Without a script for analysis, we are held to the limited resources at hand. It remains possible that a greater acceptance of Heege's Swedish-dialect characters came about based upon years of exposure to audiences and critics alike. It also could be that Sven is a more sophisticated and much-improved character construction or that Heege's performance skills demonstrated additional refinement. Much of the publicity and post-production information for *A Yenuine Yentleman,* nevertheless, remains similar to previous dialect offerings by Heege and does not offer definitive insights.

Based upon what we know, however, the *Springfield (Mass.) Union*'s assessment that "Sven Hansen [*sic*] is Yon Yonson in a different atmosphere and surroundings" must be viewed as a considerable oversimplification or simply false.[63] The key difference between these two characters is the elevation of Sven Hanson to an educated immigrant. In Sven, we are told, one finds an "elaborated and broadened" character that moves well beyond the admirable traits of Ole and Yon to an individual largely comfortable with American ways and means and also capable of making valuable and immediate contributions to society.[64]

Changes present in the lead character of *A Yenuine Yentleman* perhaps can be seen most clearly in a standard promotional image used to advertise the show. In figure 9 one views Sven in a bold and confident stance having thrust his large travel trunk upon his shoulders, readied for seemingly all contingencies with riding boots and umbrella in tow.[65] Such a visual depiction of the Swedish immigrant "type" is a far cry from those found in figures 1–3, images that range from only three to eight years earlier.

Heege as Performer

Over the years Gus Heege is cited for consistent maturation in his character delineations to his own benefit and that of his audiences. It is not entirely clear, however, whether such praise reflects refinements in his acting or refinements in the characters portrayed. While his efforts are labeled as "somewhat crude as an actor yet" during performances in Chicago in 1891,[66] the next year they are evaluated as being "a little more mellowed and softened."[67] The *Brooklyn Daily Eagle* concurs with this assessment, emphasizing that in a return visit in 1892 Heege had "subdued the sensationalism of his part, and, if anything, his characterization of a good natured Swede is nearer the actual individual as we know him in these parts."[68] By 1895 his impersonation of the Swedish character is deemed "more matured and more artistically developed."[69]

Unfortunately, additional artistic refinement in acting and playwriting was to be short-lived, as Heege died on February 2, 1898, while only in his mid-thirties (survived by his wife and ten-year-old son). At the time of his death, reportedly from kidney disease, Heege was at work on an original Swedish-American light opera, the composition of the score entrusted to Max Faetkenheuer, the music director of the Lyceum Theatre in Cleveland.[70] The opera, titled *Amalia Mora*, eventually took the stage in early August 1912 at the Garden Theatre in Cleveland. With acts laid in both Sweden and Wisconsin, the ambitious effort included Arthur Donaldson as Ole Jonson, specially engaged for the role originally intended for Heege. The *New York Dramatic Mirror* offered faint praise for the score but found genuine merit in the opera's staging and lavish costumes, warning that the work needed "considerable pruning and rewriting, after which it may prove popular as a musical comedy."[71] With the abrupt passing of Gus Heege, a significant chapter in the history of Swedish-dialect plays came to an end.

Figure 9. Publicity for Gus Heege's *A Yenuine Yentleman* in the *Brooklyn Daily Eagle*, February 21, 1897, 24.

Ben Hendricks as Ole Olson

Second in importance only to Heege as a Swedish-dialect comedian was Ben Hendricks, whose longevity in the role of Ole Olson made him a perennial favorite across this nation. Hendricks was born in Buffalo, New York, and his obituary in *Variety* claims he made his stage debut playing the role of the boy in a mounting of *Rip Van Winkle* starring Joseph Jefferson.[72] Prior to turning to dialect comedy, Hendricks played supporting comic roles for several years in productions starring Minnie Palmer, including *My Sweetheart*.

Acclaimed as a talented dialect comedian whose career spanned over fifty years, including both stage productions and motion pictures, Hendricks (1868–1930) made a livelihood performing in all three of the dialect plays written by

Heege.[73] Knowing that Hendricks was not a playwright, it is interesting to follow his publicity ploys, in which he appears to battle openly for the title of "originator" of Swedish-dialect plays. When Hendricks performing in *Ole Olson* claims to be "The Original and Greatest of All Swedish Dialect Comedy Successes" and that "All Others Are Imitators," the implied target is Heege. Regardless of appearances, though, the record extols Heege as the key pioneer impersonator of the Swedish immigrant on the legitimate stage and confirms that Hendricks and others followed.[74]

When investigating what circumstances motivated Heege's creation of his Swedish-dialect compositions, one must address various tales of origin and glean factual elements from stories seemingly created and shaped for promotional purposes. For example, concerning *Ole Olson,* one story is circulated by the author of writing the show for a specific performer, but when this individual backs out Heege is obligated to take on the part "as a matter of accident" and is forced into "hasty" preparations.[75] This story certainly seems plausible based on Heege's experience as both actor and playwright plus the intensity of negative reactions to the acting in initial performances, especially Heege's.

A more widely circulated story concerns the creation of *Yon Yonson* and centers on unexpected exposure to Swedish laborers. The oft-told tale is that while touring in Shakespearian and other legitimate roles through small rural villages and hamlets, the company in which Heege was performing disbanded, thus throwing him upon his own resources (for a period often reported as three months) among the locals, which included many Scandinavian woodchoppers. According to this account, Heege made the best of a bad situation and used the time to carefully study the dialect and habits of the logcutters.[76] During an interview for the *Atlantic Journal,* Heege offered another variation on this origin theme. He claimed that he was performing for lumbermen in the early spring months when "sturdy woodsmen come from their winter's work" with "savings in their pockets, all out for recreation and enjoyment." Following careful observation and analysis, Heege asserts, he determined that the Swede "would be a good thing to put before the footlights" and that after this experience he spent three summer months in Sweden to study the language, leading to the creation of *Yon Yonson.*[77]

Unquestionably, time spent in lumber camps and travel to Sweden should not be viewed as fanciful. In fact, the story of Heege's time in Sweden is repeated on various occasions, but such study traditionally is cited as having the purpose of aiding the writing and improving the overall quality of *A Yenuine Yentleman.*[78] In the final analysis, these evolving renditions leave many important details unsubstantiated and result in a rather suspect time line, but they are not outside the realm of possibility. At the very least, such tales of persever-ance, opportunity, and ingenuity, as well as travel to a foreign country, generate exciting promotional copy to pique curiosity and fuel interest in the theatre-going public.

It is conceivable that the appearance of an intense rivalry between Heege and Hendricks was manufactured for publicity effects and purposely height-ened when both performers toured in and around the New York City area in 1891. While Odell places Heege at the New Park Theatre in December of that year, Odell's entry concerning this time period for Holmes's Star Theatre notes that "*Ole Oleson* [*sic*] shifted us (14th–19th) into a different dialect, with Ben Hendricks, St. George Hussey and Alice Evans."[79] Although Heege and Hen-dricks were frequently projected to be competing aggressively against one an-other, Odell's annals place them side by side in *Ole Olson* at the Novelty The-atre in February 1893.[80]

In what might have been an attempt to both connect and distance him-self from Heege, Hendricks's publicity tactics frequently centered on praise by association; for example: "If Gus Heege's play, *Yon Yonson,* is, as is claimed, an imitation of this [*Ole Olson*], it has the excuse of copying something worth the undertaking."[81] Similar ad ploys were used for years, but following Heege's un-timely death his widow fully transferred the production rights of *Ole Olson* to Hendricks in 1901.[82] In this action the role of chief delineator of Swedish im-migrants onstage formally passed into the experienced hands of Hendricks. In future years he would drop any credit to Heege, and regardless of who was in the starring role, advertisements for productions of *Ole Olson* would tout "Ben Hendricks' Famous Comedy."[83]

Hendricks's acting generated frequent comparisons to Heege's, and the outcome varied seemingly in relationship to the predilections of the reviewer. While a performance in Lincoln was deemed "not as good" as the dialect por-trayals offered by Heege,[84] critical comment from the same 1892 season praised Hendricks as Heege's equal in the matter of his Swedish characterization, with the added bonus of being "a little more vivacious and certainly better looking than Gus."[85] As might be expected, the key to such performances was the in-telligibility of the dialect delivery, and Hendricks was not unique in receiving mixed reviews concerning this element. In 1892 the *San Francisco Chronicle* praised him for being "not so unintelligible as his predecessor. He speaks the quaint Swedish dialect so you can follow what he says."[86] That same year a com-mentator from Cincinnati suggested that "were his dialect not so thickly laid on as to render his utterances almost unintelligible," he might "be a most accept-able comedian."[87] Hendricks consistently earned praise for strong acting skills, which perhaps only slightly outdistanced his singing abilities,[88] highlighted, we are told, by a "broad, stolid and good-humored face."[89]

Among theatre circles and the general public, Hendricks's longevity in dialect roles was legendary. Route listings affirm consistent touring in creations by Heege from the early 1890s to at least 1912. A 1911 account praising his endurance and skill in performing the title character in *Ole Olson* declares that Hendricks had become in his particular line a parallel to Denman Thompson's creation of Josh Whitcomb in *The Old Homestead*.[90] But touring takes its toll, and following many years on the road Hendricks resorted to character parts in both film and extended runs. By 1915 *Billboard* attests to his joining a stock company in Albany, New York, to assume the principal comedy roles.[91] His final extended stage performances reportedly included two years in *Abie's Irish Rose* by Anne Nichols, followed by ninety-five weeks with Schwab and Mandel's *Desert Song*, which closed in May 1929, less than a year before his death.[92] To countless theatregoers, the face of Ben Hendricks was the face of Swedish-dialect comedy. Figure 10 shows Hendricks late in his career, complete in his traditional costume of small workman's cap, neck scarf, and homespun suit.

Common Characteristics of Swedish-Dialect Scripts

Detailed research—including a review of route listings and company reports in such trade publications as *Billboard,* the *New York Dramatic Mirror,* and the *New York Clipper*—reveals to date nearly eighty-five Swedish-dialect production titles. However, the expansive time spread of composition (late 1880s to the Depression era) and the diversity of scripts (ranging from Swedish-dialect productions in New York City to texts authored by tent repertoire and circle stock companies) clearly challenges effective characterization.[93] Indeed, a significant spread is present, ranging from Heege's initial effort of *Ole Olson* in 1889, to *Ole on His Honeymoon* in 1919 in the upper Midwest,[94] to *The Swede and the Flapper* copyrighted by Perley H. Ames in 1934. Compounding this situation, repertoire veterans report that companies promoting Swedish-dialect performances up to the immediate pre–World War II era often adapted standard Toby and G-String bills by merely changing the names of the characters, the title, and ethnicity for the territory. While an analysis of surviving Swedish-dialect scripts demonstrates a wide variance in the skillful manipulation of plot construction and character development, thus creating a considerable range in the quality of writing present, three primary plot characteristics emerge from more than forty texts in the author's possession.[95] These primary characteris-

Figure 10. Publicity image of Ben Hendricks in costume as Yon Yonson, photo courtesy of the Harvard Theatre Collection, Houghton Library.

tics include necessary English-language instruction, the demonstration of considerable physical strength by the Swedish character, and the extensive use of vaudeville specialties.

The first of these foundational elements is the English-language instruction of the Scandinavian character. In Heege's *Ole Olson* (1889) we encounter the character of Genie Dimple, who, while admitting that it is "cruel to poke fun at him in this way," defines for Ole various colloquial phrases in a deceptive manner. At one point she states that finding oneself "in the soup" means that an individual is "smart and handy." Genie soon concludes that Ole is "too green to burn" and that he has flies on him. Such crooked but comedic lessons became standard in the genre, and subsequent efforts emulated Heege's initial shaping of the exchange:

OLE: Ay gass you note know what you bene taking about. Ay note got any flies on me.

GENIE: Don't you know what that means? That means that you are bright, intelligent and industrious. When you are applying for a situation just tell them you've got flies on you and they'll hire you kerplunk.

OLE: By Yingo, I learn the English language pooty fast hare.

In Ezra Walck's *A Prince of Sweden* (1908), the character of Carl Carlson willingly parrots back the language instruction he receives from the juvenile comedy role on how to ask properly for a job:

NELSON: (Enter from Store) Good morning Carl. How would you like a situation?

CARL: No ay vant a yob. Ay been dead easy mark, ay look for something to do, ay been in soup, ay been dust with the juice squeezed out of him, ay open your letters and keep half your money orders.

Following this illogical outpouring, old Nelson concludes Carl must be crazy; Carl, in turn, flatly reasons, "Ay just tank ay no get job."

A second major staple of Swedish-dialect plays is the Swedish character's use of his size and strength to become a swift dispenser of physical justice. Normally, when language skills fail, physical ability fills the void. In Heege's *Yon Yonson* (1890) we experience the theme of action over words in this conversation between Grace and Yon (only later do we discover that they are sister and brother):

GRACE: Yon, may I ask a service of you? I am left to roam about the camp here alone the greater part of the time, as my father and Mr. Holloway are kept busy. There are a great many rough characters about the camp and I need a protector. Will you act as my chaperone?

YON: Yore vat?

GRACE: My Chaperone.

YON: Vall, ay note know vat det mane, bote ay'll be it anyhow.

GRACE: What a struggle you have with the Queen's English.

YON: English? Oh, ay note can talk English poota gude, but van et come to doing a tang—val yo know a faller can do a tang in Svedish yust abote as good as hae can in English.

In *Ole Olson*, the title character enters at one point in the opening act to hear only three lines of escalating tension between individuals before coming downstage to remove his coat, knock the apparent offending character to the ground, replace his coat, and then immediately exit without a word. Later in *Ole Olson,* physical strength is employed to bring act 1 to a rapid conclusion. When Jefferson Bassett attempts to kidnap his son Philip, whom he abandoned soon after birth, Ole swiftly throws Bassett into a nearby greenhouse. When challenged concerning his actions, Ole promptly deposits four other characters either to the ground, on top of one another, or to available furniture. The closing stage direction notes that he "strikes [a] boxing attitude" followed by the command of a quick curtain.

In Clarence Black's *The Man from Sweden* (1909), when Alice Jefferson is about to lose her farm, she states: "Oh how I wish there was a man here to punish you as you deserve." Carl happens to enter and overhear the request. He crosses immediately to Morris Doan, the play's villain, "grabs him by the throat, [and] forces Doan to [his] knees," asking, "Oh Miss Alice, skall A pound him to a yelly?" He pleads further, "Oh let me soak him just once." When instructed to let him go, Carl still throws him aggressively to the side. Act 1 concludes with another physical confrontation between Carl and Doan:

CARL: Out I go? No sir, not *out* I go, but *in* you go. (Shoves Doan in well, shuts lid) What's the meaning of this? Ding dong dell, pussy in the well. What, there bane water in there? Yas sir, about two feet. Have a drink on me. It bane dark in there? Well if it vane dark in there, here bane a match (slips match under cover, then sits on cover)

Doan is held in the well until the farm is safely purchased for Alice using the money collected by neighbors. As might be anticipated, audiences took great delight in these displays of physical strength. The *Brooklyn Daily Eagle* claims of *Yon Yonson:* "When he threw that hateful person into the river last night, very much as a longshoreman throws a bag of grain on a truck, he was applauded till the lights shook."[96]

A third chief component is the frequent inclusion of vaudeville turns or specialties. Such additions unquestionably increased the variety of entertainment provided for the price of admission and are staple elements in these texts. And while these supplements generally do not overpower the action, they can be seen to dominate some scripts. For instance, in Harry Hart's *Swan from Sweden* (1894) the entire act 4, scene 2 is described as "Specialties by Sam, ect. [*sic*]."

In some texts specialties are inserted with seemingly little or no relationship to the events of the play or with little or no preparation for inclusion in the script. In review, one may be hard pressed to see any attempt of integration. For example, the placement of Ole's specialty in Albert E. Markham and Benjamin Greenfield's *Ole, the Swede Detective* (1914) directly follows the angry outburst, "Some day aye going to push my face up against his fist so hard das— vell aye bet four dollars he will see stars." No further introduction is provided. Sometimes the setup for a specialty turn is as simple as a character desiring a song and the request being granted. This is not to ignore, however, the fact that skilled and experienced performers smoothed over a lack of introductory text with clever character action. The ability for extemporaneous stage business was seen as a necessary professional proficiency.

Although specialty turns in many instances lacked smooth and polished introductions, examples do exist of considerable integration into the text. In *A Prince of Sweden*, Thomas Jefferson White (a typical blackface role of the period) opens act 4 lonesome and depressed. An offstage musical interlude, however, causes him to respond, "I's sure got to do something or I'll bust," which leads directly into his specialty. An even more effective integration of specialties into the text takes place in *Yon Yonson* when Jennie, attempting to sell volumes of *Gillicuddies' Compendium of Universal Information*, challenges Mrs. Laflin, the Irish biddy character, concerning the book's value:

JENNIE: Is there anything she doesn't know? Oh, yes, it teaches you how to sing and dance.
MRS. LAFLIN: To sing and dance, is it? It's not to books I'll have to go to learn how to shake a foot.
ROLY: Oh, you can't dance.
JENNIE: Of course you can't. You're just saying so to get out of buying the book.
MRS. LAFLIN: Then here goes. I'll do a step or two to show you both you're wrong.

In rare situations a script will offer up the words to a song specialty. In Fred James's *That Swede* (1915), the character Ole informs the audience that "Ay tank ay sang a song, vile ay vait until he kum!!" The four verses provide Ole with considerable possibilities for comic business and with an opportunity to develop his character through additional actions related in the song:

I.
At home ay ban told en des land of de free—
Potatoes had eyes on plainly kud see—
Dot hams grow on trees, en dot ears grow on corn.
Now do you tank dem took mae fur a grin-horn?
Now do you tank dem took mae fur a grin-horn?

II.

Mae slumber von day, near a tree by de vood—
Et vas smash'd en two by a Ninny-Goat—
Vot vas nibbling on mae, vile ay sleep serene.
Now kud dot goat tank vonce, det ay vas so grin?
Now kud dot goat tank vonce, dat ay vas so grin?

III.

Yust now, as ay kom here tu see 'bout des yob—
Ay see raight behind mae, a yelling mob;
Ay yump en ay run, yust as kvick as kan be—
Ay vould laik tu know vy dem vas after mae?
Ay vould laik tu know vy dem vas after mae?

IV.

Nice gurl on de Bowry, she ask' mae last week—
Tu shange des (Bus.) tirty-five Dollar bill kvick—
Den she kiss'd mae, en sed: "Ta-ta! Mr. Green!"
Kan von of you told mae, vot det gurl kud mean?
Kan von of you told mae, vot det gurl kud mean?
(As he finishes singing, Ole looks at door L. in alarm, grabs his carpet bag, and
quickly sits on chair, assuming innocent attitude.)

On occasion newspaper reviews highlighted the importance of specialties
to the total entertainment package. Concerning a touring Swedish-dialect production, the *Logan (Utah) Journal* insists: "While the situations are clever and
unique, possibly the most interesting feature is the sweet singing of 'Strawber-
ries,' 'Memories of my Swedish Home,' and singing and dancing specialties by
'Ole' and 'Yenie' and other characters."[97] On the other hand, the *Svenska Korrespondenten*, a Swedish-language newspaper of Denver, found the inclusion
of specialties difficult to comprehend: "The plot of American comedy is in addition often inappropriately cut off, in that one actor after another comes on,
for no reason, and performs tricks exactly as in a 'tarrachim.' You sit there, wondering and questioning, not knowing what good all of that is supposed to do."[98]

Beyond these three primary characteristics, additional commonalities exist. Despite normally being the title character, the Swedish figure is found on
the whole to be incidental to the action. The character usually makes a late entrance and affects the text in sections of short duration, frequently at the end
of scenes or acts. The Scandinavian often arrives on the scene seeking employment and displays a strong work ethic. In *The Man from Sweden*, a hungry and
nearly destitute Carl Anderson turns down the offer of a monetary reward for
his heroic actions and asks only for work—for "anything." A miller by trade in
Sweden, Carl is offered a granary position and eventually becomes the super-
intendent of the local mill and acquires a controlling interest in it.

A typical first entrance of the "Ole" character seeking employment is found in Charles and Billy Hall's *The Scandinavian* (1904), found here in the voice of Neils:

FLOOD: Are you looking for anyone?
NEILS: Yas sir, I look faer work.
FLOOD: What is your occupation?
NEILS: Yaas sir.
FLOOD: No, I say what is your occupation?
NEILS: Swede.
FLOOD: (laughs) Swede. No, I mean what kind of work can you work at? Or what can you do? Mill hand, take care of horses or what?
NEILS: Yaas sir.
FLOOD: What are your politics, Democrat or Republican? One must be careful who he hires nowadays.
NEILS: Aye not look faer city job.
FLOOD: No?
NEILS: No, I look faer work.

Although the Swedish character is able to work hard, because he lacks acquaintance with modern conveniences, extended comic business is possible. In *That Swede,* Ole confronts a telephone in a traditional bit of comic stage business:

(Sees phone on table, drops paper, looks at phone from all sides in open mouthed astonishment.) Des ban great mashkine—ay herd about dem!! (Drops bag on floor, picks up phone, curiously examines it all over, takes receiver off hook, puts *transmitter* to *ear*—and *receiver* to *mouth,* listens intently.) Ay no hear anytang!! (Hangs receiver on hook upside down—puts phone on table. Phone starts to ring, he jumps back in alarm, quickly takes off cap, slams it over phone, which continues to ring, removes cap, puts it back on head, looks at C.D. and D.L. apprehensively, scratching head, has an idea, stands as far from phone as he can, reaches over, and with fingertips, lifts receiver off hook so that it falls off, upon table. Phone stops ringing. Ole laughs in childish glee, sighs with relief.) Ay ban smart faller. (Looks all around.) Ay ban en truble, ef des tang no stop!!

An act of heroism in the recent past is frequently utilized, a technique found in *The Scandinavian* when we learn that Neils once saved Marion Flood. The incident is retold in sensational fashion: "Just then I saw a manly form springing from the shadow of a tree. Then straight as an arrow from the bow he sprang to the heads of the frightened steeds, dragging them back upon their haunches scarce ten feet from that frightful precipice." The modest Swedish fellow quickly flees the scene following the heroics, and when questions arise about his nature, Neils is pictured as "A peculiarly dressed fellow with a handsome laughing face" that will likely be seen again. In addition to being newly arrived on the scene, the Swedish character is often searching to find a family member. Repeatedly one discovers that Ole has been separated from his sister, and his initial arrival is in the midst of the quest.

Once on site the male Swede might well find himself sought after by the seemingly ever-present female Irish character. Such a classic encounter is captured in a surviving Shober and Carqueville poster promoting *Yon Yonson* (fig. 11). Set in the lobby of a train station, Yon employs a full sprint to escape from the Biddy character. Not to be outdone, the stout Irish lass hikes up her long dress and apron to maintain a hot pursuit, exclaiming, "Phwat a noice husband that Swede would make!" While Ole traditionally runs from the Biddy figure, when the Swede does fall in love the audience is treated to his comic fumbling when dealing with accepted courting procedures. This exchange between Freckles and Neils from *The Scandinavian* is representative:

FRECKLES: Say Neils, was you ever engaged?
NEILS: Yas sir ree, a good many times.
FRECKLES: Oh, Neils Jennings, to who?
NEILS: To every man ay ever work faer.

Plot elements frequently center on dealings with significant amounts of property. At times the impending foreclosure of the family farm is central. Various other plots utilize the inheritance of a ranch or mine or the purchase of a large piece of land as a key dramatic moment. Very often, the crucial truth is revealed through the reading of a last will and testament.

In numerous instances the Ole character is absent from a major portion of the dialogue, only to return changed or altered, often displaying newly adopted—and usually ill-fitting—colorful attire. Of additional interest is the recurring plot device of the actual exchange of clothing. A colorful Strobridge lithograph poster (fig. 12) promotes Yon and Simpson, the latter a comic servant role played in blackface, in their swapped apparel. While this physical exchange might be viewed as simply unsophisticated comic business, the significance in these dialect plays deserves some reflection. The adoption of any "American" wardrobe, even from the character Yon refers to without malice as the "neeger faller," demonstrates the relative ease in shedding the semblance of the immigrant by taking on the trappings of the dominant culture. But Jennie admonishes Yon, stating, "It doesn't take a dress-suit to make a gentleman." Yon re-

Figure 11. *Yon Yonson* publicity poster, Shober and Carqueville Co., ca. 1899. Courtesy of the author.

sponds with insight for anyone in attendance to note: "Dan ay note bene a yentleman anyhow, and dese hare clothes note bene raight neither."

Although Ole normally appears slow and dim-witted, he consistently demonstrates that God-given abilities and native intelligence allow him to prevail in the end. Emalina, from *The Man from Sweden,* pronounces a prevailing sentiment when she concludes, "He is rather awkward, I will admit, but he has a heart of gold, and is a man through and through, and when the day of reckoning comes, I calculate he will stand just about as good a show as some of the men I know that are much better looking and wear much finer clothes."

While similar opinions about the Swedish character's general wholesome nature are regularly given voice, Ole characters occasionally demonstrate a deeply held belief in their own abilities. The sentiment of Hans Hanson in Charles Roush's 1913 version of *A Swede in Ar Kan Saw* expresses a growing personal strength: "These people here seem to think that because I'am a Swede I don't know noting. I've been pretty mum so far, but watch me from now on—see if I don't make things buzz around har!" Or as Swan's final line from *Swan from Sweden* reads: "Yes, A bane poor greenhorn, but A bane too fast for you."

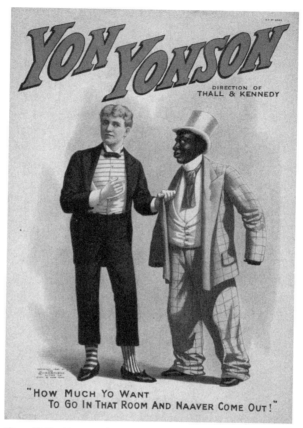

Figure 12. *Yon Yonson* publicity poster, Strobridge and Co., ca. 1899, Library of Congress, Prints and Photographs Division [POS-TH-1899.Y65, no. 1 (C size)].

Waning Years of Performances

The golden era of Swedish-dialect plays rightfully must be bracketed by the careers of Gus Heege and Ben Hendricks in the years from 1889 to roughly 1912. Swedish-dialect performances, nevertheless, continued in the United States for approximately thirty more years, until the immediate pre–World War II era, and did so largely without reliance upon Heege's original plays. This is not to suggest, however, a lack of dramatic works utilizing the Swedish immigrant caricature. Starting as early as the mid-1890s, Swedish-dialect compositions (many seemingly modeled on Heege's original offerings) regularly take to the stage, with the most productive period being the second decade of the twentieth century.

What trends can be gleaned from the existing dialect works that follow the heyday of Heege and Hendricks and continue until the final offering of Swedish-dialect plays on the American scene? Besides appreciating the strong desire of playwrights to combine contemporaneous events with popular and proven comic characters, it is apparent that Heege's creation of Sven Hanson in *A Yenuine Yentleman* did not wholly displace a reliance on the traditional greenhorn motif. Whereas the Swedish immigrant is frequently swept into current events and given a story line that speaks of an education and greater refinement, he still affects the plot in ways reminiscent of the most traditional examples of the genre. It is evident that this closing era of Swedish-dialect plays is marked by an active and willing reliance upon the blending of these two traditions.

Exploration of the greenhorn and urban/educated themes largely sets the agenda for additional research concerning popular culture caricatures of the Swedish immigrant. In striving for as complete a history as possible, effort should focus on the final years of Swedish-dialect productions that persevered through the 1930s and beyond. For example, little is known about female "Tillie" roles, so Cecil Vernon's production of *Dolly Olson* traveling from Minnesota to Utah and back in the late spring of 1941 certainly deserves attention.[99] Also of keen interest are the popular Swedish "Cowboy" plays such as those made famous by companies touring under the banner of the Ketrow Brothers in the period prior to World War II. Overall, one wants to know whether the Swedish characters of this era maintained vestiges of traditional themes or if they lost their immigrant specifics and were reduced to stock comic characters.

Investigation could also profitably center on the image of the Swedish immigrant in various entertainment entities and forums, including popular sheet music; joke and jest books such as *McNally's Bulletin, Madison's Budget,* and the various *Mack's* guides; and Swedish-dialect performances on the vaudeville stage. Such research is required and beneficial in and of itself; it could, as a bonus, reveal more about the use of the greenhorn motif and whether the Swedish immigrant and his journey of acculturation ever took on the form of an ethnic "two-act," commonly called, for example, Double Dutch or Double Hebe.[100] We need to explore if this established vaudeville and burlesque comedy format possibly advanced the placement of both Swedish character types (greenhorn and the urban/educated) opposite each other onstage as when, for instance, one learns of manager George Engesser and others promoting performances of *The Two Oles* in the 1920s. How this play fulfilled the promise of its intriguing title and whether it represents a cross-fertilization of any significance between entertainment entities is still to be discovered.

Acceptance and Impact of
the Swedish-Dialect Character

In addressing the questions of acceptance and impact of the characters of Ole and his companions, our removal in time obviously challenges complete and thorough understanding. One begins, nevertheless, by exploring the initial introduction of the character type and subsequent reactions by the general public and critics. From the onset, such dialect plays were viewed with some pointed skepticism. The newness of the Swedish-American character caused some to anticipate these plays "to be a makeshift to suit a particular dialect player." The *Providence Journal* further claims that patrons in 1891 "were not anticipating a consistent story, or a comedy of contemporaneous human interest."[101] The novelty of these plays often became the chief selling point of advance publicity in the initial years of touring. The *Boston Globe* in the spring of 1891 boasted that "something absolutely new in these latitudes is Swedish-American comedy."[102] Highlighting in publicity the "interest of novelty" or "fresh interest and the attraction of strangeness" frequently preceded early performances. Yet perhaps to distance these productions from Swedish origins and prevent negative response, the prospective audience might be assured that an upcoming performance was not a "Swedish play, as its name [*Yon Yonson*] seems to indicate, but an American comedy, with the central figure that of a Swede."[103]

While novice Swedish-dialect performers undoubtedly discovered that a pioneering stage characterization often presented various obstacles to audience acceptance, the addition of this character type was increasingly praised as novel and worthy. The *Manchester (N.H.) Union* argued in 1892 that "there have been studies of French, German, Irish, Italian, Negro and even Chinese characters without number, but until the advent of *Yon Yonson* the golden-haired, blue-eyed Swede had yet to find a place upon the stage."[104] The *Boston Globe* further reasons: "The American stage grows richer every year in original character creations, like Col. Sellers, Bardwell Slote, Josh Whitcomb, Deacon Tidd, the Senator and Hon. Maverick Brander. To this list of original creations, the offspring of our own composite national life, must now be added Yon Yonson . . . a thoroughly quaint and entertaining personage."[105] Certainly such introductions aided Swedish-dialect performances to gain greater acceptance and prominence in the early years.

Freshness amidst an overcrowded field of dialect plays, coupled with proficiency in writing and presentation, certainly proved to be of value. According to the *Omaha World-Herald* in the fall of 1892, "one reason why this play commended itself, not alone to Swedes, but to native Americans, was because the Swede was not represented as a buffoon or a semi-idiot with unearthly yells like the so-called heroes of the 'Irish drama,' now happily defunct. When another Boucicault arises he may profit by the lesson taught by the author and player of Ole."[106]

With the skillful combination of character and performance, audience response was strong—bordering occasionally on the extreme. One learns, for example, that in Buffalo "they thronged the Academy of Music last evening. After every box and every seat from orchestra to roof had been filled, there were not a few people who were obliged to lean over the foyer-rail and look at the play."[107] In Boston, "every seat and most of the standing room in the largest theatre in Boston was occupied."[108] In Brooklyn, "the audience, too, was about the same in size—packed to the doors—as when Yonson was here before."[109] Swedish-dialect plays often produced "a special clientele of their own"—many, according to one observer, "who don't go to see anything else."[110]

Despite traditional audience loyalty, evidence of hostile crowd response surfaced on occasion, such as when we learn of "a loud laughing and discouraging contingent in the audience" who "insisted on regarding [Gus Heege] as a clown."[111] While such recorded negative events largely remain rare, some were drawn to these performances by a feeling of cultural superiority. "H. B." from the *Nebraska State Journal* argues for such a general feeling in 1894: "We always like, we northern and English races, to see people of the primitive type from which we have matured. We like to see the solid Scandinavian['s] honest strength shove it[s] obstinate way through our little artificial social shams and dishonesties."[112]

Sold-out performances and enthusiastic audience feedback to these dialect texts can be confirmed. Ultimately, though, one must assess the impact of the Swedish immigrant stage characterization upon the performers involved and, more importantly, upon Swedish immigrants at large. In examining the former concern, one could reasonably inquire: What motivated playwrights and stage performers to turn to Swedish characters? As sufficiently demonstrated in previous studies, ethnic characters at this time populated the American stage in abundance and were a firmly established stage tradition. In the words of Holger Kersten, an "enormous interest in linguistic variation was displayed" at this time, and as writers experimented with language "they were recorders of the huge linguistic variety that characterized America."[113] The *Milwaukee Sen-*

tinel in 1894 argues that a timely and opportune introduction of the Swedish-dialect character had taken place and that productions such as *Yon Yonson* fit well into the general "dialect craze" without problems of overexposure: "This dialect, woven around stories that might be found in the lumber districts of the Northwest, has not yet reached any of the leading magazines, affected with the dialect craze, but some decidedly clever newspaper sketches embodying it have been written, and clippings from them are carried around in the pocket-books of any number of persons who appreciate a good thing."[114] Novelty was required to make headway in the crowded offering of performance vehicles, and the Swedish-dialect character offered a viable and valuable niche for a small group of dedicated performers, providing for a comfortable lifestyle and career. The *Louisville Commercial* in 1892 likely speaks for many when it pronounces the Swedish dialect "refreshing" after the "surfeit of German, Irish and negro dialect the theater-going public has been forced to hear of late years."[115]

As for the impact upon Swedish immigrants, various phrases to describe the stage caricature in reportorial and promotional copy deliver a mixed message. For instance, the *Baltimore American and Commercial Advertiser* in 1891 pictured the stage Swede as "ignorant and uncouth" but having behind his rough exterior a "warm, manly heart."[116] The description offered of the Swedish-American stage type a few years later by the *Brooklyn Daily Eagle*—"honest, frugal, thrifty, hard headed, slow moving, slow minded"—paints a complex ethnic portrait.[117] Unflattering images of Swedes onstage and in English-language newspapers reflected the general views of the dominant society and took hold at the expense of the ethnic group as a whole. In James Dormon's assessment, these ascriptive qualities associated with the Swedish immigrant resulted in a "we-they" polarity.[118] Any positive characteristics depicted, however, are severely compromised by the periodic admonition that "for stage purpose" the Swedish character "is made an uncommonly shrewd and heroic representative of the type."[119] In this instance a backhanded compliment for the stage character casts a general negative light upon the Scandinavian immigrant. Unquestionably, popular culture perceptions were formed or reinforced significantly by such promotional images, both print and visual, affecting how mainstream society viewed Swedes and how Swedes saw themselves.

In a few instances the press did speak out against negative elements of the caricature. The *Newark Daily Advertiser* openly wished in 1893 that Ole had been "represented as just a little less stupid" in a production of *Ole Olson*, because the "difference between his bright moments and his dull ones is too great to seem possible in the same man."[120] This call for change, however, appears exclusively for the benefit of improving the stage performance. The Swedish-language press felt compelled to voice similar concerns on occasion, but in doing so it addressed the larger implications of such negative stereotypes. A reviewer from the *Svenska Korrespondenten* of Denver found reason to view the portrayal of the title character in *Ole Olson* as moderately successful but often "too stupid": "Stupid we are, generally speaking, we Swedes, when we first come here; but we rarely look *that* stupid, nor do we find English language acquisition difficult to such a degree as Ole Olson does." In addition this commentator boasts, "it is a known fact that this language [English] is not learnt more rapidly [by any other nationality] than by us Swedes."[121]

Far less frequently we learn of opposition to the pervasive visual images used to promote these productions. On one occasion we read: "The street lithographs convey a false notion of Yon . . . Yon is not flashy, even when he blunders into flashy attire."[122] The lithograph in question was likely similar to the *Ole Olson* poster by Shober and Carqueville presented in figure 13. With the title "One Year Over," the image is of an unquestionably well-to-do Ole sporting a new line of clothing, complete with a full battery of trappings understood to be signs of success—and all this after only a short time in America. The Swedish-language newspaper *Scandinavia* of Worcester, Massachusetts, once took considerable offense at these characters' appearance in seemingly garish clothing, arguing that the mistake in having "honest Yon appear in the last act dressed in a suit giving him the appearance of a miserable fool. Yon, who earlier during the twists and turns of the play has evidenced so much tact would certainly never be guilty of such a blatant misstep." Furthermore, it is stressed, "To add insult to injury, he appears in different colored socks, which [we are told] he has bought because of their bargain price, another detail which completely contradicts his generous nature."[123] While we can appreciate the indignation voiced by this representative of the Swedish community, one must ask if these sequences involving Ole and others in loud apparel or exchange of clothing serve purposes beyond the immediate visual and comic moment. These changes do mark a clear and undeniable transformation for the character from his past to the present and, in addition, speak of foolishness in the act of imitation, as well as commenting on the dominant culture being imitated.

Despite decidedly mixed messages concerning the Swedish immigrant "type" projected through stage portrayals and promotions in print and visual forms, the record demonstrates that the ethnic comedy in question never framed the Swedish immigrant as a potential threat or danger to society. It can be argued that the comedy was placed primarily in the situation and not at the expense of character, with, according to one vocal editor, "none of the lowering and brutalizing effects, common to a great number of the farce comedies of

Figure 13. *Ole Olson* publicity poster, Shober and Carqueville Co., ca. 1890, Library of Congress, Prints and Photographs Division [POS-TH-1890.04, no. 8 (D size)].

the day."[124] As one critic articulated in 1892: "The audience laughs continuously while Ole is on the stage, but it laughs with and not at him. Awkward though he is, ungainly and slow, he is always given credit for shrewdness and mother wit; not very bright, perhaps, but sufficiently to make him adapt himself to new surroundings in a very short time."[125] Anne-Charlotte Harvey summarizes that the Swedish-American ethnic stereotype was ideal: "harmless and innocent, politically safe, socially and intellectually inferior to just about anybody, but also foreign and colorful enough to be exotic."[126] As comedy built upon stereotype, this was not humor by means of negativity or oppression.

Unfortunately, no firsthand personal testimony of the impact of these characterizations upon Swedish immigrants has yet come to light. Evidence from the Swedish-language press of the period, however, reinforces the positive reception of these productions in Scandinavian strongholds and certainly reflected commonly held beliefs of these immigrants, if not actively helping to shape such beliefs. Concerning an early production of *Yon Yonson,* the Swedish-language newspaper *Scandinavia* writes:

> *Yon Yonson* presented himself last Friday before a well filled auditorium at Worchester Theatre, where a large number of Swedes had ventured, curious to see how a Swede viewed through American eyes would appear on "these boards that represent the world." And *Yon Yonson* was indeed an acquaintance well worth making. The play, it is true, is fairly inferior as a work of dramatic art but the [audience] interest is all the time focused on the main character, the through and through honest, somewhat slow Swedish peasant boy, who under his unpolished surface hides a heart of gold. Mr. Gus Heege['s] . . . appearance, the way in which he carries himself, and his accent with its carefully reproduced Swedish cadences were all extraordinarily characteristic.[127]

The import of this critique of *Yon Yonson* appears clear to even the casual reader; namely, a skillful and faithful performance by a non-Swedish performer promotes the Swedish immigrant to the society at large as possessing valuable qualities of both mind and heart.

From advance promotion in the *Svenska Tribunen* of Chicago we learn of *Yon Yonson:* "The hero is of course caricatured when it comes to his pronunciation of the English language, his dress and his manners on arrival in America, but at the same time the Swedish characteristic traits of determination, courage, and honesty are foregrounded in a way which must appeal to every audience member of Swedish descent." The *Tribunen* further reminds its ethnic audience that "our people's more solid character traits are done full justice in the piece, so that we ought to be able to say also about Yon Yonson that 'he may deserve a little to be laughed at but still more to be honored.' Let us therefore go to the theatre, as many of us as possible, in order to hear and see—how we ourselves appear in the eyes of 'native born' Americans."[128] Here we experience once again a refrain found in the Swedish-language press of the period: stage characters present in these theatre performances provide an important glimpse into how the Swedish immigrant was viewed by the dominant culture.

As performances of *Yon Yonson* concluded in Chicago in early September 1891, the *Tribunen* reflected:

> It is, by the way, no wonder that audiences flock in masses to see this amusing piece, for in addition to song, lively and in part quite crazy dance numbers, the play

also contains scenes of a touching nature, along with a thoroughly sound and healthy spirit permeating it all. As far as audience members of Swedish heritage is concerned, it must do them good to the core to see the very best traits of their national character as powerfully and well exhibited as in the person of the hero, Yon Yonson . . . The ridiculous aspects of Yon Yonson [emphasized by the action] are so completely innocent that no one should be able to take offence at the caricature, especially considering that these aspects are more than compensated for by those [positive] traits in his character which are stressed at the expense of the representatives of all other nationalities occurring in the play.[129]

Given the response and acceptance afforded these productions in regions dominated by Swedish-American immigrants, one can argue that these performances helped such immigrants, in the words of John Lowe, "to enter laughing— using the more delightful aspects of ethnic-generated humor to win friends, acceptance, and material success."[130] As we learn concerning a performance of *Ole Olson* starring Ben Hendricks in 1892, "the genuine imported Swedes in the audience shrieked with delight last night when they saw their characteristics mirrored faithfully, but not unkindly, on the stage."[131]

Although labeled as Others, many Swedish immigrants were able to recognize and laugh at themselves through these dialect characters and were afforded an inroad to acculturation in their new society. Early advertising images, such as the one titled "An Official Reception" (fig. 14), projected the dual desired goals of acceptance and success for the immigrant, present in this instance via a warm presidential welcome to the White House. Despite the numerous hardships of adjusting to life in the United States, the Swedish immigrant found in characters such as Tilly a sense of the familiar through the comic portrayal of past and likely ongoing struggles: a yardstick against which one measured growth. Likewise, viewing the foibles of characters such as Yon assisted Swedish immigrants to define and contrast their identity in relation to the dominant culture surrounding them. "For the newly arrived," maintains historian William Linneman, "ethnic jokes served as a mirror reflecting gaucheries and greenness. These comic portrayals showed them how not to act."[132] In taking the stage, Ole Olson and companions provoked both tears and laughter for audience members expecting diversion and entertainment; in addition, they provided a mirror for Swedish immigrants, identifying both ethnic character traits of value and societal miscues to avoid. A summary by one newspaper of the period (although written in reference to the stage character) speaks to the relationship between dialect plays and new Swedish arrivals: "The object is to give the green Swede a chance to develop his precocity in catching on to American ways and mannerisms."[133]

AN OFFICIAL RECEPTION

Figure 14. Publicity for Gus Heege's *Yon Yonson* in the *Kearney (Neb.) Daily Hub,* November 5, 1892, 4.

Notes

1. Representative research includes Harley Erdman, *Staging the Jew: The Performance of an American Ethnicity, 1860–1920* (New Brunswick, N.J.: Rutgers University Press, 1997); W. T. Lhamon Jr., *Raising Cain: Blackface Performance from Jim Crow to Hip Hop* (Cambridge: Harvard University Press, 1998); Dale Cockrell, *Demons of Disorder: Early Blackface Minstrels and Their World* (Cambridge: Cambridge University Press, 1997); Gavin Jones, *Strange Talk: The Politics of Dialect Literature in Gilded Age America* (Berkeley:

University of California Press, 1999); Sean Metzger, "Charles Parsloe's Chinese Fetish: An Example of Yellowface Performance in Nineteenth-Century American Melodrama," *Theatre Journal* 56, no. 4 (2004): 627–51; William H. A. Williams, *'Twas Only an Irishman's Dream: The Image of Ireland and the Irish in American Popular Song and Lyrics, 1800–1920* (Urbana: University of Illinois Press, 1996); Kenneth J. Cerniglia, "Becoming American: A Critical History of Ethnicity in Popular Theatre, 1849–1924" (Ph.D. diss., University of Washington, 2001); Dale T. Knobel, " 'Hans' and the Historian: Ethnic Stereotypes and American Popular Culture, 1820–1860," *Journal of German-American Studies* 15, nos. 3–4 (1980): 65–74; Jennifer Stiles, "Import or Immigrant? The Representation of Blacks and Irish on the American Stage from 1767–1856," *Journal of American Drama and Theatre* 12, no. 2 (2000): 38–55; Holger Kersten, "Using the Immigrant's Voice: Humor and Pathos in Nineteenth Century 'Dutch' Dialect Texts," *MELUS* 21, no. 4 (1996): 3–17.

2.   Special thanks must be extended to Anne-Charlotte Harvey and Douglas McDermott for sharing both insights and research materials concerning Swedish-dialect plays and performers. Their generosity is deeply appreciated. All translations from Swedish, unless otherwise noted, are courtesy of Anne-Charlotte Harvey.

3.   Anne-Charlotte Harvey, "Swedish-American Theatre," in *Ethnic Theatre in the United States*, ed. Maxine Schwartz Seller (Westport, Conn.: Greenwood Press, 1983), 492.

4.   Ibid., 503.

5.   Lars Ljungmark, *Swedish Exodus*, trans. Kermit B. Westerberg (Carbondale: Southern Illinois University Press, 1979), 6.

6.   James H. Dormon, "American Popular Culture and the New Immigration Ethnics: The Vaudeville Stage and the Process of Ethnic Ascription," *Amerikastudien* 36, no. 2 (1991): 182. See also James H. Dormon, "Ethnic Semiosis in American Popular Culture, 1880–1910," *Semiotica* 83, nos. 3–4 (1991): 197–210; James H. Dormon, "Ethnic Stereotyping in American Popular Culture: The Depiction of American Ethnics in the Cartoon Periodicals of the Gilded Age," *Amerikastudien* 30, no. 4 (1985): 489–507; Lawrence E. Mintz, "Humor and Ethnic Stereotypes in Vaudeville and Burlesque," *MELUS* 21, no. 4 (1996): 19–28; and Joseph Dorinson and Joseph Boskin, "Racial and Ethnic Humor," in *Humor in America: A Research Guide to Genres and Topics*, ed. Lawrence E. Mintz (Westport, Conn.: Greenwood Press, 1988).

7.   Dormon, "American Popular Culture and the New Immigration Ethnics," 182.

8.   *Chicago Daily Inter Ocean,* March 18, 1890, 4.

9.   Robert S. Salisbury, "Swedish-American Historiography and the Question of Americanization," *Swedish Pioneer Historical Quarterly* 29, no. 2 (1978): 129.

10.   See Sture Lindmark, *Swedish America, 1914–1932: Studies in Ethnicity with Emphasis on Illinois and Minnesota* (Stockholm: Läromedelsförlaget, 1971), 321–29; and Allan Kastrup, *The Swedish Heritage in America: The Swedish Element in America and America-Swedish Relations in Their Historical Perspective* (St. Paul, Minn.: Swedish Council of America, 1975), 640–41.

11.   Rudolph J. Vecoli, "An Inter-Ethnic Perspective on American Immigration History," in *Swedes in America: Intercultural and Interethnic Perspectives on Contemporary Research*, ed. Ulf Beijbom (Växjö, Sweden: Swedish Emigrant Institute, 1993), 16.

12.   Rudolph J. Vecoli, "From *The Uprooted* to *The Transplanted*: The Writing of American

Immigration History, 1951–1989," in *From "Melting Pot" to Multiculturalism: The Evolution of Ethnic Relations in the United States and Canada*, ed. Valeria Gennaro Lerda (Roma: Bulzoni, 1990), 52.

13. George M. Stephenson, *The Religious Aspects of Swedish Immigration: Study of Immigrant Churches* (1932; reprint, New York: Arno Press, 1969), 417.

14. Lindmark, *Swedish America*, 11, 27–28.

15. Ole Olson should not be confused with John Sigvard Olsen, the "Ole" Olsen of the noted vaudeville team Olsen and Johnson. This pairing, which headlined on the Keith circuit by 1920, starred in eleven motion pictures, including *Hellzapoppin* and *Ghost Catchers*. To date, the most extensive exploration of Swedish-dialect plays is Anne-Charlotte Harvey's "Performing Ethnicity: The Role of Swedish Theatre in the Twin Cities," in *Swedes in the Twin Cities: Immigrant Life and Minnesota's Urban Frontier*, ed. Philip J. Anderson and Dag Blanck (St. Paul: Minnesota Historical Society Press, 2001), 149–72.

16. Figures range from 1 to 1.3 million. See Anne-Charlotte Harvey and Richard H. Hulan, "'Teater, Visafton Och Bal': The Swedish-American Road Show in Its Heyday," *Swedish-American Historical Quarterly* 37, no. 3 (1986): 126. See also Dag Blanck, "Growing Up Swedish in America: The Construction of a Swedish-American Ethnic Consciousness," in *Out of Scandinavia: Essays on Transatlantic Crossings of Cultural Boundaries*, ed. Poul Houe (Minneapolis: Center for Nordic Studies, 1993), 23.

17. *Nebraska State Journal*, January 12, 1895, 6.

18. *New York Daily Tribune*, December 29, 1891, 7.

19. *Daily Nebraska State Journal*, December 19, 1891, 7.

20. *Brooklyn Daily Eagle*, January 18, 1891, 13.

21. As reported in *Seattle Post-Intelligencer*, March 13, 1891, 8.

22. Cliff Ohlson to author, August 30, 1991.

23. *Jolliet (Ill.) Daily News*, September 22, 1910, 3.

24. *Omaha Bee*, December 24, 1910, 19.

25. *Murray County (Minn.) Herald*, November 15, 1917, 5.

26. An early performer on the variety stage was Swedish-dialect comedian and violinist Peter Heelstrom. "There have been other representations, though very few, of the Scandinavian dialect upon the stage . . . Heelstrom is the first to introduce the Swedish character and dialect upon the variety stage and establish it beside the German and Irish dialect character." Heelstrom was scheduled to appear in the lower theater of the Dime Museum in Minneapolis. *Minneapolis Journal*, September 6, 1890, 8.

27. To date a copy of *Rush City* has not been discovered, and while the title suggests a possible reference to the Swedish community of Rush City, Minnesota, a preview article in the *Brooklyn Daily Eagle* (December 31, 1895, 9) places the play in Oklahoma as a satire on the western land boom, with no apparent Swedish characters. In addition, for copyright purposes Frank Peel of Taunton, Massachusetts, is listed as the author of *Rush City*, not Gus Heege. It is reasonable to believe, however, that this individual is Fred Peel, who is listed as the advance agent for the 1891–92 *Yon Yonson* company starring Gus Heege (*New York Dramatic Mirror*, August 22, 1891, 9).

28. *New York Dramatic Mirror*, February 12, 1898, 9.

29. Ibid., November 22, 1890, 5.

30. *Morning Oregonian*, October 27, 1891, 5.

31. *New York Dramatic Mirror*, April 11, 1896, 13.

32. *Minneapolis Times,* November 3, 1889, 8.

33. *New York Dramatic Mirror,* April 6, 1889, 12.

34. *Stillwater (Minn.) Daily Gazette,* March 26, 1889, 4.

35. *Hastings (Minn.) Daily Gazette,* March 29, 1889, 4.

36. *Winona (Minn.) Daily Republican,* March 29, 1889, 3. One player this critic found to be of an "inferior stamp" could well have been Heege's wife, Lillie Mandeville, also originally from Cleveland. The two married in 1885 while in Canada, and when Heege began touring in his own dialect productions she took to the stage, despite having no theatrical experience. She performed alongside her husband during both the early and late stages of his career, but exact periods of trouping remain difficult to pinpoint. Following the birth of their only child (likely in 1888), it stands to reason that her value as a mother would be deemed of growing importance. While touring in 1890 the harsh evaluation of one critic perhaps hastened her taking leave of the stage: "There is one in the cast who offers a good opportunity for those who have not kept Lent and who feel that they should this week do penance in some way. Let them listen to the wearisome mouthings of Lillian Manderville [*sic*] as *Mrs. Jordan,* and their patience will be tried. She no doubt means well, but her delivery is hopelessly bad." *Milwaukee Sentinel,* April 1, 1890, 3. By 1897, nevertheless, she was touring with her husband once again, and the *Boston Herald* reported that she was "seen to excellent advantage" (February 16, 1897, 6).

37. *Winona (Minn.) Daily Herald,* March 29, 1889, 4.

38. *Saint Paul and Minneapolis Pioneer Press,* April 1, 1889, 5.

39. *Minneapolis Journal,* November 5, 1889, 4.

40. Ibid.

41. *New Orleans Daily Picayune,* February 15, 1892, 3.

42. *Arkansas Gazette,* January 1, 1893, 10.

43. Also mentioned as completing a rewrite of *Ole Olson* (starring Robert L. Scott at the time) is E. E. Kidder (*San Francisco Chronicle,* February 2, 1891, 3). Such an isolated report is not consistent, however, with the repeated references to the script work done by James A. Herne.

44. *Boston Herald,* January 10, 1893, 7.

45. *Cleveland Plain Dealer,* September 11, 1892, 11.

46. W. D. Coxey was reportedly a newspaper man formerly connected with the press in the Philadelphia area (*Utica Daily Observer,* December 29, 1890, 5). W. D. Coxey is also listed as the business manager for Jacob Litt's Standard Theatre in Chicago (Jackson and Halsted Streets) in a March 22, 1890, program for a performance of *Ole Olson.*

47. *New York Dramatic Mirror,* January 10, 1891, 11.

48. In addition to Gus Heege and Ben Hendricks, a limited number of performers are known to have headlined as the Swedish immigrant. The following introduction primarily serves as prologue to additional needed research. Robert L. Scott holds claim as one of the earliest performers to take over the Ole Olson role when Heege turned his attention to *Yon Yonson.* By January 1891 the *New York Dramatic Mirror* notes "great satisfaction of the audience" in Scott's performance at Whitney's Grand Opera House in Detroit (January 24, 1891, 9). Reportedly from San Francisco, Scott frequently is cited as having toured the country as the Old Soldier in *Muggs' Landing* and in the Chip o' the Old Block company prior to his appearances as a son of old Sweden. The *Saint Paul and Minneapolis Daily Pioneer Press* in 1890 praises a performance by Scott supported

well with "by-play and stage business" (November 17, 1890, 6). On occasion Scott is compared to Heege and found lacking, perhaps not able to "sling [the] Swedish dialect as well as his predecessor" (*Kearney [Neb.] Daily Hub,* January 25, 1891, 5). Another performer of note is James T. McAlpine, the husband of Dolly Foster, who also maintained a career as a well-known character and dialect performer. McAlpine, identified as hailing from Sioux City, Iowa, was known particularly for his ability to yodel, and this talent became a key part of his specialties. "The temptation to overdo drollery is great in this play [*Ole Olson*]," declared the *Lincoln Evening News* in 1893, stating further that he "never for one moment yields to it" (September 15, 1893, 5). Prior to appearing in productions authored by Heege, McAlpine successfully toured in the title role of *Hans Hanson* (*Sioux City Journal,* October 15, 1902, 7). Other early replacement leads touring in *Ole Olson* include Richard Baker and Edward F. Cogley. Concerning Baker's talents, the *Chicago Tribune* records, "How near his dialect comes to the Swedish is left to the many who saw the play . . . the writer not being familiar with that peculiar sing-song assassination of pure English. His acting was amusing, however, and it went well with the audience" (October 16, 1893, 4). In regards to Cogley's skills, the *Buffalo Courier* notes, "Ed F. Cogley as Ole was a prime favorite, and his comical nature, clever songs, and Swedish dialect captivated the large audience" (December 26, 1893, 6). Having once established a reputation as a Swedish-dialect performer, actors might soon find themselves headlining in new productions created to ride the popularity of the genre. The 1894 touring season found Cogley performing the title role in George H. Broadhurst's new play, *Swan Swanson* (*New York Dramatic Mirror,* May 5, 1894, 10).

49. *Erie (Penn.) Morning Dispatch,* April 11, 1892, 5.
50. *Seattle Post-Intelligencer,* November 4, 1891, 8.
51. *Minneapolis Tribune,* November 9, 1889, 4.
52. George C. D. Odell, *Annals of the New York Stage,* vol. 15 (1949; reprint, New York: AMS, 1970), 62.
53. *New York Times,* January 3, 1892, 7.
54. Ibid., December 29, 1891, 5.
55. *New York Daily Tribune,* December 29, 1891, 7.
56. *Brooklyn Daily Eagle,* January 20, 1891, 4.
57. *Boston Daily Globe,* March 10, 1891, 5.
58. *Buffalo Courier,* January 9, 1891, 5.
59. *Nebraska State Journal,* January 4, 1894, 6.
60. *Chicago Tribune,* January 10, 1897, 34.
61. Ibid., August 27, 1895, 12.
62. *Boston Herald,* February 14, 1897, 10.
63. *Springfield (Mass.) Union,* November 19, 1895, 5.
64. *Sioux City Daily Tribune,* February 13, 1896, 5.
65. *Brooklyn Daily Eagle,* February 21, 1897, 24.
66. *New York Dramatic Mirror,* September 5, 1891, 10.
67. *Morning Oregonian,* September 20, 1892, 4.
68. *Brooklyn Daily Eagle,* February 9, 1892, 6.
69. *Minneapolis Tribune,* January 1, 1895, 6.
70. Obituaries for Gus Heege are found in the *New York Dramatic Mirror,* February 12, 1898, and the *New York Clipper,* February, 12, 1898.

71. *New York Dramatic Mirror*, August 24, 1901, 2.

72. *Variety*, May 7, 1930, 76.

73. Hendricks died on April 30, 1930, in Hollywood, California. Following funeral services, his body was shipped to Flushing, New York, for interment. Hendricks was survived by his wife of thirty-eight years, Isabelle Hendricks, and his son, Ben Hendricks Jr. *Variety*, May 7, 1930, 76; see also obituary in *New York Times*, May 3, 1930, 13.

74. Swedish-dialect performers of record (in addition to those listed previously) include, to date, J. G. Anderson, Martin Bowers, Arthur Donaldson, Knute Erickson, Nelse B. Erickson, Henry Hall, Peter Heelstrom, Ben Holmes, and Charles Lindholm Sr. Of this group, Nelse Erickson was touted as having been a member of the Royal Stock Company in Stockholm and "an actor of considerably greater ability than is usually seen in the part" (*Sioux City Journal*, September 22, 1903, 3). Those performers noted as having portrayed Swedish girl roles such as Tilly Olson, as presently researched, include Aimee Common, Phyllis Daye, Emily Erickson Greene, and Agnes F. Nelson.

75. *Minneapolis Tribune*, November 9, 1889, 4.

76. *Providence Sunday Journal*, January 24, 1892, 3; *Cleveland Plain Dealer*, October 8, 1893, 6.

77. *Atlantic Journal*, October 12, 1894, 3.

78. *New York Dramatic Mirror*, October 14, 1893, 3.

79. Odell, *Annals*, 15:215.

80. Ibid., 523.

81. *Buffalo Express*, December 8, 1891, 6.

82. *New York Dramatic Mirror*, October 12, 1901, 17.

83. *Idaho Statesman*, March 23, 1911, 8.

84. *Lincoln Evening News*, August 27, 1892, 4.

85. *Cleveland Plain Dealer*, September 13, 1892, 8.

86. *San Francisco Chronicle*, March 22, 1892, 4.

87. *Cincinnati Commercial Gazette*, October 10, 1892, 8.

88. *Daily Nebraska State Journal*, August 27, 1892, 6.

89. *Boston Daily Globe*, January, 10 1893, 3.

90. *Yakima (Wash.) Morning Herald*, April 7, 1911, 4.

91. *Billboard*, March 20, 1915, 19.

92. *Variety*, May 7, 1930, 76.

93. A listing of major New York productions includes *Yon Yonson*, by Gus Heege and W. D. Coxey (1891); *Yenuine Yentleman*, by Gus Heege, with music by Percy Gaunt (1895); *Tillie's Nightmare*, by Edgar Smith and A. Baldwin Sloane (1910); and *Tillie*, by Helen R. Marin and Frank Howe Jr. (1919).

94. *Madison (Minn.) Western Guard*, August 29, 1919, 1.

95. Nearly all scripts studied were obtained from the Manuscript Division of the Library of Congress and Special Collections at Southern Illinois University at Carbondale (SIUC). The examples from the Library of Congress are scripts that have survived after being deposited during the copyright process. The scripts from SIUC are from the Sherman Theatre Collection, named after Robert L. Sherman, a theatre manager who purchased the holdings of the Chicago Manuscript Company following the owner's death. As such, the collection largely reflects the holdings of this Chicago printing company, which sold and rented play scripts from 1895 to 1922. Being from a functional play brokerage, the scripts from this source could be legitimate or pirated versions. The three-act version

of Charles Lindholm Sr.'s (1874–1936) *The Man from Minnesota,* which featured Lindholm as "Charlie Lutefisk," was obtained from Professor Anne-Charlotte Harvey. The author is also in possession of a re-created version of *Ole's Elopement,* as remembered by Cliff Ohlson more than sixty years following his final appearance in the play. Major script collections at the Museum of Repertoire Americana in Mount Pleasant, Iowa, the Popular Culture Library at Bowling Green State University, and the Russel B. Nye Popular Culture Collections at Michigan State University produced few, if any, results. For additional information on dramatic literature available in the Manuscript Division of the Library of Congress see Alan R. Havig, "Neglected Playscripts, Hidden Talent: The Vaudeville Playlet," *Journal of American Drama and Theatre* 19, no. 1 (2007): 33–56.

96. *Brooklyn Daily Eagle,* February 9, 1892, 6.
97. *Logan (Utah) Journal,* March 22, 1911, 5.
98. *Svenska Korrespondenten* (Denver), January 29, 1891. To date, no definition for "tar-rachim" has been located. The meaning within the context, however, seems clear.
99. *Bob Feagin's Bulletin,* May 28, 1941, 2.
100. Mintz, "Humor and Ethnic Stereotypes," 22.
101. *Providence Journal,* February 10, 1891, 8.
102. *Boston Globe,* March 8, 1891, 10.
103. *Rochester Union and Advertiser,* January 3, 1891, 6.
104. *Manchester (N.H.) Union,* February 1, 1892, 8.
105. *Boston Globe,* March 13, 1891, 4.
106. *Omaha World-Herald,* August 25, 1892, 7.
107. *Buffalo Express,* January 9, 1891, 6.
108. *Boston Herald,* March 10, 1891, 10.
109. *Brooklyn Daily Eagle,* February 9, 1892, 6.
110. *Ottawa (Ill.) Daily Republican Times,* September 23, 1910, 4.
111. *Brooklyn Daily Eagle,* January 20, 1891, 4.
112. *Nebraska State Journal,* January 4, 1894, 6.
113. Kersten, "Using the Immigrant's Voice," 3.
114. *Milwaukee Sentinel,* December 10, 1894, 3.
115. *Louisville Commercial,* October 25, 1892, 2.
116. *Baltimore American and Commercial Advertiser,* April 12, 1891, 13.
117. *Brooklyn Daily Eagle,* January 20, 1894, 4.
118. James H. Dormon, "European Immigrant/Ethnic Theater in Gilded Age New York: Reflections and Projections of Mentalities," in *Immigration to New York,* ed. William Pencak, Selma Berrol, and Randall M. Miller (Philadelphia: Balch Institute Press, 1991), 149.
119. *Brooklyn Daily Eagle,* January 20, 1891, 4.
120. *Newark Daily Advertiser,* February 21, 1893, 4.
121. *Svenska Korrespondenten* (Denver), January 29, 1891.
122. *Boston Daily Globe,* March 10, 1891, 5.
123. *Scandinavia* (Worcester, Mass.), April 3, 1891.
124. *Erie Morning Dispatch,* September 24, 1892, 7.
125. *Omaha World-Herald,* August 23, 1892, 2.
126. Anne-Charlotte Harvey, "Holy Yumpin' Yiminy: Scandinavian Immigrant Stereotypes in the Early Twentieth Century American Musical," in *Approaches to the American Mu-*

sical, ed. Robert Lawson Peebles (Exeter: University of Exeter Press, 1996), 69. See also Dormon, "Ethnic Semiosis," 202.

127. *Scandinavia* (Worcester, Mass.), April 3, 1891.

128. *Svenska Tribunen* (Chicago), August 27, 1891.

129. Ibid., September 3, 1891.

130. John Lowe, "Theories of Ethnic Humor: How to Enter, Laughing," *American Quarterly* 38, no. 3 (1986): 339.

131. *Omaha World-Herald,* August 23, 1892, 2.

132. William R. Linneman, "Immigrant Stereotypes: 1880–1900," *Studies in American Humor* 1, no. 1 (1974): 38.

133. *Stillwater (Minn.) Daily Gazette,* March 26, 1889, 4.

Games with Ghosts in Müller's *Explosion of a Memory*

A Study of Pre-ideology in the Müller-Wilson Collaboration

—REBECCA KASTLEMAN

> That's how it was for me working with Bob [Wilson]....
> Always it was like playing games.
> HEINER MÜLLER

When discussing his experimental drama *Explosion of a Memory,* the East German playwright Heiner Müller remarked, with characteristic irony, that he had written the piece for an audience of the dead. In producing a text that was to be performed for a congregation of ghosts, Müller asserted, he had merely adhered to the lessons of socialism: "I think it's just a democratic attitude, because the dead ones are the majority. There are many more dead people than living ones, and you have to write for a majority. This is socialist realism."[1] *Explosion of a Memory*—whose original German title, *Bildbeschreibung,* translates literally as "description of a picture"—was written as a prologue to Robert Wilson's 1986 production of Euripides' *Alcestis* and follows the attempt of an unidentified narrator to describe the violent scene he sees in an image.[2] By satirically categorizing this text as a performance of socialist values, Müller suggests an alternative context for understanding the significance of his collaboration with Wilson on *Alcestis.* In the following pages I will trace Müller's dramaturgy as it unfolds in *Explosion of a Memory* and, in so doing, outline the means by which Müller and Wilson's collaboration on *Alcestis* complicates common assumptions about the partnership between these two artists.

The production of *Alcestis* developed by Wilson and Müller, which was first staged at the American Repertory Theater in Cambridge, Massachusetts, has been largely overlooked by both critics and scholars. Although Müller's partnership with Wilson has merited extensive analysis, critics have repeatedly minimized the importance of *Alcestis* while simultaneously identifying other Wilsonian epics to which Müller contributed—such as *the CIVIL warS* and *Death Destruction & Detroit*—as pivotal events in contemporary performance. Such discussions have been too hasty in their dismissal of Müller's role in the making of *Alcestis,* which marked both a turning point in Müller and Wilson's collaboration and a milestone in the history of new American drama.

Wilson's prior productions—most of which were based on classical operas or original narratives, and which generally featured texts that Wilson himself had developed—had little in common with *Alcestis.* While it was not the first time Wilson had engaged with classical drama, *Alcestis* did mark his first attempt to stage a literary text without a full musical accompaniment. At first the director struggled with this emphasis on the written word: he was stymied by the density of Euripides' language and dissatisfied with his attempts to balance the narrative of *Alcestis* with the stage images in his design. In the initial workshops for the production in the summer of 1985, Wilson blocked the entire play "and then realized it was a mess."[3] In response he assembled his own spare adaptation, drawing upon multiple translations and drastically cutting the script, but even after these modifications he was uneasy with the text. *Explosion of a Memory,* Müller's contribution to the script, arrived at a point when the director felt that he had "almost no place to go" with his own adaptation.[4]

Müller had worked with Wilson on two occasions prior to *Alcestis:* the first was the Cologne chapter of *the CIVIL warS,* in 1984, and the second was an original opera, *Medea,* which was composed by Gavin Bryars and premiered in the same year. For *Alcestis,* Wilson initially intended to use the entire text of Müller's *Explosion of a Memory* as a prologue to the production. Ultimately, however, he used only a fraction of Müller's text in the prologue and spliced the remainder into the body of his adaptation. Thus Wilson and Müller are, in effect, coauthors of the final script, though the voices of the two artists surface in the text with more dissonance than congruity. The sections developed by Wilson are recognizable in that they are tied to the immediate action of Euripides' drama but stripped bare of linguistic complexity; meanwhile, the excerpts from *Explosion of a Memory* surface between scenes, refer to a scenario that is only thematically connected to Euripides' *Alcestis*, and rely on the texture of Müller's language to conjure a highly abstracted event.

If Wilson cultivated the interference between his own style and Müller's during the making of *Alcestis*, critics were less likely to warm to the competing elements of the production's aesthetic vocabulary. Prior to its opening, *Alcestis* had been anticipated as a major event in Wilson's artistic career; it sold out its run at the American Repertory Theater and was brought back to the theatre for additional performances in June and July 1986, shortly before the production traveled to the Festival d'Automne in Paris.[5] But American critics' response to the opening of *Alcestis* was divided and, at best, ambivalent: while a few praised the production as an exciting new turn in Wilson's work, most dismissed it as a shallow and unsatisfying take on Euripides' play. This lukewarm reception in the United States is largely responsible for the fact that *Alcestis* has been all but forgotten.

Nevertheless, *Alcestis* presents a host of unanswered questions, both as an anomaly among Wilson's productions and as an enigma for scholars interested in the collaborative development of dramatic texts. In the following discussion I will examine the ways in which Müller's self-proclaimed identity as a socialist artist, and the context of his work within the German Democratic Republic (GDR), introduced a layer of ideological tension in the creation of a production that was dominated by the fiscal and cultural conditions of the United States. Wilson's approach to staging Müller's works, as Johannes Birringer has observed, tends to "confront the frozen dialectical images in Müller's texts with all the potently rich splendor of First World theatre."[6] I will show that Birringer's claim can also be inverted—that is, Müller's socialist dramatics were a major factor in organizing his approach to Wilson's grand spectacles.

What significance did Müller attribute to his collaborations with Wilson, and how did the playwright's views of socialist ideology surface in the context of these collaborations? As David Bathrick has shown in his article "Robert Wilson, Heiner Müller and Ideology," in which he examines the Müller-Wilson collaboration by turning to Müller's influential essay on Bertolt Brecht, "Fatzer ± Keuner" (1980), Müller discovered in Wilson the "pre-ideological" dramatist that Brecht imagined in his *Lehrstüke* (learning plays). Müller says of *Fatzer*, a Brechtian *Lehrstük*, that "the text is pre-ideological; its language does not articulate the fruits of thinking but rather scans the thinking process. It carries within it the authenticity of the first glimpse of something unknown, the horror in the face of the first appearance of the new."[7] By characterizing the theatre of the early Brecht as "pre-ideological," Müller defines ideology by its opposite—the prelinguistic apprehension of the unknown. For Müller, ideology is the codification of this apprehension into an inflexible system of reference, a rhetorical process by which the possibilities of expression are limited and the authenticity of the original experience betrayed. The prelinguistic "glimpse of something unknown" that Brecht's *Lehrstüke* provide unhinges the ideological systems that organize and regulate social understanding. Following his reading of Brecht, Müller felt that the dreamlike naïveté of Wilson's images freed the theatre from the constraints of totalizing systems of representation and opened it up as a space of aesthetic free play.[8]

In the making of *Alcestis,* the figure of the ghost—which served both as a literal representation of the sacrificed Alcestis and as a metonym of the theatre itself—became a pivotal sign through which Müller called attention to the ideological disconnects that both frustrated and animated his collaboration with Wilson. That the theatre is intimately bound up with the concept of ghosts and ghostliness has been convincingly explicated by Marvin Carlson in *The Haunted Stage: The Theatre as Memory Machine,* in which Carlson argues that "one of the universals of performance, both East and West, is its ghostliness, its sense of return, the uncanny but inescapable impression imposed upon its spectators that 'we are seeing what we saw before.'"[9] Not only does the theatre's continuous recycling of ephemeral images recall so many "ghosts" onstage, but any appearance of a ghost in a theatrical production renders visible the invisible, reminding the audience that what they see onstage is made possible only by dramatic design and thereby partially exposing the mechanism of the play. In Müller's oeuvre, the ghost not only assumes these dramatic functions but also occupies a privileged ideological position: it serves to facilitate a mode of remembrance that resists the dogmatic optimism of socialist utopias. In the context of *Alcestis,* the ghost both enabled a critique of the easy aestheticism of Wilson's production and resisted the conversion of that critique into dogma. The ghost reveals, through a series of ironic gestures and partially voiced arguments, that Müller embedded his resistance to ideology in a production that did not appear to have "political" content. In the process, Müller called into question the boundaries between aesthetic and political experimentation.

I begin with a brief review of the history of Müller and Wilson's collaboration and its critical interpretations before examining how their partnership unfolded in the making of *Alcestis.*

The Müller-Wilson Collaboration:
Complementarity or Contradiction?

Critic Andrzej Wirth has described the collaboration between Müller and Wilson as an "unlikely convergence," one as improbable as it was inevitable.[10] By training and temperament, the two had little in common. Müller made his home in East Berlin, at the heart of a socialist nation that lauded him as the greatest German playwright since Brecht even as it banned the publication of his controversial texts. Wilson, schooled as a visual artist, made a name for himself as an iconoclast in New York City's avant-garde theatre scene of the 1960s before turning to freelance projects predominantly based in Western Europe. The two artists differed in their preferred style and form: Müller's dramatics reflect his fraught relationship with language, celebrating the abstract and cerebral, while Wilson's theatre is defined by the psychological magnetism of its images. For critics seeking to make sense of this partnership, the question was—as John Rockwell phrased it in his review of *Hamletmachine* in the *New York Times*—"what brought this visually oriented Texan and this doom-laden East Berliner together?"[11]

American reviewers' responses to this query have tended to rely upon a straightforward typing of Wilson's theatre as formal and visual and of Müller's work as language-based and thematically heavy. As Gordon Rogoff writes, "In Wilson, Müller has found the perfect director for unearthing the form behind the scribble, and in Müller, Wilson has at last found the dramatist who can give textual weight to his stunning, impalpable visions."[12] Though they at first appeared to be an unlikely pair, Rogoff explains, "once seen, nothing could be simpler" than the collaboration of the two artists.[13] According to this model, the relationship between Wilson and Müller expresses a basic complementarity: Müller's dense text anchors Wilson's astonishing images.

This simplistic equation not only minimizes the imagistic quality of Müller's texts and the psychological depth of Wilson's staging but also belies the complexity of their partnership. Müller had worked as a director as well as a playwright, and Wilson often wrote or adapted the texts used in his productions; the dynamics of the collaboration were continually parsed and revised, marked by shifts and changes in the work of both artists over a period of more than ten years. Most importantly, however, the complementarity model incorrectly assumes that each artist strove for the same dramatic objectives, and it falsely implies that Wilson's and Müller's contributions to a given production were intended to act in concert rather than play against each other. I will show that their collaboration depended not upon a straightforward pairing of the literary and the visual but rather upon the productive dissonance between their total views of the theatre. To account for this dissonance we must examine each artist's aesthetic logic not as an independent phenomenon but as a language intimately bound up with the political and cultural milieu in which he found himself.

Wilson and Müller met in 1979 in West Berlin, where Wilson was developing *Death Destruction & Detroit* at the Schaubühne. This production, which examined the life of the prominent Nazi Rudolph Hess, opened at a time when the division between East and West was entrenched in German culture. During this period, West Germany struggled to reconcile itself with its violent past—Wilson's production being one such attempt—while the GDR pretended to forget it.[14] For both Wilson and Müller, the differing historical narratives typical of the East and the West, as well as the crosscurrents that connected these two realms, were a source of artistic fascination. While Wilson mined dramatic material from German history, Müller found inspiration in the prerevolutionary Americas: upon meeting Wilson, the playwright had just penned *The Mission,* a text that explored the colonial consciousness in the New World through a treatment of socialist exile Anna Seghers's novel *The Light in the Gallows.*[15] Set in the French West Indies, *The Mission* traces the problems of the socialist revolution back to the failed revolutions in the colonies. It was no coincidence that, in the year that Wilson and Müller met, Wilson was exploring the patterns of ideology, nationalism, and identity in German history, while Müller investigated similar themes in the Americas. A preoccupation with the dominant ideologies of East and West and a concern with probing and deconstructing these categories were at play from the inception of their artistic partnership.

Indeed, the first collaboration between the two artists—the multimedia opera *the CIVIL warS,* for which Müller coauthored the Cologne segment—thematized the idea of national difference and explored the grand sweep of global history by experimenting with the rhetoric of nationalism and internationalism. Scheduled to tour six nations, incorporating segments from each country into a twelve-hour epic, *the CIVIL warS* was an unprecedented theatrical and financial spectacle. But the production was upstaged by a real-life drama that unfolded against the backdrop of the global capitalist economy: unable to secure funding for the final performance at the 1984 Olympics in Los Angeles, Wilson's flamboyant pageant of international artistic solidarity was never completed. In the project's aftermath, some critics expressed ambivalence about Müller's participation in the production—an apprehension that Birringer has traced to the "well-publicized ease with which the plays of a Marxist writer travel from Berlin and the GDR to New York and the US, where they seem to have been seamlessly assimilated into the advanced capitalist formalism of Robert Wilson's lavish 'theater of images.'"[16] Wilson's treatment of Müller's texts seemed to collapse the particularity of national and political identities, subsuming the specific cultural currency of Müller's writing to Wilson's mythologized, and fatally uncritical, internationalism.

Later in 1984, Wilson and Müller worked together on an operatic *Medea*, composed by Gavin Bryars and staged at the Opéra de Lyon. Unlike *the CIVIL warS*, the political valence of the production was introduced largely by Müller, whose textual contribution to *Medea*—a prologue entitled *Waterfront Wasteland/Landscape with Argonauts/Medeamaterial*—reveals preoccupations with ideology and history similar to those that had characterized his earlier work. *Waterfront Wasteland* provides a snapshot of a post-utopian war zone, the defeated revolutionary Medea left abandoned in a devastated landscape. Wilson's decision to incorporate *Waterfront Wasteland* as a prologue rather than in the body of *Medea* emphasized the discreteness of the text against the backdrop of Euripides' drama and Bryars's opera, carving a space of relative autonomy for Müller's voice in the context of the production.

The inclusion of *Waterfront Wasteland* in *Medea* informed the incorporation of *Explosion of a Memory* in *Alcestis*, as well as later works in which Müller's prologues provided a counterpoint to the principal text and action in Wilson's productions. This "prologue" stage of the Wilson-Müller partnership constitutes an early form of the collaboration and was later revised for Wilson's seminal productions of *Hamletmachine* (1986) and *Quartet* (1987), in which Wilson staged complete productions of Müller's preexisting plays. During the making of *Alcestis*, however, these patterns of collaboration had not yet been clearly defined. As the third production that Wilson and Müller created together, *Alcestis* offers an important glimpse at the collaboration at an intermediary moment, a point at which the terms of the partnership were articulated but the dynamics still flexible. *Alcestis* is thus a curious anomaly: although the piece does not resemble Wilson and Müller's work in its later incarnations, it is a significant departure from their first two productions.

How did the two artists conceive of Müller's contribution to *Alcestis* at the inception of the project? On the surface it appears as though Müller's involvement in the production was relatively circumscribed. The playwright had little connection with the production process leading up to *Alcestis*, although he communicated with Wilson by telephone and received videotapes of rehearsals once they began. Moreover, while Wilson specifically commissioned a text from Müller for use as a prologue to *Alcestis*, *Explosion of a Memory* had a life outside Müller's collaboration with Wilson: the text was completed before it appeared in *Alcestis* and premiered independently in Germany in 1985.[17] Indeed, Müller attributed his original inspiration for the piece not to Euripides but to an unfinished drawing by a Bulgarian art student. As Jonathan Kalb emphasized in a 2005 interview, the fact that Müller's initial concept for *Explosion of a Memory* was unrelated to *Alcestis* must be taken seriously, because the playwright's later identification of the piece with *Alcestis* and with other classical and modern texts may have been intended to frustrate rather than facilitate its interpretation.[18]

Despite the indications that *Explosion of a Memory* and Wilson's production of *Alcestis* were not mutually dependent, there can be no question that the text was composed with Wilson himself in mind. As Matthew Griffin successfully argues, *Explosion of a Memory* is "a text written expressly for Wilson and his theater."[19] In its style and content the piece chronicles Müller's evolving attempt to understand and control the role of his texts in Wilson's productions, using the story of *Alcestis* to expose and refigure the issues at stake in their partnership at a critical moment in their collaboration. More specifically, it records Müller's attempt to negotiate his ideological position with respect to Wilson's dramatics. Although *Explosion of a Memory* does not feature the overt interrogation of ideology and nationalism that is characteristic of *the CIVIL warS* and Müller's prologue to *Medea*, these concerns have hardly vanished from Müller's work. To examine more closely the strategies through which ideological tensions between the cultural realms of "East" and "West" are managed and deconstructed in this text is to witness the sophistication and irony of Müller's game with Wilson, with *Alcestis,* and with himself.

Pre-ideological Theatre in the Müllerian Imagination

Reviewers might have insisted on describing Wilson and Müller as complementary opposites that fused together to create an aesthetic unity, but the artists themselves stressed the impossibility of assimilating their aesthetics and methods. Wilson praised the impenetrable, "rock-like" quality of Müller's language, claiming that he was unable to understand the texts and uninterested in interpreting their meaning through his staging.[20] Instead, he preferred to allow Müller's words to unfold independently of the images onstage as a kind of aural texture—a language-score that paralleled, and only selectively aligned with, the visual elements of the production. Müller praised the director's approach, which he believed to facilitate a productive discord among text, image, and action. Wilson, he wrote, "never interprets, a text is simply there and it is served up, and not tainted in any way and not explained."[21] The critical dramaturge must ask why the artists explained their work according to this "commensurability" model of collaboration, which is so uncharacteristic of projects undertaken separately by Wilson and Müller in which each artist strove to leave his mark on every aspect of the production.

In fact, neither the complementarity model offered by critics nor the explanation put forward by Wilson and Müller fully accounts for the dynamics of the partnership. The fact that Müller praises Wilson for refraining from interpreting his texts is a vital clue to Müller's perception of their collaboration. Here we turn again to Bathrick's argument that Müller was drawn to Wilson because the director seemed to be a truly pre-ideological dramatist, one who was more true to Brecht than Brecht was to himself. Müller wrote that although the writings of the early Brecht envisioned a pre-ideological theatre, Brecht later became too entangled in the intellectual snares of postwar Leninism to continue developing the playful dramatic idiom that he had imagined. Müller viewed himself as a successor to Brecht, and his texts perpetuate the dream of the pre-ideological theatre; like Brecht, however, Müller found himself estranged by his own erudition. Müller found in Wilson an artist whose childlike imagination had not been captured or limited by ideological rhetoric and who offered "the experience (*die Erfahrung*) of a different way of working; a letting go of something; a lightening up."[22]

Bathrick suggests that Wilson and Müller's partnership enabled the production of a dreamlike landscape—the dream being a space of imaginative possibility—in which texts were "opened up for reflection."[23] The visual grandiosity of Wilson's direction did not lead to the depoliticization or dehistoricization of Müller's writings, Bathrick argues, but rather exposed and liberated them. Wilson treated the text as "furniture" that was to be isolated and, to some extent, resisted,[24] an approach that distanced Müller's language from its own ideological undertones. As Bathrick writes, "While working in the extreme hermetic spaces of the Wilsonian no man's land Müller is released momentarily from the cultural 'civil wars' of Germany's east-west misere of the 1970s and 1980s, mired as they were in tired and overly ideological mantras."[25] Müller's text remained affiliated with the political and historical milieu in which it was written, but those facets of his work that might otherwise have been overdetermined by their political or historical connotations—and thus ensnared in ideological constructs—were destabilized by Wilson's interventions, which continually violated expectations and imagined new paradigms. According to this argument, the play of Wilson's directorial eye permitted a certain flexibility of interpretation that liberated Müller's words. His language loosed from pre-established meanings and associations and allowed to stand on its own terms, Müller found in Wilson's theatre a space of absolute freedom.

Bathrick provides a convincing analysis of Wilson's ties to the early Brecht and the attraction Müller felt to Wilson's pre-ideological directorial style. However, one assertion requires further elaboration: the claim that Müller fully believed that ideological baggage could be effectively purged from his texts through Wilson's choice to refrain from interpreting them. Certainly, Müller had great admiration for the images Wilson was able to produce through the treatment of language as "furniture." Furthermore, there is no question that Müller preferred Wilson's approach to the conventional theatre of narrative, which, he argued, circumscribes all action under a single monolithic interpretation and therefore may become both dogmatic and dangerous. But in suggesting that Müller wholeheartedly endorsed Wilson's interpretive "no man's land" on the grounds that it enabled a pre-ideological dramatic language, Bathrick minimizes the self-referential irony of Müller's praise for Wilson. Müller was sincere in his respect for Wilson's cultivated naïveté and willing suspension of interpretive acuity, but the erudition and historical sensibility of Müller's own work calls into question whether pre-ideological drama is even possible. In fact, it displays an acute cultural and historical specificity and becomes fully legible only in the context of East German society. Müller walked a fine line in his collaborations with Wilson: he hoped to "open his texts for reflection" while preserving certain themes and historical details on which the audience was invited to reflect.[26] The danger of pre-ideological theatre, Müller recognized, is that as it becomes increasingly "liberated" from the ideology of language—as it proposes, in effect, an end to the trappings of historical specificity—it sidesteps history's inexorable continuation and begins to bear an unpleasant resemblance to the socialist utopias that Müller so vociferously resisted.

Müller explores this problem in his prologue to *Alcestis.* The ghostly woman, one of the central figures in *Explosion of a Memory,* becomes a means of recalling the weight of history. Through this figure, Müller raises a sidelong critique of Wilson's method insofar as it signals a rash disregard for the particulars of historical time and place. The ghost calls attention to the historical sensibility that is missing from Wilson's work by drawing upon reservoirs of recent collective memory that were common to both East and West, enjoining the audience not to succumb blindly to the aesthetic escape provided by Wilson's spectacles. Müller's resistance to Wilson's style is, therefore, not merely a question of the director's treatment of Müller's texts but a methodological critique that Müller has preemptively inscribed in his contributions to the director's productions. Yet Müller's criticisms are always allusive rather than explicit: Müller seeks to remain in a playful, pre-ideological mode, disguising and destabilizing his own claims. In staking his arguments as gestures and games rather than definitive assertions, Müller avoids ensnarement in his own ideological position and ensures that his words will offer lively, adaptable resistance to Wilson's method.

Overpaintings of *Alcestis:*
Disappearing History, Raising the Dead

Explosion of a Memory, Müller later explained in his epigraph to the published edition of the piece, "may be read as an overpainting of Euripides's *Alcestis* which quotes the Noh play *Kumasaka,* the Eleventh Canto of the *Odyssey,* and Hitchcock's *The Birds*... an explosion of a memory in an extinct dramatic structure."[27] The text contains no explicit references to Euripides' drama, but it captures *Alcestis* in a picture that has been "painted over," its dominant themes obscured by the deconstructive interventions of Müller's writing. Müller responded to central elements in Euripides' *Alcestis*—most notably, a woman's sacrifice and her troubled resurrection—but transported them to an entirely different context and situation. His "overpainting" opened *Alcestis* to exposition and revision while preserving an allusive structure in which all references to the classical drama were suggestive, ironic, or incomplete.[28]

The titular event of *Explosion of a Memory*—the "description of a picture"— is the conversion into language of an image seen by an unidentified narrator. As cultural historian Arlene Teraoka observes, "the activity of seeing is intimately connected with the violence of the scene."[29] But Müller is not interested in what the eye observes when it is open; rather, he describes the scene perceived in the space of a blink, that is, "what is visible between glimpse and glimpse, when the eye HAVING SEEN IT ALL squints itself closed over the picture."[30] As the speaker reports the elements he sees, the text twists and doubles back on itself as it proposes an unending chain of alternatives for the events captured in the image, revealing the obfuscations and ambiguities of the picture. In the continuously shifting constellations of the elements in the description—whose three principal characters are identified only as a man, a woman, and a bird— each configuration of events ends with the murder of the woman. The recurring depiction of the woman's death serves as a pivotal moment that is common to all interpretations of the picture, calling to mind the centrality of Alcestis's sacrifice to Euripides' drama.[31]

The instant of the blink in which the narration unfolds captures the "horror in the face of the first manifestation of the new" that Müller associated with the pre-ideological theatre. The picture that is apprehended behind closed eyes is an illusion that exists apart from the realm of literal representation, and the description captured in *Explosion of a Memory* extends the duration of the blink to enable the pre-ideological play of the imagination. In Müller's writings, the idea of the blink is explicitly bound up with Wilson, and also with the political conditions of reunified Germany, as outlined in a 1995 essay: "When Robert Wilson talks about his work, he always comes back to blinking. What do you see in the blink of an eye? Blinking continually creates a new image of the world, or reality. This image is always forgotten. That is exactly what is happening in Germany now. In the new Germany no one is blinking any more."[32] The blink that frames *Explosion of a Memory* suggests that, in Müller's imagination, Wilson is already implicated in the text.[33] In its deconstruction of the image, the piece attempts a literary experiment with pre-ideological dramatics, paralleling and parodying Wilson's directorial approach. The experiments in representation that characterize *Explosion of a Memory* are not merely an aesthetic feature of the text, however—they also gesture toward a space of political possibility. While Müller explains that the world, and the new Germany in particular, is inclined to forget the fresh visions contained in the imaginative moment of the blink, *Explosion of a Memory* preserves and elevates that ephemeral creative moment. The blink reveals a rupture in history, a "gap in the process" that is a "hole in eternity, the potentially redeeming MISTAKE";[34] this break in the teleological progress of history offers an opportunity to create "a new image of the world."

The manner in which Müller imagines the pre-ideological landscape he explores in *Explosion of a Memory* reveals both the danger and the possibility of this mode of expression. The process of description enacts a form of violence, destabilizing the image and calling the events of the picture into question through a narrative that operates in the subjunctive mode. German scholar Florian Vaßen has referred to this voice as the "or-structure" of *Explosion of a Memory*, a system produced through the introduction of a series of possible conditions that are given equal weight, reflecting a "seeming uncertainty of the onlooker in the act of describing."[35] At the inception of the piece, the or-structure permits a certain hermeneutic flexibility, a free play of interpretive possibilities; as the description continues, however, it triggers accelerating scenarios of escalating urgency and destruction. The or-structure extends the encounter with the pre-ideological unknown, revealing the open-ended interpretations of each element of the picture. But it also builds with deadly momentum toward the collapse of all boundaries between characters, events, and objects, until, in the final lines of the text, the speaker becomes almost indistinguishable from the picture. It is only through the obsessive recollection of the woman's death, the sole point in the description that marks something "other" than the speaker, that the narrator can be distinguished from the picture he describes.

That the death and reappearance of the woman in the picture determine the rhythm of *Explosion of a Memory* reveals the centrality of this ghostly woman to the text. Robert Scanlan and others have written that the events recounted in *Explosion of a Memory* may be intimately connected to the suicide of Inge Müller, Heiner Müller's first wife.[36] While a biographical reading by no means exhausts the interpretation of Müller's text, it may illuminate the psychological gravity attached to the figure of this particular ghost. The woman in the picture periodically returns—as Teraoka writes, "like an obsession"[37]— suggesting a traumatic memory and perhaps recalling the many suicide attempts that preceded Inge Müller's death.[38] The playwright, who seldom spoke publicly about his wife's suicide, admitted that *Explosion of a Memory* "has very much private material in it, too, for sure," although he never explicitly connected the text to the loss of his wife.[39] The event of Inge Müller's suicide may also have influenced Heiner Müller's rendering of the text's narrator, whose guilty complicity in the scene is suggested by his role as a spectator and confirmed through the escalating description, revealing the extent to which the playwright himself was "haunted" by the image he describes.

The ghost of the woman occupies a privileged position with respect to the image, as she exists at multiple points in space and time. Müller said of *Explosion of a Memory* that "there is one point that I'm really interested in, the question of what is after death. . . . So I tried to write a text about the world on the other side of death."[40] The woman in the picture, trapped between the earth and the underworld, is able to glimpse this other side. Her murder and resurrection occur in the same fixed moment in the picture, and her appearance reflects her liminal position between the world of the living and the world of the dead. The woman's affect is wan and uncanny, and she bears the scars of prior violence: "the face is gentle, very young, the nose far too long, with a swelling, the result of a punch perhaps from a fist of knuckles; she looks to the ground, as if there were an image she cannot forget and/or another she does not want to see."[41] The unforgettable image of the past, which threatens to reproduce itself in the present, imprints itself on the woman: her body carries the traces of traumas that only she can witness.

The figure of the ghostly woman is thus a harbinger of a time in which the past will violently resurface. The woman's backward gaze registers the rising number of ghosts that have accumulated throughout history. Through her eyes, we witness "rock sliding triggered by the wanderings of the dead in the inner earth": there is no more room under the ground for the dead, and they threaten to return to the world of the living.[42] The speaker suggests that the woman is the marshal of these underground soldiers—an "angel, hollow underneath her dress," who holds her finger into the wind as an army of resurrected corpses blows a storm into the picture.[43] Like Walter Benjamin's Angel of History, the woman is caught in the storm of progress, staring at the accumulated ruins on the surface of the earth while unable to stop the accretion of debris.[44] She bears witness to the effacement of the landscape imagined in *Explosion of a Memory,* which "is a space of collective history, but it is a history at a standstill."[45]

The woman in *Explosion of a Memory* offers a study of the ideological significance of the ghost, a figure that frequently surfaces in Müller's dramatics, featuring prominently in *Hamletmachine, Germania Death in Berlin,* and *ABC,* among other dramas. Müller's spectral characters bring the afterworld perilously close to the world of the living; Müller imagines his theatre as a vast cemetery, a landscape of death in which ghosts appear and disappear from view. Müller writes that his drama envisions a "theater of resurrection" that "naturally presupposes daily death"; it enacts a "raising of the dead, the ensemble recruited from spirits which must return to the grave after the performance, until the final performance, a premiere of the third kind, the set a travel guide through the landscape beyond death."[46] By imagining the theatre as a site for the "raising of the dead," Müller reveals his belief that theatre has an obligation to confront the reality of time's passage—that is, the reality of historical change. In his article "Heiner Müller's Spectres," Hans-Thies Lehmann argues that the importance of the ghost in Müller's oeuvre is based in the relationship of the spectator to the actual ranks of the dead in history. The ghost "refers to an uncanny dimension (*Unheimlichkeit*) in time and history: consciousness demands memory. Without the immersion in death there can be no well-founded viewpoint on life. Without remembering there can be no utopia."[47] The ghost, therefore, is a necessary reminder of the burden of the past, a memory of the untold dead of history that holds open the possibility of a better future.

This element of the figure reveals its importance in the context of Müller's political thought. By facilitating a mode of remembrance that resists the blind optimism of ideology, the "heavy" ghost provides a concrete link to the past that anchors the present and guides the future. Lehmann summarizes the importance of the ghost in Müller's works: "Memory and the retaining of history as a burden and even as ghostly nightmare are the sole form of utopia. Ideology is, on the contrary, a seduction precisely because it allows one to throw off the burden. The image of heaviness opposes ideology and the reduction of experience to the present and to the world of consumption. The dead that leap onto the backs of the living provide consciousness with the all too necessary weight of its history."[48] The weight of the ghostly woman in *Explosion of a Memory*—a weight that, at the moment of her murder, crushes a chair, upends a table, and sends objects in the room flying—provides a necessary reminder of the inescapable burden of the dead in history. At the same time, the ghost's continually recycled form threatens to dematerialize and disappear, stranding the future in a directionless ocean of forgetting.

The ghost is removed from the pre-ideological free play that propels the description; her gaze extends beyond the moment of the blink, looking backward into the past to affirm the presence of history and the necessity of retrospection. The metonymic repetition of her death exposes a past that cannot be forgotten, even as representations of that past are effaced by Müller's words. The result is a game that Müller plays with the ghost, a contest in which the act of writing both necessitates and resists the act of remembering.

Writing with One Eye Open

As Müller might have predicted, Wilson's staging of *Explosion of a Memory* in *Alcestis* largely sidesteps the issues raised by Müller's self-referential battle with the dead.[49] The director's somber, ritualized treatment of the text—with its stylized action and intoned narration—leaves little room for the exploration of Müller's literary irony. Throughout the production, the text of *Explosion of a Memory* spews from the mouth of a mummy who is suspended above the stage in the arms of a Cycladic statue. In the prologue this live recitation of Müller's text is overlaid with a homemade cassette recording of Christopher Knowles, Wilson's adopted autistic son, reading through the material.[50] The images onstage, which bear only an associative connection to Müller's text, unfold like the landscape of a dream—a man lies in a pool of blue light on the floor; Herakles appears in the distance, holding his club aloft; a woman who carries a handbag stands perfectly still, her back to the audience; the figure of Death, his body suspended in the air and resembling the thorax of an enormous white moth, extends his enormous wings. Meanwhile, a woman in a white dress, who seems to represent the woman in Müller's text, runs gracefully toward a man who stands at the opposite end of the stage; midway through her advance, she stops in her tracks and turns away from him. The surprising and inscrutable configurations of the elements in Wilson's collage of images generate an independent visual vocabulary that playfully jettisons all reference to the world outside the "blink" in which Müller's picture was apprehended.

While Wilson's staging choices were consistent with the pre-ideological aesthetic Bathrick describes—demonstrating a naive free play with theatrical forms and embracing the pre-representational space of the blink—Müller always kept one eye open, such that *Explosion of a Memory* was not a blink but a *wink* at his audience. In the performance of this ironic gesture, Müller intended to conspire with the production's spectators while preserving a sense of play. The text of *Explosion of a Memory* poses a half-voiced challenge to call Wilson's images into question and to consider the implications of Müller plotting against Wilson, against the play, and even against himself. Far from displacing the interrogation of ideology that was central to *the CIVIL warS* and *Waterfront Wasteland/Landscape with Argonauts/Medeamaterial*, *Explosion of a Memory* hypothesizes a world in which history is "painted over" and language achieves a "pre-ideological" freedom. Through this thought experiment, Müller arrives at a critique of Wilson's method. Elinor Fuchs has called Wilson's interpretation of *Alcestis* "an imaginative work-through to the end of western culture."[51] Müller's tactics, however, resist the possibility of an end to history, opening the eyes of the audience to the hidden presence of the dead and relying on the voices of ghosts to critique the codification of ideology through a return to memory. Even in his collaboration with Wilson, Müller remained wary of severing his writing from its particular position in culture and history. In this way, *Alcestis* offers a glimpse of the evolving process by which Müller negotiated the political and ideological stakes of his partnership with Wilson through a series of tricks and games.

Müller's construction of the ghost not only allowed him to raise a playful critique of Wilson's theatre but also exposes a central framework of his dramatics in its relation to GDR politics. The figure of the ghost presents a dilemma for a culture that turns its back on the past, serving as a reminder of the extent to which history can be suppressed and overwritten. By ironically suggesting that he had written *Explosion of a Memory* for an audience of the dead, Müller revealed not his literal adherence to socialist realism—as he explained, "the dead ones are the majority . . . and you have to write for a majority"—but his desire to rehabilitate socialism through reflection on the past, without which there can be no cognizance of present possibilities. The figure of the ghost, to

which Müller attended closely in *Explosion of a Memory,* enjoins us to interrogate those stories and ideologies that have slipped from view. Müller's "theater of resurrection" ironically exhumes the disappearing dead in an effort to
resuscitate the future. Accordingly, in the making of *Alcestis,* Müller kept one
eye shut to dream, and one eye on what was missing from the picture.

Notes

1. Bonnie Marranca, ed., *The PAJ Casebook: "Alcestis,"* 10, no. 1 (1986): 96–97.
2. Müller intended that the title *Explosion of a Memory* be used for the English translation of his drama *Bildbeschreibung.* See "Explosion of a Memory/Description of a Picture" in *Explosion of a Memory: Writings by Heiner Müller,* ed. and trans. Carl Weber,
   (New York: Performing Arts Journal, 1984), 93–102. In the American Repertory Theater
   production of *Alcestis,* however, the text was referred to as *Description of a Picture.* I use
   the title *Explosion of a Memory* throughout this analysis for the sake of consistency, even
   though Wilson and his other collaborators might have known the text only as *Description of a Picture.*
3. Alisa Solomon, "Theatre of No Ideas: A Conversation with Robert Wilson and Heiner
   Müller," *Village Voice,* July 29, 1986.
4. Ibid.
5. In 1987 the production was staged in German as *Alkestis,* which opened in Stuttgart in
   April.
6. Johannes Birringer, *Theatre, Theory, Postmodernism* (Bloomington: Indiana University
   Press, 1991), 62.
7. Heiner Müller, from 1980 "Brecht vs Brecht" ("Fatzer ± Keuner"), in *Germania,* ed.
   Sylvère Lotringer, trans. Bernard and Caroline Schütze (New York: semiotext(e), 1990),
   131.
8. David Bathrick, "Robert Wilson, Heiner Müller and Ideology," unpublished translation
   by the author. Originally published as "Robert Wilson, Heiner Müller und die Ästhetik
   des Präideologischen" in *Die Insel vor Augen,* ed. Michael Opitz (Berlin: Theater der Zeit,
   2004), 12.
9. Marvin Carlson, *The Haunted Stage: The Theatre as Memory Machine* (Ann Arbor: University of Michigan Press, 2001), 1.
10. Andrzej Wirth, "Heiner Müller and Robert Wilson: An Unlikely Convergence," in *Heiner
    Müller, Contexts and History: A Collection of Essays from the Sydney German Studies
    Symposium 1994,* ed. Gerhard Fischer (Tübingen: Stauffenburg Verlag, 1995), 213–19.
11. John Rockwell, "Wilson and Müller and NYU," *New York Times,* May 12, 1986, C14.
12. Gordon Rogoff, "Hamletmachine," *Performing Arts Journal* 10, no. 1 (1986): 54.
13. Ibid.
14. Ian Buruma provides a clear analysis of the problems of postwar remembrance in *The
    Wages of Guilt: Memories of War in Germany and Japan* (London: Vintage, 1995), in
    which he describes a "peculiar state of innocence in the GDR" (156) with respect to

crimes committed during World War II, a perspective legitimated by the socialist teaching that the Communist Party had contributed to the resistance against fascism.

15. For more on Anna Seghers's influence on Müller's dramatics, see Helen Fehervary, "Landscapes of an 'Auftrag,'" *New German Critique* 73 (Winter 1998): 115–32.

16. Birringer, *Theatre, Theory, Postmodernism,* 55.

17. Ginka Cholakova, Müller's second wife, directed the premiere of *Bildbeschreibung,* which opened in Graz in October 1985 (Matthew Brett Griffin, "Text and Image in Heiner Müller's Theater Collaborations with Robert Wilson" [Ph.D. diss., New York University, 1999], 343). Today, *Explosion of a Memory* is staged as an independent text in both its English and German incarnations.

18. Jonathan Kalb (Hunter College Theatre Department chair) in discussion with the author, October 29, 2005.

19. Griffin, "Text and Image," 204.

20. Wirth, "Unlikely Convergence," 214.

21. Bathrick, "Robert Wilson, Heiner Müller and Ideology," 1.

22. Ibid., 9. Wirth supports Bathrick's assessment of the affiliation between Wilson and Brecht in Müller's understanding, showing that "the last dream of Brecht was to reach a level of epic 'naiveté' in theater. Müller inherited the dream, but he is intellectually too cerebral, too complicated to be able to dream it. Unexpectedly in Wilson's theater Brecht's/Müller's dream came to life" ("Unlikely Convergence," 215).

23. Bathrick, "Robert Wilson, Heiner Müller and Ideology," 4.

24. Ibid., 18.

25. Ibid., 12.

26. Jonathan Kalb, "Resisting Müller," in *Free Admissions: Collected Theatre Writings* (1990; reprint, New York: Limelight Edition, 1993), 193–95. He discusses the paradox of Müller's relationship to his texts in production: "It's as if he [Müller] committed a sort of provisional suicide, disclaiming authority in the production process like a good post-Artaudian corpse but cherishing the thought that privileged subtexts do exist in his work and will be discovered by future generations" (195).

27. Müller, *Explosion of a Memory,* 102.

28. Many of Müller's plays operate as deconstructions of major dramatic works in the literary canon, but *Explosion of a Memory* is unique in that the body of the text does not explicitly reference its source material.

29. Arlene Akiko Teraoka, "Writing and Violence in Heiner Müller's *Bildbeschreibung,*" in *Vom Wort zum Bild: Das neue Theater in Deutschland und den USA,* ed. Sigrid Bauschinger and Susan L. Cocalis (Bern: Francke Verlag, 1992), 189.

30. Müller, *Explosion of a Memory* (1984), in *Theatremachine,* ed. and trans. Marc von Henning (London: Faber and Faber, 1995), 134. In this and subsequent citations from *Explosion of a Memory,* I quote from Marc von Henning's translation of the text, which is more faithful to the original German and to the flow of Müller's language than is Weber's.

31. Teraoka, "Writing and Violence." Teraoka has observed that "the silent woman of Müller's text . . . recalls Euripides' *Alcestis*" (183).

32. Müller, "The Less We See the More We Describe," interview montage, in *Theatremachine,* xx–xxi.

33. David Sterritt, "Robert Wilson: Orchestrator of Theatrical Images," *Christian Science Monitor*, March 12, 1986, 25. Wilson himself hoped that his work would cause his audience to blink: "blinking changes our perceptions, and that's what I want."

34. Müller, *Explosion of a Memory*, in *Theatremachine*, 137–38.

35. Florian Vaßen, "Images Become Texts Become Images: Heiner Müller's *Bildbeschreibung* (Description of a Picture)," in Fischer, *Heiner Müller, Contexts and History*, 171.

36. Robert Scanlan, "Post-Modern Time and Place: Wilson/Müller Intersections," in *Art and Design Profile No. 45*, ed. Nicholas Zurbrugg (London: Academy Group, 1995), 79.

37. Teraoka, "Writing and Violence," 182.

38. The recollection of Inge Müller also seems to haunt other texts by Heiner Müller: in *Obituary* he gives a semi-autobiographical account of discovering his wife's body (*Germania*, 180–83). In the poem "Yesterday on a Sunny Afternoon," contained in the drama *ABC*, he speaks of the "desire / to exhume my wife from the cemetery" (*ABC: A Collage of Poetry and Prose*, in *Theatremachine*, 23).

39. Marranca, *The PAJ Casebook*, 96.

40. Ibid.

41. Müller, *Explosion of a Memory*, in *Theatremachine*, 133.

42. Ibid., 136.

43. Ibid.

44. Walter Benjamin's description of the Angel of History, a figure inspired by Paul Klee's painting *Angelus Novus*, imagines an angel staring back at the ruins of history. His face is "turned toward the past. Where we perceive a chain of events, he sees one single catastrophe which keeps piling wreckage upon wreckage and hurls it in front of his feet. The angel would like to stay, awaken the dead, and make whole what has been smashed. But a storm is blowing from Paradise." Benjamin, "Theses on the Philosophy of History," *Illuminations* (New York: Schocken, 1968), 257.

45. Vaßen. "Images Become Texts Become Images," 176.

46. Heiner Müller, *Dove and Samurai: A Heiner Müller Reader*, ed. and trans. Carl Weber (Baltimore: Johns Hopkins University Press, 2001), 114.

47. Hans-Thies Lehmann, "Heiner Müller's Spectres," in Fischer, *Heiner Müller, Contexts and History*, 87–88.

48. Ibid., 93.

49. However, Scanlan has suggested that the proliferation of ghosts in *Alcestis* may have had special significance for Wilson as well. He has argued that *Alcestis* enabled Wilson, a private homosexual, to confront the spread of HIV at the height of the AIDS epidemic. Robert Scanlan in discussion with the author, October 14, 2005.

50. In addition to that of Knowles, three other voices are audible on the recording: actor Harry Murphy, playing a newscaster; a young child; and actor Rodney Hudson in his role as Death.

51. Marranca, *The PAJ Casebook*, 85.

On the Emergence of European Avant-Garde Theatre

—ANTONIS GLYTZOURIS

Introduction: A Problem of Theatre Historiography

When historians of theatre examine bibliographical sources concerning the genesis of European avant-garde theatre, they usually find exceptional works on the major artistic movements, including monographs on artists as well as anthologies of theoretical texts and manifestos, but they are unable to accomplish the goal of tracking down a comprehensive historical study dealing with the phenomenon of the emergence of the theatrical avant-garde.[1] This short essay does not set out to accomplish this immense goal; rather, it seeks to put in order the pieces of a puzzle in order to provide an overview, to map an existing situation, and to put forward a working hypothesis on the rise of theatrical avant-garde.

Even the preliminary problems historians have to confront are complex and thorny. In the final analysis, the most serious of these problems has to do with the way historians of the theatre must connect the art of the theatre with avant-garde art so that they neither disassociate the art from the general discourse on the history and theory of the avant-garde nor apply to the field of theatre history general theoretical constructions, which are derived from aesthetics, literature, or the fine arts.[2] Additionally, one must bear in mind the contemporary dispute between theatre studies and performance studies.[3] Problems of this kind usually appear when researchers do not make an effort to avoid projecting current ideological quarrels into the past. As a consequence, they put forward extremely restrictive theoretical schemata that may be convenient and fascinating but which, historically speaking, remains arbitrary and distortive.

As historians do not begin their research based only on theoretical tools but, primarily, based on evidence, they cannot ignore the fact that the terms related to avant-garde theatre appeared not with futurism or constructivism but much earlier: in the context of the first independent theatres, naturalism, and symbolism.[4] Theatre historians do not start their job with present theories of avant-garde performance, with a theoretical definition of what avant-garde theatre is. For their purposes, avant-garde theatre is simply what a given society at a given time regards as such. This happened for the first time in the history of European theatre in the last quarter of the nineteenth century.

If one adopts the perspective of post–World War I avant-garde aesthetics, one will characterize the pioneers of the first modernist wave as mere reformers or innovators and not as eclectic avant-garde artists. In its effort to define the concept of avant-garde and in order to come close to current beliefs, much theatre historiography does not listen to anything from the past but instead the echo of its own voice. The far-reaching consequences of this approach are that it reproduces another prejudice: in order to read the past, it adopts (and is confined within) the perspective of the neo-Darwinist ideals of avant-gardism.[5] In this way, it continues to think a priori of avant-garde not as a historical form but in terms of its own self-definition, that is, within and yet outside bourgeois society: living behind a shield that protects it from the abuses of modernity and mass pop culture of the twentieth century. Pop culture is usually denounced and rejected as the revolting producer of a "cheap" form of industrialized entertainment created for a mass market. This approach seems to ignore that commercialization of the avant-garde movements had already begun in the years of its emergence, just because it was the lawful (albeit somewhat irregular) child of a modern society. It carried in its chromosomes some of the paramount values of modernity: radicalization, experimentation, and innovation, even if the latter sometimes meant destruction. As Adorno put it, "the new in art is the aesthetic counterpart to the expanding reproduction of capital in society. Both hold out the promise of undiminished plenitude."[6]

From the above sample of problems it becomes clear that the complex phenomenon of avant-garde theatre is a matter of degree, associated always with a specific set of historical circumstances. It would be better for historians to avoid holding a monolithic notion of the avant-garde and instead speak of a diversity of avant-gardes.[7] On the other hand, historians must not ignore the theoretical speculations that have been formulated in relation to the art of the avant-garde, because the danger that lurks in this case is an unproductive historical relativism that abolishes the avant-garde theatre as a historical unity. Furthermore, it would be extremely productive for one to bear in mind that the first systematic theoretical studies on the avant-garde began at a time when the phenomenon was drawing to its close, when artists such as Cocteau and Ionesco had become members of the French Academy and one in five French theatres was dubbed "d'avant-garde."[8] As one can appreciate, the contribution of postmodernism was important, with the consequent demystification of the highbrow art of the modernist tradition. Today it has become clear that avant-garde art does not automatically mean good, better, or worse art, and this offers a significant advantage to modern historiography in its effort to provide a fresh historical reading of the recent past by denouncing older prejudices. Since historians begin their project knowing for certain that they do not discover an "objectivity" positively somewhere in the past but that they must construct it while inventing it, their construction should be nearest to the complex, fluid, fragmentary, and conflicting "disorder" of the past, without being monolithic, incomplete, inconsistent, or untidy.

Theories on the Genesis of the Avant-Garde

In general terms, the term *avant-garde* brings to the historian's mind challenging, anti-bourgeois artistic movements that appeared in the context of modernism.[9] The avant-garde is a basic ingredient of modernism, but semantically speaking it is not concomitant with it, since modernism (even in the period 1890–1940 when it was at its height) was not limited solely to the "innovations" of the avant-garde.[10] If modernism signified awareness of the present "as the womb of the future," a vehement break from the past, then the avant-garde was its battering ram. It was that constantly evolving section of bourgeois culture which was its vanguard in the search for new territories and which, in order to discharge this duty, rose up against the very culture that gave birth to it. To this end, the avant-garde remains the child of a bourgeois society but at the same time signifies a challenge to the bourgeois status quo.[11] Thus, avant-garde artists, in their effort to experiment with new styles of expressions in modern society, were also cut off from the general public, while their artistic conventions largely expressed differentiation and innovation and, like the Pataphysics of Alfred Jarry, laid down the laws that proved the exception and not the rule.[12] Eventually, from this perspective, the common denominator for all avant-garde movements was a deep feeling of dissociation in the relationship between the artist and his public. From another perspective, however, the avant-garde contributed to a deeper, more organic inclusion and incorporation of art into the world of the capitalistic mode of production: no matter how or how much the avant-garde artists reacted to capitalism, the experimental and innovative nature of their work was frequently found to be in tune with the agendas of "big business" that made their appearance in Europe at the time the avant-garde was starting to emerge.[13] What is more, the commercialization of the avant-garde had already begun in its infancy.[14]

As noted earlier, the term *avant-garde* has no static, fixed theoretical meaning; the avant-garde was the result of a historical process, a result of the various ways in which the term has been used in various societies and epochs. For the same reason, the avant-garde has not always existed. Its influences lie in romanticism, and one certainly cannot talk about related concepts before the Sturm und Drang movement.[15] Romanticism was the first revolutionary movement against tradition, against the ancien régime and its neoclassicism and, from a certain point onward, against capitalism itself.[16] Nonetheless, avant-garde art only effectively emerged between the last quarter of the nineteenth century and World War I.[17] Only after the end of romanticism was the basic historical condition that gave birth to the avant-garde met: the triumph of bourgeois industrial culture, something which in the field of art meant the gradual autonomy of aesthetics in terms of the process of artistic production and the predominance of the realistic ideal in terms of the artistic end product. In effect, the avant-garde arose along with the first fundamental crisis (or for others, decline) of bourgeois society and art in the last quarter of the nineteenth century (especially at the period of the major depression, between 1873 and 1895) and found expression in naturalism, primarily in symbolism at first, and in the avant-gardes that followed thereafter—that entire range of -isms that appeared in the years around World War I. It was then that the art of the avant-garde shaped its own special nature and was transformed into an overall self-critique of bourgeois society art. It reached its triumphant zenith, taking on its well-known vehement, intensely anti-realistic manifestations. Yet, approaches vary. Others place the first major period of the avant-garde between 1905 and 1938 and identify its influences in naturalism and symbolism, while others talk simply about the second phase of the avant-garde, considering this second phase to be an integral part of modernism. Theorist Peter Bürger, finally, makes an innovative distinction between modernism as a mere reaction to traditional artistic techniques and the avant-garde as a violent attack that sought to change the social function of art in bourgeois society. However, in reality, the problem is again a historical one: in this last case we have a change in the *target* of the avant-garde from the ideological content of art to its social function as an institution in bourgeois society.[18] Nonetheless, in all cases the avant-garde remained the flesh and bones of the bourgeois class for another reason: the historical processes—

which led to such conduct historically—presupposed aestheticism. This development indicates an initial achievement of autonomy for art and its theory, a process that has its roots in the emancipation of the bourgeois class and in the aesthetics of Anthony Ashley Shaftesbury, Immanuel Kant, and Friedrich Schiller.[19] Given that in aestheticism form and content coincided under the dogma of "art for art's sake," certain artists realized that modern art had been transformed into a "sacred refuge" within bourgeois society; the next step in the self-critique of bourgeois art was to be the most radical, since it was opposed not only to this "sanctification" of art but also to the aesthetic experience itself as a private sphere that had lost its social function.[20] In this way the avant-garde artists not only retained a basic element of aestheticism but also sought to incorporate art and life or attempted to organize life *via* art. Nevertheless, the rift between the avant-garde movements and bourgeois society must not mislead us into approaching them in the absence of their real place in history. The scientific and technological discoveries that followed the second industrial revolution were the driving force for this huge storm of experimentalism in new artistic modes of expression and made a decisive contribution to the emergence of the avant-garde, regardless of the intentions of the individual artists and movements involved.

Naturalist and Symbolist Theatre and the Avant-Garde

A basic problem facing theatre historians who deal with this issue is the simple absence of theatre as an art form in the aforementioned theories of the avant-garde, theories that rest almost exclusively on the fine arts and literature.[21] Historians should take into consideration the differences presented by the special features of theatrical art (e.g., in the case of theatre one must consider public, more socially institutionalized products, which, additionally, were fleeting performances). Nevertheless, historians should not overlook the similarities between theatre and other forms of art. One could perhaps identify the inklings of an avant-garde approach in the premiere of Schiller's *Die Räuber* (1782) in the Royal Theatre of Manheim or *Hérnani* (1830) at the Comédie Française or, more so, in Wagner's *Gesamtkunstwerk*. However, in the world of the theatre, the naturalistic movement set in operation the mechanism for the rise of the avant-garde as a conscious and systematic reaction to the conventional realism of the "pièce bien faite" and the "pièce à thèse."[22] The naturalistic movement is key to understanding this issue, since it is a maturation of bourgeois realism and *at the same time* an initial critique of it; thus the avant-garde began to emerge via a revolutionary movement that, although never turning against the realistic ideal, nonetheless did, via stinging criticism of bourgeois society, lead to the birth of modernist drama. It is no coincidence that among the explorations of artists who were placed in the midst of naturalism, cracks began to emerge in the European bourgeois consciousness from which sprang first symbolism and later expressionism. The works of Ibsen, Hauptmann, Strindberg, or Lygné-Poe and Meyerhold, both with naturalism and the anti-realistic reaction, are symptoms of a deep-seated crisis but also critiques of bourgeois culture that rise above the individual features of these movements. The first cracks started with naturalism condemning the "dark" aspects of bourgeois society while at the same time insisting on its more "developed" aspects. Since almost all avant-garde movements that followed naturalism were anti-realistic, they turned against it as they saw realism as concomitant with a non-creative, photographic depiction of reality. Many researchers of avant-garde theatre also adopted this stance.[23] However, naturalism was the major revolutionary movement in Germany at the end of the 1880s and the beginning of the 1890s, as it was directed against the art of Gründerzeit or the bourgeois formalism of Gustav Freytag's dramatic theory.[24] The pre-expressionist plays of Wedekind or Sternheim were closely associated with naturalism, even though they were opposed to it.[25]

In general terms, avant-garde theatre emerged fully when it met symbolism or neo-romanticism: the first reaction not only to bourgeois art but also to its realistic ideals.[26] By the beginning of the twentieth century symbolism had stopped being an avant-garde movement and had begun to be assimilated by the rest of modern theatre. Maeterlinck in *Monna Vanna, Sœur Béatrice,* and *Marie Magdeleine* had become the "comme il-faut" Nobel laureate of 1911 and was no longer the avant-garde playwright of *L'intruse, Les aveugles,* and *Pelléas et Mélisande.*[27] In the first decade of the twentieth century, moving through complex channels, with its roots in the realm of neo-romanticism, one part of avant-garde theatre led to its completion, became more violent, more nonrepresentational, and more experimental, and took other dimensions when it encountered futurism, Dadaism, expressionism, Bauhaus, surrealism, and so on.

The Rise of the Independent Theatres and Modern Stage Direction

Avant-garde theatre emerged when modern theatre production had liberated itself and become independent as a special discipline, a trend that characterizes bourgeois art in general. Were one to search for the makeup and constitution of avant-garde theatre, one would have to turn to the very venues within which the gradual liberation of the world of theatre took place: the independent theatres movement, those new powerhouses generating the art of the avant-garde that appeared along with the first major depression or decline in the robust theatre industry of the nineteenth century.[28] With few exceptions these were pitiful minorities, exceptionally short-lived and marginal efforts that were established after a share of spectators interested in their new "experimental products" had appeared. It was a public not at all unlike that of the small artistic journals which emerged after the triumph of mass journalism.[29] As theorist Jiří Veltruský rightly points out, the experiments of the avant-garde theatre had an impact on the development of theatre precisely when they started to lose their private character and operated with more stable theatre troupes capable of forming their own clientele. Amid all that, the avant-garde theatre experiments became historical reality and their existence created a completely new social phenomenon, a new way of integrating theatre into society.[30] Théâtre Libre paved the way for various paths in the following decades, and the independent theatres were transformed in the laboratories of Sturmbühne, Galleria Sprovieri, Cabaret Voltaire, or the Bauhaus stage workshop. The fact that the latter underlined their experimental character meant simply that their experimentalism was of a different kind and degree from that of Antoine's theatre, that they were descending from the archetype born in 1887.

Nonetheless, we must bear in mind another factor: the emergence of theatrical avant-garde was a clear break from the past precisely because it was the result of a deep-seated crisis in the European bourgeois drama of the nineteenth century and an innovative attempt to overcome that crisis.[31] At first this occurred in an effort to reinstate the role of the playwright, but (via an exceptionally interesting historical paradox) it actually led to the emergence of the modern director as the new artist of the theatre, which on its own was an ontological change of classification in the history of theatre. It is not a coincidence that Edward Gordon Craig, in the context of neo-romanticism, first announced this discovery in his famous essay "The Art of the Theatre: The First Dialogue" (1905). Thus guided by the modern directors, we move from aestheticism to theatricalism and to the search for a new autonomous essence, that is, theatricality, as something sharply different from dramatic poetry. That means that the avant-garde stage artists attempted to overcome the crisis by rebaptizing the art of the theatre in the holy water of this new essence, which they considered had been interred under the realistic stage. The theatricalist trend, which marks a large section of the avant-garde theatre in the years before and after World War I, sought to do away with bourgeois theatre, a theatre without theatricality[32] in its view, although in many cases it ended up searching for a "teatralitá senza Teatro," to use Marinetti's words. Of course, we must keep in mind several reactions to these trends that took place within the modernist tradition.[33]

However, the major break had already occurred: modern avant-garde theatre performance emerged when theatre decided to liberate itself from drama. This began with the new dynamic concept of the naturalistic "milieu" and its consequences in the art of stage direction. It matured with the poetic theatre of symbolist suggestiveness and imagination and the work of such visionaries as Appia. Up until the end of the nineteenth century the theatre was viewed as an art form in the service of literature. Only thanks to the first experimental stages, and within the wider context of neo-romanticism, did the revolutionary transformation of dramatic poetry into stage poetry begin to take place—an osmosis of text and performance so important that it became the cornerstone of modernist theatre.[34] The establishment of experimental stages was a revolutionary act not only because it called into doubt the academic art of the royal or state theatres or the conventional realism of the theatre industry but primarily because within these small theatres the aforementioned transformation started to take place within the context of symbolism. It is no coincidence that this process occurred at a time when another debate was raging: the crisis of prose theatre in the last quarter of the nineteenth century.[35] In this perspective, the avant-garde theatre artists served as a response to the crisis in the theatre industry and contributed to creating a way out: smaller but more inventive and flexible theatre businesses.[36] In the first decades of the twentieth century, the avant-garde movements modernized theatre production when they wanted to take a stance against a new (still) popular art form of cinema. After the new shape of the market emerged, prose theatre had not only stopped being popular entertainment but had to turn its attentions to an even more specialized bourgeois public of intellectuals and artists. With the discovery of "theatricality" and the new stage language, a new world came to light that offered unlimited opportunities for creative expression onstage and provided a modern complicated theatre culture to the theatre audience. Actually, it was the beginnings of the "postdramatic theatre."[37] It was a new powerhouse for generating "pure theatrical energy" with an as yet unpredictable dynamic in areas such as the modern interpretation of the "classics" (and of course the consequent decline of traditional playwriting). The most radical aspects of this process led to futurist synthetic theatre and, generally speaking, performance art, a total prevalence of spectacular elements. This entirely new dynamic of stage poetry which emerged from the revolutionary slogan "theatricalize the theatre" meant simply that the older production and consumption standards of the theatre industry had been exhausted at a time when cinema brought the arts of spectacle into the age of "technical reproducibility."[38]

Avant-Garde Theatre and the Rise of Theatricality

Inside or outside the context of the history of the theatre, one can trace "the idea of theatricality in its various manifestations throughout many periods."[39] However, one fact steadily remains: the term *theatricality* did not exist prior to 1837, when Thomas Carlyle introduced it in his *French Revolution*. In a strictly historical perspective we cannot speak of theatricality in the Roman theatre in the same way that we cannot speak of "drame" bourgeois or "metteur en scène." *Theatricality* denotes, once more, a significant break with the past that took place in the post-Enlightenment era, and it was formulated at about the same time as both the emergence of aestheticism and the concept of avant-garde. As Tracy Davis puts it, the inventor of this neologism simply "coined a word for a concept that was articulated by Edmund Burke and Adam Smith in the eighteenth century."[40] Perhaps the most interesting notion is that Carlyle already used the word as synonymous "with a theatrical matter, or performance" in his *Reminiscences* (1866) after a night at Drury Lane.[41] But, generally speaking, in the Victorian era *theatricality* denoted mainly artificiality with all those negative connotations of insincerity and inauthenticity. These connotations became gradually positive when they were spirited off to another planet, to the environment of aestheticism and symbolism.[42]

As had happened with the case of avant-garde art, the contributions of symbolism and aestheticism were catalytic. One prior major step was the modernist invention of theatricality in Wagnerian aesthetics, a clear forerunner of the modern mise-en-scène.[43] Even though one can speak safely of significant trends of a "modernist anti-theatricalism," there seems to be unanimity for "avant-garde theatricalism." And that's because there is a main division between attacks on the theatre motivated by a celebration of the value of theatricality and those motivated by a resistance to it.[44] In the context of symbolism a "theatricalization of literary discourse" also took place firstly as "a realization of an artistic concept in everyday life" that gave rise to the dandy as an avant-garde artist.[45] The next major step was the transformation and further specification of aestheticism to theatricalism. This term alludes to "an unprecedented celebration of the theatre and of theatricality," to "those turn-of-the-century reformers and revolutionaries of the theater who made it their business to rescue the theatre from what they thought of as its accelerating decline."[46] Besides Edward Gordon Craig, among these artists one can mention not only the major stage directors of the era but also avant-garde artists like Marinetti, who shared this state of "theatrocracy," manifested in his famous phrase "tutto è teatrale quando ha valore" ("everything valuable is theatrical").[47] In fact, "there is a metatheatrical dimension in the avant-garde experiments where the familiar reality is represented as theatrical." But, here again, the major developments took place in the Russian avant-garde, beginning with Meyerhold and his transition from his early symbolist "plasticity" to the formation of his experimental "theatricality"; later with Russian futurism; and, mainly, with the work of Nikolai Evreinov, who combined extreme "theatricalism" not only in the stage of his experimental Ancient Theatre but also with his *Theatre in Life* (1913) and *Theatre for One-self* (1915–17).[48]

It is no coincidence that from the late 1920s until the early 1970s this avant-garde Russian artist was gradually pushed out of the limelight and that his name made a dynamic comeback during postmodernism—or, better, late modernism—when the notion of theatricality started to diffuse into the "cultural performance" and became a fundamental concept of the new field of performance studies as a "conditio humana."[49] In the world of the illiterate bourgeois class, one century after Carlyle's neologism, the word *theatricality* lost its negative connotations and became a fundamentally positive concept of the new field of performance studies, as an almost anthropological category. However, from a certain point of view the above development was a product of the formation of the avant-garde theatre that took place in the 1900s and 1910s as a reaction to the crisis of the theatrical system of the nineteenth century.

Epilogue

Theatricality was from the beginning (directly or not) connected with the development of the experimental stages. The ephemeral character or financial failure of the latter did nothing to contradict the association between the appearance of avant-garde theatre and the modernization of the theatrical business faced with the new needs of the public, a modernization in which the avant-garde artists played the role of not only revolutionaries but also innovators. That is why, when the avant-garde directors of the beginning of the twentieth century asked the theatre to reexamine its relationship with the public, they did not mean that it had to acquire a new content but rather a new aesthetic role, to become a celebration, a ritual, a paratheatrical spectacle, a happening, a political meeting, and so on.[50] They emphasized this aspect just because they wanted theatre to acquire a new function within the newly emergent mass culture, a function that, as noted, naturally presupposed aestheticism. However, even though these experimenters remained within the confines of aestheticism, they continued another, much more enduring tradition that breaks through the art of avant-garde as well as that of the elite.[51] That is to say that the boundaries between avant-garde theatre and mass culture were not so strictly defined. This finding becomes clearer when theatrical historiography moves away from the study of major "personalities" (i.e., from the traditional romantic historicism of the nineteenth century); when it turns more to quantitative data, measurements, comparisons, and averages in its effort to identify the content and style of the avant-garde ritual that certain "priests" created for the numerically meager audiences of the twentieth century; and when it finally examines thereinafter the relationship of avant-garde theatre with other aspects of modern culture, such as commercial theatre, cinema, and television. This need is even more pressing when one recalls that the emergence of avant-garde theatre through the aforementioned revolutionary transformation gave birth to the modern historiography of the theatre as a separate discipline.[52]

Notes

1. See also the notion of Jiří Veltruský in "Semiotics and the Avant-Garde Theatre," *Theatre Survey* 36 (1995): 90–93. In the last fifteen years a more systematic discourse has been developed. The most recent case is Günter Berghaus's *Theatre, Performance and the Historical Avant-Garde* (New York: Palgrave/Macmillan, 2005). Berghaus discusses the formation of modernism and avant-garde theatre (1–54) but actually offers a new and detailed presentation of the four major prewar avant-garde movements (expressionism, futurism, Dadaism, and constructivism), bringing new and significant evidence to bear on the history of avant-garde performance. Earlier, in 1998, David Graver, in *Aesthetics of Disturbance: Anti-Art in Avant-Garde Drama* (Ann Arbor: University of Michigan Press, 1998), treated the same question theoretically in the starting chapters of his study ("Defining the Avant-Garde" and "Negotiating the Artistic Material," 1–63), but his focal point was the relationship between the avant-garde and five major playwrights (Oskar Kokoshka, Gottfried Benn, Raymond Roussel, Roger Vitrac, and Wyndham Lewis). Even earlier, Christopher Innes, in his pivotal *Avant Garde Theatre, 1892–1992* (London: Routledge, 1993), did not pay any attention to the problem of the genesis of avant-garde theatre. Finally, Arnold Aronson's *American Avant-Garde Theatre: A History* (London: Routledge, 2000) discusses the case of the American avant-garde.
2. John Henderson's pioneering book *The First Avant-Garde (1887–1894): Sources of the Modern French Theatre* (London: George G. Harrap, 1971) avoids correlating theatre

history with the phenomenon of the avant-garde (9–18). Contrarily, Berghaus begins to study theatrical avant-garde with a "conventional schema" (*Historical Avant-Garde,* xii), taken from the history of the visual arts and literature, which he then tries to apply to the history of the theatre of the nineteenth and twentieth centuries. It is not a mere co-incidence that he focuses mainly on "the key role" (xv) played by painters, poets, and musicians in avant-garde performances. When one finishes reading the first chapter, one feels that the great absence is the art of the theatre itself. At this point the meager presence of theatre as an art form in the major theories of the avant-garde must be noted; i.e., Renato Poggioli, *The Theory of the Avant-Garde* (Cambridge: Harvard University Press, 1968), and Peter Bürger, *Theory of the Avant-Garde* (Minneapolis: University of Minnesota Press, 1987).

3. In this context one must examine Berghaus's decision to deal with avant-garde performance and to exclude from his scope European theatre and drama in order to define as theatrical avant-garde primarily the four artistic movements composing the object of his study. There is no doubt that performance art has its roots in the above-mentioned artistic movements, and since the late 1970s its relation with postwar avant-garde has been defined. See RoseLee Goldberg's *Performance Art: From Futurism to the Present* (London: Thames & Hudson, 1990), first published as *Performance: Live Art 1909 to the Present.* But these movements were only a significant aspect of theatre avant-garde (those associated with the major developments in literature and fine arts) and, of course, have to do with a particular historical phase, which is not associated with the genesis of theatrical avant-garde but with its triumph around World War I. It is the moment when they challenged the theatre as an institution or, as Berghaus puts it, "abolished the product-oriented working method of institutionalized theatre" (*Historical Avant-Garde,* 46). In this way, the author seems to restrict the concept of avant-garde to what Poggioli had characterized as the "antagonistic moment" hereof (*Theory of the Avant-Garde,* 25–27).

4. Henderson, *First Avant-Garde,* 9–18.

5. On this subject as well as on the downgrading of the historical study of the popular theatre of the twentieth century, see Allan Woods, "Emphasizing the Avant-Garde: An Exploration in Theatre Historiography," in *Interpreting the Theatrical Past; Essays in the Historiography of Performance,* ed. Thomas Postlewait and Bruce A. McConachie (Iowa City: University of Iowa Press, 1989), 166–76.

6. Theodore Adorno, *Aesthetic Theory* (London: Routledge, 1984), 31.

7. Here lies another danger of a strict schematization. In the mid-1990s, Richard Schechner famously spoke of five avant-gardes, but the topography he offered was not that of a historian; his main concern was the "future of the ritual," not its past. Schechner, *The Future of the Ritual: Writings on Culture and Performance* (London: Routledge, 1993), 5–22.

8. Henderson, *First Avant-Garde,* 13. On the decline of modernism and the avant-garde, see the different approaches of Jürgen Habermas, "Modernism versus Postmodernism," *New German Critique* 22 (1981): 5–6; and Daniel Bell, *The Cultural Contradictions of Capitalism* (New York: Harper Collins, 1978), 3–30. The most important theoretical contributions to avant-garde art are those of Poggioli and Bürger (see note 2), which appeared first in 1962 and 1974 in Italian and German, respectively, before being translated into English. Among the immense bibliography on this issue, note also the essays

of Raymond Williams collected in his posthumous *The Politics of Modernism: Against the New Conformists* (London: Verso, 1990). For a bibliography on the avant-garde see Matei Calinescu, *Five Faces of Modernity: Modernism, Avant-Garde, Decadence, Kitsch, Postmodernism* (Durham: Duke University Press, 1987), 371–74; and Berghaus, *Historical Avant-Garde,* 283–97.

9. As far as terminology is concerned, a useful starting point is Calinescu, *Five Faces of Modernity;* for the avant-garde theatre see Bert Cardullo, "En Garde! The Theatrical Avant-Garde in Historical, Intellectual and Cultural Context," in *Theater of the Avant-Garde, 1890–1950: A Critical Anthology,* ed. Bert Cardullo and Robert Knopf (New Haven: Yale University Press, 2001), 3–5.

10. Gene H. Bell-Villada, *Art for Art's Sake and Literary Life* (Lincoln: University of Nebraska Press, 1996), 125–26. See, too, the position taken by Miklos Szabolcsi in his essay "Avant-Garde, Neo-Avant-Garde, Modernism: Questions and Suggestions," *New Literary History* 3 (1971): 50–51; and Peter Bürger's critique of Habermas and Adorno in "The Significance of the Avant-Garde for Contemporary Aesthetics: A Reply to Jürgen Habermas," *New German Critique* 22 (1981): 21–22.

11. Thomas Bishop, "Changing Concepts of Avant-Garde in 20th Century Literature," *French Review* 38 (1964): 34–41; Calinescu, *Five Faces of Modernity,* 119; Habermas, "Modernism versus Postmodernism," 3–14; Poggioli, *Theory of the Avant-Garde,* 216–18; Williams, *Politics of Modernism,* 32, 49–56. See also the very useful introductions in the anthologies *Contours of the Theatrical Avant-Garde: Performance and Textuality,* ed. James Harding (Ann Arbor: UMI Research Press, 2000), 1–11; and *Not the Other Avant-Garde: The Transnational Foundations of Avant-Garde Performance,* ed. James Harding and John Rouse (Ann Arbor: UMI Research Press, 2006).

12. Poggioli, *Theory of the Avant-Garde,* 57.

13. Bell-Villada, *Art for Art's Sake,* 145–46, 155–56.

14. Jost Hermand, "The Commercialization of Avant-Garde Movements at the Turn of the Century," *New German Critique* 29 (1983): 71–83. According to Berghaus, "many of the items produced by Futurists and Constructivists for the everyday use of ordinary citizens affected the future history of production design.... In the first quarter of the twentieth-century, many of the innovative traits and achievements of the avant-garde were adopted by the Modernist movements ... the capitalist consumer market successfully colonized Modernist art and integrated it into its portfolio of commodities. By the mid-1920s many ideas originally propagated by the avant-garde had become assimilated by the mainstream" (*Historical Avant-Garde,* 43–44).

15. Poggioli, *Theory of the Avant-Garde,* 14, 51–54, 213; Bell, *Cultural Contradictions of Capitalism,* 16–18.

16. It is not mere coincidence that the term *avant-garde* was introduced in the context of French romanticism, as it intersected with the first tentative steps of the socialist and anarchist movement, initially by Saint-Simon in 1825 and then by Proudon. See Donald D. Egbert, "The Idea of 'Avant-Garde' in Art and Politics," *American Historical Review* 73 (1967): 342–45.

17. According to Poggioli (*Theory of the Avant-Garde,* 13–14), terms related to the avant-garde then became established and disseminated.

18. Szabolcsi, "Avant-Garde, Neo-Avant-Garde, Modernism," 53–54; Poggioli, *Theory of the Avant-Garde,* 227–28; Bürger, *Theory of the Avant-Garde,* 22–27.

19. Bürger, "Significance of the Avant-Garde," 21. The romantic movement first used the phrase "l'art pour l'art," which was coined by Benjamin Constant (1804) while he was in Germany under the influence of Kantian aesthetics (Egbert, "The Idea of 'Avant-Garde,'" 344). To be precise, it was a romantic misinterpretation of Kantian aesthetics that was disseminated during the French Restoration (Bell-Villada, *Art for Art's Sake,* 35–56).

20. Bürger, *Theory of the Avant-Garde,* 22–27, 47–49.

21. The first major theoretical approaches to avant-garde theatre came from representatives of the Prague School; see Veltruský, "Semiotics and the Avant-Garde Theatre," 87–95.

22. Henderson, *First Avant-Garde,* 19–25; Cardullo, "En Garde!" 5. The above-mentioned dramatic forms, due to later preference for the anti-realist avant-garde art among modernist theatre critics, were supplanted by modern historiography, even as topics for study, being ignominiously dubbed "boulevard." However, this paints a misleading picture, since we should not underestimate the decisive impact of these forms in shaping modern drama. See, too, Michael Hays, "Declassified Documents: Fragmentations in the Modern Drama," *Boundary* 17 (1990): 102–28.

23. Innes, for example, saw the par excellence unifying element in avant-garde theatre only in the irrational primitivism of the ritual (*Avant Garde Theatre,* 2–3). It is indicative that his book was first published under the title *Holy Theatre* (1981).

24. Hermand, "Commercialization of Avant-Garde Movements," 72–74.

25. On naturalism as the heir to bourgeois realism and the first step toward modernist theatre see also Williams, *Politics of Modernism,* 84–85.

26. Veltruský, "Semiotics and the Avant-Garde Theatre," 87–95; Jindrich Honzl, "Dynamics of the Sign in the Theater," in *Semiotics of Art: Prague School Contributions,* ed. Ladislav Matejka and Irwin R. Titunik (Cambridge: MIT Press, 1976), 92; Cardullo, "En Garde!" 5–6; Harding, introduction to *Contours of the Theatrical Avant-Garde,* 1–11; Frantisek Deak, *Symbolist Theatre: The Formation of an Avant-Garde* (Baltimore: Johns Hopkins University Press, 1993), 2.

27. This is something that two recent monographs about the theatre of this half-forgotten Belgian playwright suppress in their effort to praise his role in the shaping of modern theatre. See Linn Konrad, *Modern Drama as Crisis: The Case of Maurice Maeterlinck* (New York: Peter Lang, 1986); and Patrick McGuinness, *Maurice Maeterlinck and the Making of Modern Theatre* (Oxford: Oxford University Press, 2002).

28. See Frederick W. J. Hemmings, *The Theatre Industry in Nineteenth-Century France* (New York: Cambridge University Press, 1993), 4.

29. Poggioli, *Theory of the Avant-Garde,* 22–23; Henderson, *First Avant-Garde* 13–15.

30. Veltruský, "Semiotics and the Avant-Garde Theatre," 87–90.

31. Peter Szondi, *Theory of the Modern Drama* (Cambridge: Polity Press, 1987), 11–12, 45–46.

32. I use the term *theatricality* here in a historical sense. Of course, one can discuss its meaning in a philosophical (namely, theological) context, as William Egginton does excellently in his *How the World Became a Stage; Presence, Theatricality and the Question of Modernity* (Albany: SUNY Press, 2003), or with a special concern in the public sphere, as does the classical work of Richard Sennett, *The Fall of Public Man* (New York: Norton, 1974).

33. The anti-theatrical prejudice that various forms of modernism cultivated is worth mentioning, since they saw in it an "unorthodoxy" by modernist values, a survival of the

mimetic arts next to the figurative arts. On the relationship between theatricalism and the modernist tradition of anti-theatrical prejudice and the insistence of the latter in the leading place in a text (dramatic or theatrical), see Jonas Barish's *The Anti-theatrical Prejudice* (Berkeley: University of California Press, 1981), 350–477, and especially Martin Puchner's *Stage Fright: Modernism, Anti-Theatricality and Drama* (Baltimore: Johns Hopkins University Press, 2002).

34. On this transformation, which commenced by subjecting all elements of the theatrical art to language, resulting in the birth of an independent, liberated "stage language" and "stage poetry," see Veltruský, "Semiotics and the Avant-Garde Theatre," 88–92; Deak, *Symbolist Theatre,* 10; Henderson, *First Avant-Garde,* 5–11; Christopher Innes, "Text/Pre-Text/Pretext: The Language of Avant-Garde Experiment," in Harding, *Contours of the Theatrical Avant-Garde,* 58–75.

35. Deak, *Symbolist Theatre,* 14–15. Most interesting is the theoretical debate in the context of Russian symbolism, not only on the relations between dramatic poetry and stage poetry (the famous "Crisis of the theatre," 1908) but also the dispute that was provoked by Yuly Aikhenvald's essay "Rejecting the Theatre," first published as "The End of Theatre" (1913). See the chapter "Symbolism and the 'Crisis in the Theatre,' 1902–1908," ed. and trans. Laurence Senelick, in *Naturalism and Symbolism in European Theatre, 1850–1918,* ed. Claude Schumacher (Cambridge: Cambridge University Press, 1996), as well as *Russian Dramatic Theory from Pushkin to the Symbolists,* ed. Laurence Senelick (Austin: University of Texas Press, 1981), li–liii.

36. As Hemmings points out, the theatre industry of the nineteenth century "did not so much collapse as shrink from being big business to being what was called 'show business,' a more inventive but perhaps a more inverted form" (*Theatre Industry in Nineteenth-Century France,* 4).

37. On this subject see the recent theoretical discourse in Hans-Thies Lehmann, *Postdramatic Theatre* (London: Routledge, 2006).

38. Walter Benjamin, *Das Kunstwerk im Zeitalter seiner technischen Reproduzierbarkeit: Drei Studien zur Kunstsoziologie* (Frankfurt am Main: Suhrkamp, 1968), 25–27.

39. Thomas Postlewait and Tracy C. Davis, "Theatricality: An Introduction," in *Theatricality,* ed. Thomas Postlewait and Tracy D. Davis (Cambridge: Cambridge University Press, 2003), 2.

40. Tracy C. Davis, "Theatricality and Civil Society," in Postlewait and Davis, *Theatricality,* 127.

41. Ibid., 144.

42. Naturally, the notion of theatricality in nineteenth-century Victorian theatre is far more complex and paradoxical, as suggested in Lynn M. Voskuil's *Acting Naturally: Victorian Theatricality and Authenticity* (Charlottesville: University of Virginia Press, 2004). Nevertheless, due to these historical contradictions, aestheticism finally emerged.

43. Puchner, *Stage Fright,* 31–55.

44. Ibid., 7.

45. Deak, *Symbolist Theatre,* 248–63.

46. Puchner, *Stage Fright,* 6.

47. Ibid., 7.

48. Silvija Jestrovic, "Theatricality as Estrangement of Art and Life in the Russian Avant-Garde," *Substance* 31 (2002): 42–56.

49. See, for example, Anne-Briff Gran's "The Fall of Theatricality in the Age of Modernity," which follows up on "Evreinov's contention that modernity is an anti- or non-theatrical period," *Substance* 31 (2002): 252. See also Davis, "Theatricality and Civil Society," 130.

50. Erika Fischer-Lichte, "The Avant-Garde and the Semiotics of the Antitextual Gesture," in Harding, *Contours of the Theatrical Avant-Garde,* 81–82.

51. Poggioli, *Theory of the Avant-Garde,* 51–54.

52. Ronald W. Vince, "Theatre History as an Academic Discipline," in Postlewait and McConachie, *Interpreting the Theatrical Past,* 6–7; Erika Fischer-Lichte, "From Text to Performance: The Rise of Theatre Studies as an Academic Discipline in Germany," *Theatre Research International* 24 (1999): 168–78; Erika Fischer-Lichte, "*Quo Vadis?* Theatre Studies at the Crossroads," in *Modern Drama: Defining the Field,* ed. Ric Knowles, Joanne Tompkins, and W. B. Worthen (Toronto: Toronto University Press, 2003), 66. See also Woods, "Emphasizing the Avant-Garde," 174–75.

BOOK REVIEWS

The Enchanted Years of the Stage: Kansas City at the Crossroads of American Theater, 1870–1930. By Felicia Hardison Londré. Columbia: University of Missouri Press, 2007. 327 pp. $34.95 cloth.

It is rare, even for theatre historians, to pick up a theatre history book and experience the kind of page-turner presented in Felicia Hardison Londré's *The Enchanted Years of the Stage.* While this is clearly a serious study of one American city's touring production experience, it is very hard not to be caught up in the marvelous tale Londré weaves about the perils and pleasures of the turn-of-the-century road shows and repertory companies that graced the Kansas City theatre scene from the 1870s until the slow death of legitimate theatre in Kansas City in the 1930s. Though objectivity in the writing of theatre history has always been something of a Holy Grail, this book's author is clearly in love with, and very much a part of, Kansas City theatre history as both a professor at the University of Missouri at Kansas City and an important dramaturge for the Missouri Repertory Theatre (now Kansas Repertory Theatre). It is just that sense of being a Kansas City insider that gives this book a kind of delicious authenticity and a feeling of peeking behind the curtain of fin de siècle American theatre to see it in its glory—and its very human frailty.

What is even more enchanting about *Enchanted Years* are the sidebar annotations of the *Kansas City Star* critic David Austin Latchaw, whose sixty installments of his column, "The Enchanted Years of the Stage," have been gleaned by Londré in order to paint a complex, dramatic, heartbreaking, and at times hilarious depiction of a bygone era. Latchaw's front-row musings become a kind of contrapuntal theme to Londré's more dispassionate accounts of historical events. What with backstage stories of glorious stars like Sarah Bernhardt (who allegedly attacked a stage carpenter after a snafu onstage), Maude Adams, and

Edwin Booth, and the kind of low-life, cowtown hijinks of farm boys and fancy women taking in the cheap dime-show entertainments of the time, all of the warts and glamour of Kansas City's bygone theatre culture are revealed.

The book is structured chronologically for the most part, starting with early history of Kansas City, touching upon important early entertainments performed in frontier venues like Long's Hall and Frank's Hall, which were also occasionally frequented by figures such as Bill Ryan, a member of the James Gang. *Enchanted Years* occasionally leaves strict chronology behind, exploring some of the larger-than-life characters of the Kansas City theatre, including Colonel Kersey Coates, founder of the Coates Opera House; Colonel George W. Warder, founder of the Warder Grand Opera House; Abraham Judah, the beloved theatre manager of the Grand Opera House; and Judah's partner of many years, Melville Hudson, manager of the Coates Opera House. These owners and managers successfully booked and presented the greatest talents of the day, including entertainers such as Eddie Foy (who unfortunately died in Kansas City), Lotta Crabtree, Lawrence Barrett, Robert B. Mantell, Sir Henry Irving, Ellen Terry, Oscar Wilde (who didn't impress Kansas City audiences), and even Edwin Forrest, who performed in Kansas City toward the end of his career—oddly enough touching off a race incident. In the shadow of these larger figures in Kansas City theatre history, Londré touches upon the economic and social realities of ordinary theatregoers. She notes the separate entrances and other forms of discrimination suffered by African-American audiences, and the geographical and social divisions of Confederate—and Union—sympathizers. Londré notes also the lower-brow entertainments of the Theatre Comique and other variety saloons and the burgeoning vaudeville and burlesque performances at places like the Orpheum and Century theatres. These are contrasted with the highbrow expositions and Priest of Pallas parades at Kansas City's dazzling Crystal Palace; later, Londré documents the performance of Max Reinhardt's important spectacle, *The Miracle,* at its enormous Convention Hall.

At play here also are the forces of New York's big-business theatre world as played out among the locals in Kansas City theatre. Notable are the local battles between the representatives of the Theatre Syndicate (Klaw and Erlanger) versus the Shubert Brothers, the competing rivalries of the Syndicate's Willis Wood Theatre versus the Sam E. Shubert Theatre, which eventually went to federal courts. Caught in the middle of these battles was the stalwart theatre reviewer Austin Latchaw, who was denied entry, along with his daughter, to a performance by David Warfield at the Shubert Theatre—all because of the frictions between these outside forces.

It is difficult to read this book without keeping in mind, as I did, that the author herself is an important figure in the Kansas City theatre, and as such is as much a part of its history as the history she presents here. And so, even as one chuckles at the vanity of theatregoers who go to the theatre to be seen rather than to see theatre—the appendix on the campaign to have women remove their "merry widow" hats is particularly amusing—one cannot help but be moved by the connections made here. By the end of the book, the past melds with the present, with the major American theatre performances given by road-show stalwarts like Joseph Jefferson, Bert Williams, George Walker, and the important local repertory companies like the Woodward Stock Company reverberating with the revival in 1964 of professional repertory theatre in Kansas City. It was at this point that Dr. Patricia A. McIlrath of the University of Kansas City founded the Missouri Repertory Theatre, bringing back professional repertory theatre in Kansas after its slow demise in the 1930s. This connection the author makes herself, and in doing so she opens the possibility for other scholars to continue to deepen our understanding of the impact and importance of these early regional theatres on the regional theatre that exists today.

—**DAVID A. CRESPY**
University of Missouri, Columbia

Messiah of the New Technique: John Howard Lawson, Communism, and American Theatre, 1923–1937. By Jonathan L. Chambers. Carbondale: Southern Illinois University Press, 2006. xv + 268 pp. $55.00 cloth.

Arguably the most notable American playwright of the literary left of the 1920s and 1930s, John Howard Lawson has been omitted from almost all full-length (and period-specific) studies of American theatre. Known merely as a member of the notorious "Hollywood Ten," as a second-rate playwright, or perhaps for his text *Theory and Technique of Playwriting*, Lawson has remained ostracized by mainstream critics and historians for decades.

When I read Rosemarie K. Bank's essay "The Doubled Subject and the New Playwrights Theatre, 1927–1929" (1992), I hoped the work of the New Playwrights (Lawson in particular) would be recuperated into American theatre history studies and vigorously reexamined. More than a decade later, Jonathan L. Chambers's study of Lawson reviews the playwright's "hybrid," "mixed form," or what I call "production-dependent" texts, within an appropriate theoretical framework and from a cultural perspective. Placing Lawson at the center of his study, Chambers addresses ways in which dramatic form and style were debated, how theatre in the United States comprised a more intricate maze of theory, practice, and politics than previous studies indicate.

More important than his deliberate act of recovery scholarship in *Messiah of the New Technique*, Chambers employs critical tools that allow the reflexivity and intertextuality of Lawson's work (and life) to reverberate against and through the sociopolitical energy of the 1920s and 1930s—and beyond. His choice to scrutinize Lawson's corpus and criticism of the playwright's work through the lenses of New Historicism, poststructural Marxism, and cultural materialism, under the umbrella of a clearly defined organizing principle that utilizes Tony Bennett's notion of "reading formations," frees Chambers from the bonds of biographical study. This narrative pliability allows him to achieve his goal of simultaneously offering "a critical and political biography" and a "cultural and social history" (8).

Beyond considering the "originating conditions" (10) under which Lawson matured, Chambers reexamines the ways in which plays and productions were initially misread in print and onstage. He addresses Lawson's culpability in this interpretative dilemma, suggesting, also, that subsequent readers, critics, and historians are, in turn, inculcated by the dominant reading formations of their lived experiences. By embracing the "variable nature of reading/consumption," acknowledging the "maneuverability" of texts, and recognizing a "cyclical theory of exchange" (12), Chambers advocates a more open reading of Lawson's plays (and career). He resists the reductive readings of earlier Lawson scholars, who viewed "text" as fixed and pronounced Lawson a failure for not conforming to traditional content and dramatic form.

At crucial junctures in the text his methodologies are systematically interjected into the narrative structure, where Chambers acknowledges indebtedness to Stephen Greenblatt, Frederic Jameson, and others, and where he deftly parses difficult critical concepts, applying them to Lawson's thinking and writing. Rather than interrupting the flow, these theoretical (sometimes historical) sidebars explicate and reiterate the principles that constitute the underpinnings of Lawson's plays as well as Chambers's analyses of them.

Consistency in structure is integral to the study's success, for the linear presentation of Lawson's life grounds the work as biography and permits Chambers to manipulate his (and Lawson's) theorizing around and through it. This is not a book for the theoretically faint of heart, as some of the writing is dense; but Chambers carefully guides his reader, and the effort exerted in digesting the theoretical with the biographical is well rewarded. Chambers's methodologies complement Lawson's aesthetic and political concerns as the author traces the playwright's move to an "inquisitive tone and dialectical impulse" (117) with deleterious effects on the critical reception of his plays.

Messiah of the New Technique is divided into five chapters in which phases of Lawson's life and career are examined in the light of the playwright's metamorphosis from socially conscious community member to activist to revolutionary. Chapter 1, "The Awakening," sets the critical backdrop ("art theatre" *versus* literary left) against which Lawson's early plays emerge. Chapter 2, "Break Down the Walls of the Theatre," establishes the influences of the European avant-garde and American popular entertainment idioms on Lawson's early work. The playwright's theorizing, his goals for the theatre, and his scripts that defy the modernist's penchant for categorizing and creating binaries such as "high" and "low" or "psychology-or-physics" (69) distinguish Lawson's work from mainstream dramaturgy. These early chapters establish Chambers's conceit and set the tone for the rest of the book.

Subsequent chapters ("To Beat the Drums of Rebellion," "The Thorny Path to Commitment," and "Lost Like Hamlet in His Inner-Conflict") chronologically follow Lawson's progression to political commitment and ultimately Communism. Lawson's artistic and political agendas merge in his final play, *Marching Song,* but, frustrated with the medium of theatre as a vehicle for social change, he abandoned playwriting altogether for political action.

Messiah of the New Technique includes a cogent and masterful discussion of Lawson's plays, placing them within the context of their time(s), situating them in Lawson's oeuvre, and viewing them as "social currencies" (78). For those unfamiliar with the scripts, Chambers's lively descriptions and analyses may spawn further study. For those who have contemplated them before, Chambers offers fresh insights—Dada in *Processional; Nirvana*'s relationship to the schism between psychology and science; *Success Story*'s character Sol as a more fully developed Roger Bloomer; *The Pure in Heart* as a throwback to the jazz era.

The book's epilogue provides a fitting conclusion to Chambers's study as it not only repositions Lawson and reclaims his place in the American theatre but also expresses the author's interdisciplinarity, his relationship to his subject, and the interplay of methodologies across American studies, performance studies, and theatre history as we accept that there is no Holy Grail of objective truth.

Chambers's command of his subjects—Lawson and the primary sources attendant to biographical investigation, American culture and politics, performance theory and criticism—enables him to relate biographical material to literary output, theatrical production, dramatic theory, and criticism, all under the reading formations rubric.

Chambers answers Bruce McConachie's recent call (*Theatre Survey,* May 2007) for historian/theorists' reevaluation of the field in the light of interdisciplinary studies. *Messiah of the New Technique* is a welcome addition to the history/theory conversation and is valuable to anyone who researches United States theatre, American theatre, and American studies—or anyone who delights in questioning accepted narratives or joining Chambers in his desire "to not only write but to right the historical record" (205).

—ANNE FLETCHER
Southern Illinois University, Carbondale

Liberty Theatres of the United States Army, 1917–1919. By Weldon B. Durham. Jefferson, N.C.: McFarland, 2006. viii + 219 pp. $35.00 paper.

As the United States prepared in 1917 to enter World War I—a time of turmoil and often chaos—the War Department's Commission on Training Camp Activities decided that along with troop mobilization should come entertainment. To facilitate this, a collection of theatre venues would be needed with the stated intent of offering "morally uplifting" plays, movies, and variety entertainments. Consequently, during 1918 and 1919, forty-two Liberty Theatres were designed, constructed, or found, and, for a brief time, managed in virtually the same number of training and debarkation camps throughout the United States.

As even Weldon Durham, author of this fascinating investigation, admits, the Liberty Theatres have been little more than a footnote in histories of the home front in the Great War. Indeed, the story of Liberty Theatres as related by Durham might still be a footnote to both military and theatre history (and certainly its brief history might justify such a position) if it were not for the full context of the phenomenon and the intriguing behind-the-scenes portrait vividly presented in minute detail by Durham. What began as a very good 1973 dissertation has evolved over the past decades into a much better book—mature, well crafted, clearly written—a study that illustrates why this aspect of military theatre deserves its place in our history. The dissertation was more tightly (and narrowly) focused; the book provides much more context and places these two years in the bigger picture. It is also a far more up-to-date and multi-layered piece of scholarship than its predecessor, one that makes an important addition to the literature on the military and the theatre.

In reality, little of a serious nature has been written about military theatricals in the United States (and even less about theatricals by U.S. troops abroad during wartime). Only the USO shows of World War II have received much attention, and most of the books on that subject are largely anecdotal, such as the 1993 *Over Here, Over There: The Andrews Sisters and the USO Stars in World War II,* coauthored by Maxine Andrews and Bill Gilbert. The earliest military theatricals have been chronicled by Jared Brown's *The Theatre in America during the Revolution* (1995), and Charlotte Canning's *The Most American Thing in America: Circuit Chautauqua as Performance* (2005) introduces the role of Chautauquas in World War I theatricals, which Durham's covers in considerably more depth.

Durham has expanded his earlier study to include an excellent opening chapter that effectively places in context the theatre in both the United States and the U.S. Army, emphasizing the rapidly changing times and the varied forces that converge to help create camp theatres. A second chapter provides a historical overview of pre–World War I military theatre, followed by two chapters that analyze factors affecting the reformation of military camp life at the onset of the U.S. involvement in the war. Chapters 4 and 5 introduce what for me is the most engrossing and dramatic aspect of the Liberty Theatre phenomenon and the explanation for the ultimate modest success and a large degree of failure of this experiment. This theme then permeates the rest of the study. In a nutshell, the crux of most problems, especially during 1918, was the tension (and often ego-driven dissension) between the Commission on Training Camp Activities (those from the field of recreation) and the commercial entertainment world (most visibly Marc Klaw, a prominent member of the Theatrical Syndicate), the latter charged with the responsibility of supplying much of the entertainment fare. The intricacy of the dealings of these two groups and the motives of each—requiring great care in the telling by the author—supplies much of the interest in reading Durham's book.

However, most of the book is devoted to a thoroughly researched (good use especially is made of unpublished material from the National Archives and camp newspapers) and carefully reported and judiciously analyzed series of chapters on the operation of the theatres. These central chapters cover the physical spaces built or found; funding of the theatres; ongoing discord and internal problems; management choices and changes; the types of shows offered (tent Chautauqua, musical comedy, tabloid revues and burlesque, comedies and melodramas, minstrel shows, vaudeville, stock companies, specialty performers, motion pictures, and "soldier" shows); and three final chapters that return to the theme of conflict (i.e., the federal government and the entertainment industry), examine briefly military theatre since World War I, and a most effective summary that provides in a scant six pages a wonderful profile of the successes and failures of the Liberty Theatres, emerging "from a thicket of twisted motives and stumbling down a crooked path" to its initial openings, momentum in the spring of 1918, and final demise. Four appendixes, copious notes, and effective illustrations complete this superb effort (an excellence expected from the editor of the extraordinarily useful three-volume *American Theatre Companies*, 1986–89).

—**DON B. WILMETH**
Emeritus Professor, Brown University

Vaudeville Wars: How the Keith-Albee and Orpheum Circuits Controlled the Big-Time and Its Performers. By Arthur Frank Wertheim. New York: Palgrave Mac-Millan, 2006. 332 pp. $75.00 cloth.

Although the history of American vaudeville has been reasonably well examined, no work has focused so directly on the economic and managerial aspects of the industry as Arthur Frank Wertheim's *Vaudeville Wars: How the Keith-Albee and Orpheum Circuits Controlled the Big-Time and Its Performers*. Using a combination of first-person accounts, primary source materials, and exhaustive financial data, Wertheim tracks the rise, merger, and fall of the two dominant forces in big-time vaudeville. The resulting narrative is a compelling and insightful look into the inner workings of an American entertainment monopoly.

Wertheim begins in the mid-1880s, tracking the course of the young Benjamin Franklin Keith and his first theatre in Boston. The small venue began as a dime museum, featuring a mixture of variety acts and sideshow attractions such as "Boz, the Canine paradox, described as a 'dog with a human brain'" (15). In July 1885, in an effort to maximize his profits, Keith shifted his performance schedule to a continuous, repetitive rotation of acts, becoming one of the first to embrace the format that would become the defining characteristic of vaudeville. Wertheim's narrative then details the addition of Edward Franklin Albee to Keith's managerial staff, thus cementing the pairing that would become the foundation of the eastern vaudeville circuit.

As the Keith-Albee story unfolds on the East Coast, Wertheim introduces the history of the rise of the Orpheum circuit on the West Coast. German immigrant Gustav Walter's Orpheum Theatre in San Francisco opened in 1897, featuring acts imported from the East as well as from Europe. Walter's combination of popular and high culture appealed to a wide range of customers, achieving a profitable respectability that would later become the model for his Orpheum circuit.

From these beginnings, Wertheim tracks the expansion of each circuit throughout the 1890s, including exhaustive details about key players, economic data, marketing strategies, and management structure. Under the shrewd financial direction of Morris Meyerfield, the Orpheum circuit added venues in Los Angeles, Kansas City, Omaha, and Denver, eventually opening a booking office in Chicago in 1889. Keith and Albee first added New York to their empire, successfully challenging the great Tony Pastor with their Union Square Theatre in 1893. They also followed the Orpheum's notion of broad cultural appeal, with ticket prices at one of their Boston locations ranging from 15 cents to $1.50. By 1899 the circuit constituted four large theatres, one each in Boston, New York, Providence, and Philadelphia, with the Boston theatre alone averaging twenty-five thousand customers per week.

Having detailed the origins of the Keith-Albee and Orpheum circuits, Wertheim then outlines the various attempts of vaudeville performers to organize resistance to the increasingly strong-armed tactics of management. Beginning with the formation in 1900 of the White Rats of America, the rapidly expanding circuits on both sides of America faced organized challenges to their employment practices. The middle portion of Wertheim's book focuses on the continued consolidation of both circuits, the inner workings of their business operations, and the overall failure of the White Rats and other organizations to make any significant gains in rights for vaudeville performers. Keith and Albee joined with several other eastern managers in 1907 to form the United Booking Offices of America (UBO), and by 1913 the UBO had established a formal relationship with the Orpheum management to centralize control of a vast number of vaudeville bookings. Through a variety of tactics, such as blacklisting, hiring of scabs, the creation of its own managers union, and economic targeting of specifically resistant individuals, the UBO and Orpheum circuits maintained a stranglehold on performer salaries and rights for the duration of vaudeville, rarely making significant concessions on any key issues.

Vaudeville Wars closes with several chapters detailing the collapse of the big-time circuits. Wertheim attributes this decline to a combination of the rise of cheaper vaudeville venues (known as "small-time"), the economic impact of film and radio, and the talent drain that resulted as these new modes of entertainment drew stars away from the major circuits. These factors, as well as an unwillingness to adjust to the new economic landscape, resulted in the eventual disintegration of the monopolies. As with the preceding sections, Wertheim provides exhaustive financial data and first-person accounts of this demise, concluding his narrative with the death of Edward Albee in 1930.

Wertheim's account of the rise and fall of the Keith-Albee and Orpheum circuits is entirely straightforward in its approach, eschewing any theoretical underpinning. This sort of history doesn't necessarily need that foundation, however, as its reliance on hard economic data and primary- and secondary-source accounts creates a clear and thorough narrative of a key period in American popular entertainment. Wertheim also declines to give any substantial analysis of the actual content of the acts that were being performed on the Keith-Albee and Orpheum stages, but again, this limitation is in keeping with the goal of the study. *Vaudeville Wars* ultimately overcomes its potential drawbacks by serving as a strikingly in-depth and comprehensive accounting of the economic history and managerial structure of big-time vaudeville.

—TYLER AUGUST SMITH
University of Illinois at Urbana-Champaign

Susan Glaspell and the Anxiety of Expression. By Kristina Hinz-Bode. Jefferson, N.C.: McFarland, 2006. 292 pp. $45.00 cloth.

Susan Glaspell (1876–1948), Pulitzer Prize winner, playwright, and novelist, was a founding member of the Provincetown Players and undoubtedly a significant figure on the theatrical scene in early-twentieth-century America. However, in the early 1980s she was virtually unknown to specialists of American theatre and American literature alike. In spite of the work done in the last thirty years by scholars intent on recovering the names of writers silenced by the patriarchal canon, and in spite of the surge of interest in Glaspell (see www.susanglaspell.org for recent publications and performances), Glaspell is still generally known only for the play *Trifles* or the short story "A Jury of Her Peers," a rewrite of the earlier piece. Kristina Hinz-Bode's *Susan Glaspell and the Anxiety of Expression* is a significant addition to Glaspell studies: it goes beyond not only *Trifles* but also the until recently dominant feminist approach to her work. The year 2006 also saw the publication of two volumes of essays, *Disclosing Intertextu-*

Reconstruction America in flux" (51). According to Brooks, the frightening con-
flation of monstrous identities produced by the abolition of slavery (the merg-
ing of Jekyll into Hyde) was redressed through Jim Crow laws and culture,
which reinstated at least a de jure separation of white and black identities and
underscored the need for "a re-assertion of superior Anglo-American performative skills" (64).

Chapters 2 and 3 focus on two very different performers—escaped slave
Henry "Box" Brown and theatrical star Adah Isaacs Menken—who are linked
for Brooks by a common gift for "self-invention" (132). Brown's "performative resistance" emphasizes the problem at the heart of the transatlantic slave
movement—that the escaped slave perpetually reenacts through performance,
lecture, or narrative his or her own slavery. Thus even in freedom, the African
fugitive character was alienated from both a new identity as a free person and
from any geographical home or site that he or she might claim (Afro-alienation
is a theme Brooks raises in her introduction). Brown challenged these reductive tropes by literally creating his own landscape in the form of a panorama
entitled the *Mirror of Slavery*. Through this self-created spectacle he renegoti-
ated the role of the escaped slave in nineteenth-century America.

As another iconoclast, Adah Isaacs Menken looms as both a "morally am-
biguous maverick" who manipulated her own racial identity and as a character
transformed by successive generations of scholars, based on the prevailing historiographical trends of the day (132). Brooks questions what constitutes "evidence" in placing a character like Menken in the "racial imaginary" (135). She
compares Menken's "metaphorical racialization" to the "blackening" of women
such as Sojourner Truth (155). Truth, like Menken, used her performative body
to stage spectacles of resistance against white images of black(ened) female
identities. While Brooks's argument here is as persuasive as elsewhere, it might
also have been interesting to juxtapose Menken with other black female figures who "bodied forth" complex notions of racial and gender identity (such
as Harriet Tubman, who won contests for her master by pulling heavily loaded
sledges farther than male slaves did). Dissecting Tubman's performance—and
a white audience's seeming inability to fathom that her physical strength was as
much a danger as an asset—might have offered an intriguing contrast to Menken's often equally oblivious spectators.

Chapters 4 and 5 bring Brooks past the Civil War and into an age of spectacle, when performance redefined black identities in the transatlantic imagination. Chapter 4 focuses on *In Dahomey,* which baffled transatlantic audiences by its erasure of a colonial/fantasy/white Africa and its reinscription of

a *black* Africa that "dared to couch new images of African American culture within the old" (207–10). Brooks describes the show as a kind of "Afro-diasporic alienation effect" through which the "dissonant multivocality" of black identity might find expression (224). Parts of this chapter echo Brooks's Jekyll-and-Hyde theme—for example, the scene in which "Straight" demonstrates a miracle potion that transforms black skin to white (and vise versa). Straight's creation of a *half*-black/*half*-white character parodies white anxieties about artificial racial divisions and reveals black awareness of fluid racial boundaries.

Chapter 5 explores the careers of Aida Overton Walker and Pauline Hopkins and their "veiled" creations (Salome and Dianthe Lusk, respectively). Brooks examines how female artists mapped "individual as well as communal desire" in what she terms the "undertheorized genealogy of postbellum black women's theatrical performance" (287). Brooks demonstrates an admirable ability to return to her scholarly themes without cloying through repetition, and in this chapter she revisits the notion of how the development of a black (feminist) aesthetic intersected with contemporary visions of racial and gender identities. For Brooks, Hopkins's controversial novel *Of One Blood* fuses spiritualism and the new psychology into a potent mixture that reveals both black nationalism and black diasporic longings—all embodied in the female character of Dianthe Lusk.

By focusing on the black performative experience, Brooks challenges the perception that art transforms merely its spectators (301). For her, the black feminist art of the postbellum period transforms its creators as well. Walker, for example, "used the realm of dance and her costumed body to foreground blackness and female corporeality" (328). This chapter leads Brooks to her epilogue—a reflection on the 2004 Tony Awards, which honored an unprecedented number of African-American actresses. Yet she also criticizes the glib stereotypes of award-winning shows such as *Avenue Q*, which suggest a regression back to earlier forms and debates. While her critiques may be apt, in some ways this seems an odd note on which to end a study that has been so innovative and sweeping in its scope. By focusing on the 2004 Tony Awards, Brooks may reduce the realm of spectacular performance she has created to the comparatively narrow world of mainstream Broadway theatre. However, this is a minor argument with an extraordinarily erudite work that will make a lasting contribution to American theatre scholarship.

——**HEATHER S. NATHANS**
University of Maryland

The Plays of Georgia Douglas Johnson: From the New Negro Renaissance to the Civil Rights Movement. Edited and with an introduction by Judith L. Stephens. Urbana: University of Illinois Press, 2006. 195 pp. $40.00 cloth, $20.00 paper.

Judith L. Stephens carefully assembles all twelve of the dramatist's extant plays in *The Plays of Georgia Douglas Johnson,* and with a thorough introductory essay she contributes an insightful study of Johnson's dramatic oeuvre. This work enriches existing scholarship in two important ways: by rescuing from oblivion two previously unpublished scripts and by examining Johnson's place in "cultural history and provid[ing] insight into her rich and complex dramatic vision" (1).

Although Johnson wrote twenty-eight plays, her race and gender limited their publication during her lifetime. Despite these challenges, Johnson figured prominently in the national black theatre movement and was an important "cultural sponsor" in the early twentieth century, assembling and inspiring the intellectuals and artists who generated the next cadre of black theatre and emergent scholarship (16). As Stephens argues, "the leadership Johnson provided in building a community of black artists and intellectuals in Washington is an accomplishment that equals and complements her own contributions as a playwright, poet, and composer" (13).

Johnson's "originality and versatility as a playwright are reflected in the dramatic genres she created to organize and preserve a record of her productivity" (19). Johnson divided her work into distinct categories: "Primitive Life Plays," "Historical Plays," "Plays of Average Negro Life," "Lynching Plays," and "Radio Plays." This classification informs Stephens's division of the anthology into four parts (excluding the radio plays), placing Johnson's remaining scripts into their respective genres. While each of the first three sections features two representative plays, the lynching category presents six of Johnson's dramas, including two different versions of *A Sunday Morning in the South* and two previously unpublished manuscripts, *And Yet They Paused* and *A Bill to Be Passed.* Also included in this section is a recently discovered companion piece, *Kill That Bill!* written by Cleveland NAACP representative Robert E. Williams. Johnson's and Williams's short skits were created for the NAACP's 1938 anti-lynching campaign.

The first section, "Primitive Life Plays," features *Blue Blood* and *Plumes,* which were published and produced during Johnson's lifetime. Stephens argues that these plays "shift the focus away from black *people* as 'primitive,' toward a consideration of the uncivilized (primitive) institution of slavery, its far-reaching effects, and of how post-emancipation African Americans must deal daily with its consequences" (22). In part 2, "Historical Plays," Johnson illustrates antebellum responses to slavery with plays that serve as "model history lessons taught in an engaging and memorable way" (23). Johnson submitted *Frederick Douglas* and *William Ellen Craft* to the Federal Theatre Project between 1935 and 1938 but received ambivalent reader reviews, and neither play was produced. However, both texts were published in *Negro History in Thirteen Plays* (1935) and may have been staged by local Washington, D.C., schools (22).

Although Johnson wrote several dramas in the category of "Plays of Average Negro Life," only two scripts remain, *Starting Point* and *Paupaulekejo*, featured in part 3. *Paupaulekejo* imparts an ironic view of Christianity and its inability to negotiate "racial and sexual boundaries" (31), while *Starting Point* illuminates the struggles of an urban black family. The former is also one of the "earliest Harlem Renaissance plays to be set in Africa" and treats the miscegenation theme in a unique way, pairing an African male with the daughter of a white missionary (29).

According to Stephens, Johnson was the first dramatist to identify a dramatic genre focusing on the atrocities of lynching and its impact on the community, which is showcased in part 4. Stephens not only collects all of Johnson's lynching plays, including *Safe* and *Blue-Eyed Black Boy*, but also provides the anthology's greatest contribution: the recovery of the manuscripts of *A Bill to Be Passed* and *Yet They Paused* (previously lost in the NAACP Papers at the Library of Congress). In her introductory essay, Stephens deftly highlights correspondence between Johnson and members of the NAACP, providing a rare glimpse of the creative process, the social history behind the plays, and the playwright's struggle to fuse protest and art. Besides illuminating Johnson's political premise, the plays and the NAACP correspondence offer the best context for understanding the playwright as a woman, suggesting the tenuous place of a female dramatist confronting highly charged subject matter in a turbulent time.

Using songs, prayers, and discourse from the black community, in contradistinction to the didactic arguments of the anti-lynching bill, Johnson wields a compact and powerful missive in *And Yet They Paused*, while *A Bill to Be Passed* demonstrates the cumulative and degenerative effects of lynching on the entire black community, and finally the entire nation. These newly found dramas illustrate clearly the ways in which Johnson not only incorporated propaganda but also utilized aspects of the folk art tradition, such as spirituals. And, by focusing on the humanitarian reasons against mob rule, Johnson develops her most notable lynching dramas, which reconceptualize lynching as a permanent scar on American national identity. Though similar, *Yet They Paused* and *A Bill to Be Passed* deliver different endings to demonstrate the stalling and filibustering that contributed to "Congress's failure to pass a federal antilynching bill" (37). When Johnson defines lynching as not simply a "racial problem" but an "*American* problem," she integrates the identity of whites and blacks as Americans fighting injustice for all (187). This universal call to arms suggests a new element in Johnson's lynching genre.

If her blatant protests against lynching and her concern with miscegenation underscore Johnson's place as one of the more revolutionary, political female dramatists of the Harlem Renaissance, then it is precisely this position as a black woman activist in this era that jeopardized her reception. As Stephens points out, Johnson's lynching dramas "reflect her role as an outspoken critic of racial violence as well as her vision of theatre as a tool for social change" (39). For this reason, this collection is a tremendous resource for scholars, artists, and students of American theatre, African-American studies, and gender studies and ideally will ensure greater visibility for Johnson's under-recognized theatrical contributions through discussion and production.

—ADRIENNE C. MACKI
Tufts University

Performing Glam Rock: Gender and Theatricality in Popular Music. By Philip Auslander. Ann Arbor: University of Michigan Press, 2006. xii + 260 pp. $60.00 cloth, $24.95 paper.

With *Performing Glam Rock: Gender and Theatricality in Popular Music,* Philip Auslander has solidified his role as one of the most important scholars of a small but growing field focusing on the visual elements of music performance. Although scholars have largely ignored glam rock—the outrageous, spectacle-driven music genre popularized in the 1970s by David Bowie and other musical acts—Auslander argues that glam not only gave peripheral identities agency but also made it possible to perform queerness in public. Auslander's knowledge of and passion for glam rock and other music (e.g. psychedelic and punk rock) infuse the study.

In chapter 1, Auslander traces the evolution from psychedelic rock, in which the "antiocularity was particularly acute," to a distinctly new genre of rock music that privileged the visual (15). According to Auslander, whereas psychedelic rock stars (Jimi Hendrix notwithstanding) largely ignored spectacle, glam rock stars placed as much importance—if not more—on the spectacle as they did the music and lyrics. In this chapter, even more fundamental to his argument is the concept of "persona" inherent in glam rock: "defined by three layers: the real person (the performer as human being), the performance persona (the performer's self-presentation) and the character (a figure portrayed in a song text)" (4). Auslander further illustrates glam rock's distinction from psychedelic rock with a comparison of live performances by John Lennon, exemplifying psychedelic rock, and by Sha Na Na, a band that anticipated glam.

In chapter 2, Auslander provides more background on the birth of glam rock, highlighting the importance of queerness to glam. He defines glam "queerness" as a subversive sexual or gender identity: "glam masculinity, like Mod masculinity before it, alluded to the possibility of homosexuality or bisexuality" (60–61). Auslander argues that glam is not solely a musicological category but also a sociological one: "Socially, glam represented a rejection of countercultural values, particularly with respect to sexual identity" (50). These first two chapters help clarify how exploring peripheral identities became central to glam.

The remainder of the book is a series of case studies on glam rock stars. Chapter 3 focuses on glam's first star, Marc Bolan, the lead singer and guitarist of the rock band T. Rex. This chapter includes an examination of three different filmed performances of the same song, illustrating the evolution of glam. Auslander further affirms Bolan's role as glam's architect with a comparison of guitar solos by Jimi Hendrix and Bolan, both of whom simulated masturbation with their instruments. While the very act is theatrical, Bolan's version incorporated a tambourine in the deed, which he threw into the audience after he finished. In the section on psychedelic rock in this chapter, Auslander offers many instances in which the musicians turned their backs to the audience while performing, an act that became antithetical to the performance of glam. Bolan's stage act served as the foundation for future glam artists to take experimentation with identity to even greater lengths.

Chapter 4 focuses on David Bowie, the creator of Ziggy Stardust and clearly Auslander's favorite glam artist. Auslander roots this exhaustively researched case study in a "theatricalization of rock," in which "Bowie not only envisioned the rock concert as a staged, costumed, and choreographed theatrical performance, he understood his own performing and his relationship to his audience in actorly terms" (106). Auslander reveals that Bowie planned to mount a production starring Ziggy Stardust on the West End and that he wanted another actor to step into the role eventually. This chapter includes a fuller exploration of Auslander's concept of "persona," as Bowie switched characters regularly in performance and recordings. Auslander relies on Judith Butler's theories of gender as performance in this section, insisting that Bowie's performance of Ziggy was feminine and that "behaviors coded as feminine can be enacted by men as well as women" (140). Noting that guitarist Mick Ronson was once forced to play long enough to allow Bowie to change costumes, Auslander concludes that "the music served the spectacle rather than the other way around" (145).

Chapter 5 examines the glam careers of Bryan Ferry and Roy Wood, the lead singers of Roxy Music and Wizzard, respectively. Auslander emphasizes Ferry's use of multiple voices on individual albums and sometimes even within the same song. He identifies the song "Sea Breezes," in which Ferry used two different voices, as "a vocal version of glam rockers' transvestite play with visual signifiers of gender and sexuality in their costuming and makeup" (166). Similarly, Wizzard used multiple sounds on the same album and the same songs, experimenting with different musical styles. Auslander also cites Wood's use of elaborate makeup in performance as significant in creating the theatrical visualization of glam, especially in influencing the makeup of Kiss. The consideration of both glam performers strengthens Auslander's argument that glam provided a venue for marginal identities not previously represented in mainstream music.

Chapter 6 spotlights Suzi Quatro, the only female glam rock star in the study. Auslander reads Quatro through the lens of Judith Halberstam's "female masculinity," an unleashing of masculine behaviors, which includes Quatro forcefully thrusting her pelvis up against the bass guitar she is playing. Quatro continues her gender-bending act in her refusal to change the gender of characters in cover songs. When she sang a cover of "I Wanna Be Your Man," for example, she did not change the lyric to "Woman." Auslander reinforces Quatro's "female masculinity" by referring to her as a "cock rocker," a rock star who is aggressive, loud, lustful, and in control. Quatro's early success, Auslander concludes, paved the way for future cock rockers Joan Jett, Chrissie Hynde, and P. J. Harvey.

With his concise, jargon-free style, Philip Auslander takes a topic once ignored by scholars and makes it both accessible and vital. *Performing Glam Rock:*

Gender and Theatricality in Popular Music proves an excellent model for future investigation of this fascinating but little-researched aspect of performance.

—**STEPHEN HARRICK**
Bowling Green State University

Notebooks. By Tennessee Williams. Edited by Margaret Bradham Thornton. New Haven: Yale University Press, 2006. xxvii + 828 pp. $40.00 cloth.

In 1936, Tennessee Williams began writing a journal that eventually filled thirty composition books, ledgers, and spiral tablets. Although he apparently abandoned the project in 1958 for two decades, the notebooks resumed with occasional entries from 1979 to 1981. Margaret Bradham Thornton has gathered all of Williams's known journals from widely scattered collections, faithfully transcribing the hundreds of pages and annotating the playwright's entries with remarkable thoroughness. The 1,090 notes make frequent reference to letters from archival holdings and other unpublished sources; Thornton also corresponded extensively with several of Williams's friends, including Donald Windham, Frances Kazan, and William Jay Smith. Her four pages of acknowledgments hint at the scope of this research, as do the four pages of credits for the stunning array of images reproduced in this volume.

Thornton frames the compiled *Notebooks* with views of the curly haired toddler Thomas Lanier Williams and Tennessee Williams's 1983 death mask; other illustrations include set designs for his plays, sketches from his letters, pictures of his homes, snapshots of friends and family members, several of Williams's paintings, typescripts of his poems, reproductions of journal covers and selected entries, postcards from Williams's travels, and even the ID badge from his brief service with the War Department's "U.S. Engineers" in 1942. While journal transcriptions are printed on the right-hand pages, and notes appear opposite the appropriate entries, the scores of images are reproduced on both the left and the right, enhancing the book's visual appeal. Like the annotations, these illustrations are keyed to Williams's relevant remarks. Thus, his account of rehearsals for *Cat on a Hot Tin Roof* in late February 1955—"Bel Geddes improved but Burl Ives acted like a stuffed turkey" (665)—appears above a photo of Ives and Barbara Bel Geddes in costume as Big Daddy and Maggie. Thornton pairs this stage view with a photograph of Jordan "Big Daddy" Massee, the model for Williams's character; readers can't miss Ives's striking resemblance to Massee. On the opposite page, beneath notes on Ives and Bel Geddes, Williams is pictured with his agent Audrey Wood, who attended the rehearsal on February 26.

The notebook transcriptions are a major contribution to future studies of Williams. "Unlike his letters, where he modulated his tone and style to suit the recipient," Thornton suggests, "the journals reveal Williams' authentic voice—genuine and unadorned" (ix); they "allow glimpses into Williams' secretive world" (xvi). Helpful though it is to have this new autobiographical resource, Thornton's additional material greatly increases the volume's usefulness to scholars and theatre professionals, and to fans as well. The annotated *Notebooks* is an editorial masterpiece, an accomplishment that belongs on the same shelf with Albert J. Devlin and Nancy M. Tischler's *Selected Letters of Tennessee Williams* (New Directions, 2000 and 2004).

In high spirits at the start of his undertaking on March 6, 1936, the twenty-five-year-old Williams salutes the moon and ambitiously labels the text "a writer's journal" (3). In mid-January 1939, however, soon after his move from the Midwest to New Orleans, he makes a harsh assessment: "When I read through this book I'm *appalled* at myself—what a *fool* I am!" (133). His journal, he says, "is valuable as a record of one man's incredible idiocy," an account of "abominable dullness" relieved by an occasional "glimmer of intelligence" (133). Sick, depressed, and down to his last dollar in St. Augustine, Florida, a few years later, Williams observes that "I use this journal mostly for distress-signals and do not often bother to note the little and decently impersonal things which sometimes have my attention" (327). "Mes Cahiers Noirs" is the bleak heading for his reflections in the spring of 1979; in these "Black Notebooks," drama critics are "potential assassins" (747), and longtime friends are remembered as betrayers. "Distress-signals" appear with alarming frequency throughout the journals: drugs, nightmares, alcoholism, poverty, depression, one-night stands, grief for his institutionalized sister Rose, writer's block, actual and imagined illnesses, and a desperate yearning for love. Yet, Williams repeatedly reminds himself that endurance is imperative; "*en avant,*" his hallmark phrase, becomes a refrain as he pushes himself forward, beyond the debilitating panics, the rejection letters, and the failed relationships.

In many ways, the *Notebooks* is indeed "a writer's journal." Williams frequently names authors who are important to him; some, like Carson McCullers and William Inge, are his friends. Hart Crane, cited in the epigraph to *A Streetcar Named Desire,* is paramount among poets, but Williams also loves Emily Dickinson. He praises Katherine Anne Porter's short stories highly, and he says D. H. Lawrence's *Sons and Lovers* "should have moved the earth to pity. It reminds me of my own heartbroken home" (639). Reading Lawrence's letters in July 1939, Williams "conceived a strong impulse to write a play about him—his life in America—feel so much understanding & sympathy for him—though his brilliance makes me feel very humble & inadequate" (155). On August 20, 1939, Williams is in Taos, New Mexico, "of all improbable places" (163), where he goes to meet Lawrence's widow, Frieda. Thornton cites Williams's colorful memory of the former Frieda von Richthofen from a fragment in the Harry Ransom Humanities Research Center, and she summarizes Williams's several attempts to write plays about both Lawrences, including the one-act "I Rise in Flame, Cried the Phoenix." A picture of Frieda, Mabel Dodge Luhan, and Dorothy Brett, circa 1938, accompanies Williams's journal entry on the Lawrence ranch.

The *Notebooks* mentions many drafts for which no known manuscripts exist. From Williams's descriptions it is clear that some of these drafts (occasionally in the form of poems or short stories) are early starts on *The Glass Menagerie, A Streetcar Named Desire, Summer and Smoke, Cat on a Hot Tin Roof, The Rose Tattoo, The Night of the Iguana,* and other full-length productions. Often, Williams worked for many years, through many revisions, before a work reached the stage. In 1948, with three play manuscripts under way, he said that, despite many false starts, "So far I have never failed to push a thing through to some kind of completion if I determined that I should" (489). Surprisingly, the journals have gaps at most points where readers would expect a detailed account of premiere performances. Possibly Williams was too nervous to record these climactic events, and Thornton succinctly fills the gaps with key information. The largest gap, though, falls between 1958 and 1979, a period for which no notebooks have been discovered. Thornton cites Williams's late remark that he quit writing a journal in the 1950s, and she notes that the volume of his correspondence declined over the same period.

Thornton also points out, however, that Williams was a productive (if less honored) playwright through the 1970s. "*En avant*" remained his call. Even in a dark mood in the "Black Notebooks" of 1979, he muses: "Perhaps I was never meant to exist at all, but if I hadn't, a number of my created beings would have been denied their passionate existence" (739). Painfully and movingly, *Notebooks* records the long drama of the creator's passionate existence.

—**JOAN WYLIE HALL**
University of Mississippi

The Performing Set: The Broadway Designs of William and Jean Eckart. By Andrew B. Harris. Denton: University of North Texas Press, 2006. 256 pp. $37.95 cloth.

With the use of floating, flying, rolling, and rotating scenery, the husband-and-wife design team of William and Jean Eckart created scenery and choreographed scene changes for nearly fifty years of American theatre. Andrew Harris lauds the Eckarts' scene shift as part of the theatrical performance: hence his adoption of the term "performing set" to describe their unique achievement in American scenic design.

Harris's major purpose is to recognize the Eckarts' contribution to American theatre, a contribution heretofore neglected. Although their work has been the subject of occasional newspaper and magazine articles and an occasional mention in the memoirs of notable theatrical figures, Harris's book offers the most thorough (and only book-length) survey of their careers. Not to be taken as a coffee-table book (though it is a feast for the eyes), this career retrospective is a serious study of a theatrical collaboration that flourished in the golden age of American musicals of the 1950s and 1960s. Relying on a wide range of primary and secondary sources, including an interview with the Eckarts' son, Peter, Harris chronicles the Eckarts' path from their meeting at Tulane University through their final professional collaboration in 1970 and Bill's last production in 2000. Harris recounts the lows as well as the highs, the failures as well as successes, that the Eckarts experienced as set, costume, and lighting designers. In the process he crafts a subtext that is never far from the surface: the fight for survival in an uncertain profession.

Following a foreword by Carol Burnett and a preface by Sheldon Harnick, the book is organized in chronological sections, each covering significant career developments during a particular year or span of years. The ninth section's title, "Riding the Broadway Roller Coaster," offers a metaphor that could perhaps represent their career as a whole—a career that Harris illuminates with verbal descriptions, photographs, interviews, and anecdotes featuring such theatre luminaries as Harold Prince, George Abbott, Jerome Robbins, Stuart Ostrow, Cheryl Crawford, Robert Lewis, Michael Kidd, Theron Musser, Mary Rogers, and Carol Burnett.

In the first section, "Getting Together," Harris surveys the Eckarts' meeting at Tulane University in the late 1920s, their time together at Yale immediately following World War II, and the beginnings of their career through 1953.

As protégées of Robert Edmond Jones and Donald Oenslager, they embraced Jones's credo that a designer should give expression to the essential quality of a play, its dramatic core (10). Of their work at Yale, Oenslager observed, "Jean worked practically while Bill had the quality of the visionary" (11). According to Harris, the melding of practicality and vision was a powerful combination, and their combined achievements strongly influenced the evolution of theatrical scenery: "They saw scenery as integral, not decorative, and they saw themselves as storytellers.... With storytelling in mind, they experimented with, developed, and perfected a variety of innovative scene change systems ... and the adaptation of a minimalist style which utilized a sophisticated modern art shorthand for communicating ideas" (2). From 1951 through 1953 the Eckarts designed sets and lights for ten significant productions, including Cheryl Crawford's production of *Oh Men! Oh Women!*

Harris devotes the second section to the Eckarts' first musical, *The Golden Apple,* which was also the first musical to move from off Broadway to Broadway, in 1954. Harris includes a fourteen-page homage to the Mondrian and Grant Wood–inspired set, quoting Harold Clurman's assertion that "great credit is due to the airy, delicate, and precise coloration of William and Jean Eckarts' settings—which employ some of the decorative discoveries of the non-objective painters with handsome theatrical effect" (36).

Harris allocates four sections to the Eckarts' Broadway projects in 1955 and 1956, including an unsuccessful Broadway vehicle for actress Jennifer Jones (*Portrait of a Lady*), the 1956 production of *Li'l Abner,* and the 1955 hit *Damn Yankees,* which marked their first collaboration with director George Abbott and producer Hal Prince. *Damn Yankees* was also their first Broadway project to include costume design along with sets and lights. The *Damn Yankees* narrative is rich with insider stories about the evolution of costumes and leading characters (performed by Gwen Verdon and Ray Walston) and the open sexuality of the production, heightened by the choreography of Bob Fosse.

Subsequent sections continue to trace the Eckarts' Broadway experiences as well as notable ventures into television and film. Harris considers the 1957 live CBS television production of *Cinderella,* the star vehicle developed for a twenty-one-year-old Julie Andrews, as a prime example of the Eckarts' artistry and ingenuity. The candid photos of the set mechanics as well as the gorgeous costume renderings document the production that drew an audience of 107 million viewers, a record at that time.

Once Upon a Mattress, the 1959 production that propelled Carol Burnett into stardom, was the Eckarts' only foray into the role of producer, nurturing Mary Rogers's idea based on *The Princess and the Pea* from a concept to the off-Broadway hit that launched Burnett's career. In addition to helping raise money for the show and collaborating on the script, they designed the set and costumes, assigning the lighting design to the now-legendary Theron Musser.

Perhaps the quintessential performing set designed by the Eckarts was that created for the 1966 Broadway production of *Mame*. Its stage manager, Terry Little, described its effect: "The scenery was choreographed to flow with the music and the lyrics. It was absolutely integral to the show" (178). According to Bill Eckart, "With *Mame* we weren't doing anything new. It was just a distillation of all the things we'd done before. Only this time, we were doing them with more authority" (181). Following this high point, however, the Eckarts experienced what Harris identified as three years of "Disenchantment" (183), during which time they designed twelve stage productions and one film, with no major hits and culminating in a significant career change.

In 1971, with the authority earned by a career forged in the theatres of New York, the Eckarts joined the faculty of the Meadows School of the Arts at Southern Methodist University in Dallas, a major coup for the university. Seeking a respite from the instability of employment in New York City and a safer environment for their two preteen children, they stepped into the world of academia—a goal they had set for themselves at Yale before their twenty-year postgraduate work on Broadway.

Harris expands his account of the Eckarts' design legacy to include the stories, the political workings of their career, the network of people and events that tie one production to the next. While providing more than 350 photographs that speak for themselves, Harris writes the backstory of the work being illustrated rather than a description of the images. Employing a clear and conversational style of writing, Harris weaves a verbal and visual creation for Broadway musical aficionados as well as students of American theatrical design history.

——**PHIL GROESCHEL**
University of Missouri, Columbia

Acting: An Introduction to the Art and Craft of Playing. By Paul Kassel. Boston: Pearson Education, 2007. 224 pp. $58.00 cloth.

In his preface to the teacher and coach, Paul Kassel admits that acting textbooks cover pretty similar territory. "What has changed," he writes, "is our understanding of human beings" (xi). Kassel examines these changes through the flux of acting/voice/movement theories and methods developed over the course of the last century. Throughout the book he strives to synthesize basic concepts from such great teachers and theorists as Stanislavski, Laban, Feldenkrais, Brook, Grotowski, Chaikin, Linklater, Spolin, and others. He also foregrounds the Asian concept of ki or chi—an energy or life force that is as inextricably connected to performance as it is to living.

Acting is steeped in exercises ranging from the well known (such as zip-zap-zop) to the original. Kassel has documented the source of the exercise when known and has contextualized exercises with theoretical underpinnings with the intent of marrying theory to practice. His target audience (beginning undergraduates) might initially be perplexed by the variety of sources within the book, but for teachers Kassel provides a welcome synthesis of material in an orderly fashion. Progressing through the entire book, the reader comes away with a gestalt of the art and craft of acting.

The organization of the book makes it quite accessible, allowing teachers to pick and choose sections as needed. Part 1, "Preparation for Playing," introduces acting, the creative environment, and the concept of ki as an energy force. In part 2, "The Tools for Playing," Kassel divides chapters into body, voice, imagination, feeling, and action. Part 3, "Playing," helps the actor integrate his or her tools into a scene or production and includes chapters on tasks, dramatic structure, character analysis, and basic integration into the rehearsal process. The bulk of each chapter is composed of exercises, contextualized with a brief synthesis of theory. User-friendly components of the book include a separate index of exercises, an appendix of action verbs and other aids, and a bibliography for further study. Visual learners will appreciate the diagrams of postures, positions, and conceptual maps; they will also appreciate the Web addresses sprinkled throughout the book for further information on specific topics. For example, the chapter about voice has a "boxed" section on vocal technique, with print or Web sources about Kristin Linklater, Cecily Berry, Patsy Rodenberg, Catherine Fitzmaurice, and Arthur Lessac. Also included are Web sites addressing the vocal (physiological) mechanism itself.

One chapter might raise eyebrows among acting teachers: the one on feelings. Kassel is quick to acknowledge the controversy of such a term as it relates to actor training. "With advances in neuroscience, genetics, and in imaging technology," he writes, "our understanding of feeling has developed tremendously in the last decade or so. As the nature of feelings begins to unfold, the mystery of how feeling functions in art, theater, and acting is beginning to unravel as well. This chapter attempts to summarize current thinking about feeling, and the relationship between feeling and actor training" (82). He goes on to clarify the separate yet interconnected qualities of feeling, sensing, and emotion. Although other chapters include historical references to the subject at hand, Kassel never specifically addresses Delsarte or other systems of physicalizing emotion, which would provide an interesting sidebar to his discussion. Instead, he focuses on clarification of concepts, in part through an illustration, "The Feeling Pyramid." At the end of the chapter he gives much-needed advice on how the actor can "step out" of character—a topic of special importance to beginning actors.

In terms of pedagogy, Kassel's approach is avowedly student-centered, with an emphasis on process over product. That being said, there are plenty of guidelines (not rules, he states) written in the imperative: trust in the process, attend to the task at hand, be in the moment—a veritable to-do list. Perhaps a sense of the imperative is unavoidable given the task at hand. In any case, Kassel hands the reins back to the student by grounding the acting exercises with reflective writing and thought, always encouraging the actor to discover his or her own style and technique of playing.

In the final chapter, "Curtain Call—The Spirit of Playing," Kassel gives the student a taste of the elusive elements of a good actor: a sense of presence, a sense of service (to the play and to fellow actors), and a sense of openness. These overarching ideals provide an excellent conclusion to the book, bringing the arch of performance back into a whole—a sum of the many parts explored in the previous chapters.

In his preface Kassel freely admits that he is indebted to others who have written acting books—specifically, Viola Spolin, Robert Cohen, and Robert Benedetti. Although he covers similar territory, he aims to offer "a different perspective and emphasis" on actor training. As such, *Acting: An Introduction to the Art and Craft of Playing* provides easily accessible, well-articulated text and a valuable tool for the classroom.

——**ANNE FLIOTSOS**
Purdue University

Kenneth Burke on Shakespeare. Edited by Scott L. Newstok. West Lafayette, Ind.: Parlor Press, 2007. 368 pp. $32.00 paper, $65.00 cloth, $18.00 Adobe eBook.

Newstok has collected fourteen essays, including three heretofore unpublished items: "Shakespeare Was What?" a lecture given at Kearney (Nebraska) State

College in 1964; "Notes on *Troilus and Cressida*," a response to a graduate student paper written when Burke was a visiting professor at Washington University (St. Louis), 1970–71; and "Notes on *Macbeth*," composed in the 1970s and 1980s.

Burke's "*Othello:* An Essay to Illustrate a Method" (1951), surely his most widely read and influential writing on Shakespeare, acts as a fulcrum for the chronologically organized collection. "Antony in Behalf of the Play" (1935) and "'Socio-Anagogic' Interpretation of *Venus and Adonis*" (1950) are the most notable compositions leading up to it. Burke's penetrating exegeses of *Timon of Athens* (1963), *Antony and Cleopatra* (1964), *Coriolanus* (1966), and *King Lear* (1969) follow.

To these fourteen essays Newstok adds an elegant and perceptive introduction offering "a series of entry-points to Burke's project (xvii)" to induce readers to read or reread Burke. He discusses the basic questions Burke asks in a critical engagement, Burke's abiding focus on beginnings, some of his key terms and recurring strategies, and the apparent lack of a critical "standard" in his writing. Threaded through these discussions is Newstok's sensitive and informed placement of Burke in the contemporary critical scene, a task he accomplishes without forcing the Irish renegade into a diminishing mold.

Newstok teases out with special effectiveness the manifold significance of the fact that Burke's impact is felt as inspiration as much as influence, a condition manifesting as acknowledgment "through *indirection*" (xxiii). Burke is at once lionized and avoided. Newstok argues that this response suggests a "complicated resistance among American intellectuals to come to terms with their native theoretical roots" (xxi). Burke was essentially self-taught. His career included many visiting professorships, but his perspective is non-academic, and his critical essays have appeared in periodicals, not in the mainstream of academic publishing: *Guardian, Dial, New Republic, Bookman, Southern Review,* and so on. Burke, he notes, has been widely read, but the size and complexity of the corpus of his work (about five hundred items, including fourteen books and numerous essays, reviews, poems, and works of fiction) eludes the grasp of any but the most dedicated readers. Scholars referencing Burke seem to strike tangents off some aspect of his work, adapting and using strategies such as "prophesying after the event" or "Pentadic analysis" but seldom displaying a grasp of the function of the kit from which they select their tools.

Newstok also deals briefly with recurring concerns about the profusion of critical terms deployed somewhat "slantwise" in Burke's writing about Shakespeare. Burke rather thoroughly redefines "titles," "audience," and "character," for instance, and Newstok points out that Burke's profligate neologizing further contributes to his reputation as brilliant but idiosyncratic.

Burke's career-long engagement with Shakespeare is niftily encapsulated in an appendix listing in chronological order over eighty "Additional References to Shakespeare." This persistent recourse to the language and situations of Shakespeare's plays explicitly illustrates Newstok's most basic perception: "Shakespeare serves as a kind of test case for the whole of 'language as symbolic action'" and the "core motivation . . . for his theory of 'Dramatism'" (xxv), Burke's most significant contribution is to social and literary theory. Although these conclusions seem to me to exceed the warrant of Newstok's arguments and examples, his introduction and the collected essays and excerpts amply suggest that Burke's commentary on Shakespeare nests near the heart of his grand project of exploring the implications for the study of behavior of the fact that humans are "symbol-using animals."

Students of both Burke and Shakespeare will be grateful for Newstok's thorough and exhaustive collection. Some readers will find the endnotes useful for identifying persons of note mentioned in the essays. Others (and I am one of this band) will wish the notes might have referenced more completely Burke's theoretical writings and the salient secondary scholarship most accurately characterizing it. For instance, the phrase "pointing the arrows of expectation" occurs in a number of critical essays, as Newstok correctly notes. But this reader would have appreciated a note grounding that phrase in Burke's "Lexicon Rhetoricae" and "The Philosophy of Literary Form." I had similar longings upon encountering terms and phrases such as "paradox of substance," "order," and "socio-anagogic criticism." That those needs were not met in the book may be an indication that Newstok's larger aim—to stimulate an appetite for engagement and reengagement with Burke—has been achieved in my case.

Readers of *Kenneth Burke on Shakespeare* might note that Parlor Press, founded in 2002 as an alternative scholarly, academic press, announces on its Web site that it has ten Burke books in process, four of which have been published, including Newstok's.

——**WELDON B. DURHAM**
University of Missouri, Columbia

Codifying the National Self: Spectators, Actors, and the American Dramatic Text. Edited by Barbara Ozieblo and María Dolores Narbona-Carrión. Brussels: P.I.E.–Peter Lang, 2006. 299 pp. $38.95 paper.

The seventeen essays in this volume originated as and were selected from presentations given at the Second International Conference on American Theatre at the University of Málaga, Spain, in 2004. *Codifying the National Self* is unique among edited collections in that it presents the reader with a transatlantic conversation among dedicated U.S., Canadian, and European scholars of American theatre past and present. That American drama generates a good deal of interest abroad comes as no surprise for most theatre practitioners; what might be surprising, however, is that a good number of European scholars have managed to keep pace with American scholarship despite lacking the access to resources available to their American colleagues. What results here is a high-quality collection of essays.

Barbara Ozieblo's introduction reminds us that this European interest in American theatre—which includes an interest in American history and American culture—is not merely an academically quaint undertaking but that the issues which so obsess the American consciousness today are not unique to Americans. The tragedy of 9/11 in New York City has its counterparts in Europe: 3/11 in Madrid and 7/7 in London. And the recent string of earthquakes and tsunamis, wars and acts of terror, sexual, ethnic, and racial strife bring us all closer together as we strive to maintain or reclaim a sense of humanity in a world seemingly bent on self-destruction.

David Savran opens the collection with "Making Middlebrow Theater in America," looking at the American theatre during the formative 1920s and seeing a continued trend toward intellectual pretense buried in commercial aspirations. Serving (or trying to serve) these two masters continues to problematize American theatre and in many ways continues to plague American culture. Susan Harris Smith's "Reading Drama: Plays in American Periodicals 1890–1918" introduces the subgenre of American drama written for magazine publication and for consumption by a middle class looking for a collective identity during a time of national turmoil and anxiety not altogether different from our own times.

Wendy Ripley's "Anna Cora Mowatt: Player and Playwright" and María Dolores Narbona-Carrión's "The Woman Artist as Portrayed by Rachel Crothers and Heather McDonald" remind us of the strategies that women of talent used as they struggled to voice their visions in a culture determined to privilege male identity. Sharon Friedman's "Feminist Revisions of Classic texts on the American Stage" extends the point by looking at the rewritings of classical texts undertaken by Ellen McLaughlin, Paula Vogel, and Suzan-Lori Parks. Savas Patsalidis's "Charles Mee's Intertextual and Intercultural Inscriptions: *Suppliants* vs *Big Love*" presents Charles Mee's revisionary sensibility, challenging the classical notions of logic and coherence that American culture clings to even as those foundational elements seem to be crumbling about us.

Miriam López-Rodríguez's "Sophie Treadwell, Jung, and the Mandala: Acting a Gendered Identity" and William S. Haney II's "Artistic Expression, Intimacy, and Primal Holon in Sam Shepard" take two very different playwrights from different generations and backgrounds and suggest that alternative systems of coherency—drawing upon the idea of a mandala and the holon, respectively—may offer hope in reconnecting a world grown wary of the failed logic of dominant culture. Claus-Peter Neumann's "Theo/teleological Narrative and the Narratee's Rebellion in Tony Kushner's *Angels in America*" reminds us that Kushner likewise challenges what he sees to be a failed teleological and theological vision of American history, suggesting that realizing the error of these ways is the first step to a more harmonious adaptation to the world around us. Marc Maufort's "'Captured Images': Performing the First Nations' 'Other'" shows us that Native American theatre likewise challenges the conventional linearity of dominant American culture. And Noelia Hernando-Real's "*E Pluribus Unum:* From a Unifying National Identity to Plural Identities in Susan Glaspell's *Inheritors*" finds a related urge to loosen an American dominant inclination toward enforcing conformity and homogeneity, suggesting a new motto altogether, *E Pluribus Plurum*. Thierry Dubost's "Politics in Paratextual and Textual Elements in *Fences*" reminds us that even as these challenges to dominant American culture build steam, one element in the American cultural consciousness remains fundamentally unchanged, and that is a resistance to radical, revolutionary confrontation. Dubost uses August Wilson to remind us that "politics" in America has a social and moral dimension that advocates internal and personal change rather than legislative mandate. Esther Álvarez-López's "Food, Cultural Identity, and the Body: New Recipes for Latinas' Emerging Selves" looks at plays by Latinas who work to reclaim their identities amid myriad discriminations imposed upon them by dominant culture. Staging their lives and their bodies, they join the growing chorus of disenfranchised and underrepresented intent on exacting a more fully embracing change in American culture even as that culture seems to be moving in the opposite direction.

Natalie L. Alvarez's "Authenticity and the 'Divinely Amateur': The Romantic in Richard Maxwell" takes on a related topic, looking for authenticity in a culture increasingly attracted to simulation. Theatre, of course, is the perfect venue for such an undertaking, and Richard Maxwell's art draws us back to a longing for the authenticity found in the true amateur, recalling a time when politics, soldiering, and countless other public services were conducted by citizens rather than paid professionals. Jerry Dickey's "Mamet's Actors: *A Life in the Theatre* and Other Writings on the Art of Acting" brings Mamet into a similar discussion. Mamet longs for an authenticity in acting that the deliberate deception of American method acting prevents.

Jon D. Rossini's "The Contemporary Ethics of Violence: Cruz, Solis, and Homeland Security" reminds us that virtually all the matters discussed above are far more than merely academic issues. Recalling the government custody of José Padilla and the self-refuting argument that he must be silenced in order to preserve freedom, Rossini reminds us that violence originates from and is propagated through such twisted logic. Rossini uses works by Octavio Solis and Nilo Cruz to argue that participation in the American narrative, rather than exclusion, is the only effective way to overcome cycles of violence.

Along those lines, understanding the world about us and properly acting on that understanding are what is needed during these tumultuous times. Bonnie Marranca closes the collection with "The Solace of Chocolate Squares: Thinking about Wallace Shawn," presenting Shawn's unique passion for values that combines the moral, political, and aesthetic.

Codifying the National Self is a solid addition to the sorts of discussions necessary in a world grown closer together and torn further apart than at any time in recent memory.

—**WILLIAM W. DEMASTES**
Louisiana State University, Baton Rouge

Fantasies of Empire: The Empire Theatre of Varieties and the Licensing Controversy of 1894. By Joseph Donohue. Iowa City: University of Iowa Press, 2005. xi + 290 pp. $44.95 cloth.

The real question here is, will Professor Joseph Donohue forgive Wilde fans for not remembering that in act 1 of *The Importance of Being Earnest,* Algernon suggests to Jack that after dinner they might "trot round to the Empire at ten"? After all, for his award-winning 1995 book *Oscar Wilde's* The Importance of Being Earnest: *A Reconstructive Critical Edition of the Text of the First Production, St. James's Theatre, London, 1895,* Donohue painstakingly researched the reference and contextualized Algy's remark in a footnote for readers of the play. *Fantasies of Empire: The Empire Theatre of Varieties and the Licensing Controversy of 1894,* Donohue's new work, owes its genesis to that very footnote.

One of Victorian London's favorite music halls, the Empire Theatre of Varieties offered its patrons a lively series of entertainments, including popular song, ballet, and living pictures. When stage offerings became wearisome and thirsts demanded slaking, patrons could retire to the promenades. "American bars" dispensed alcoholic refreshments, including "Port Wine Sangaree," "Corpse Revivers," and "Bosom Caressers" (44). Patrons of manager George Edwardes's Leicester Square edifice also took pleasure in the opportunities for social interaction, conversation, and ogling—both of stage performers and theatregoers—that were facilitated by the Empire's promenades. Ultimately, those promenades would become the source of contention.

In the summer of 1894, moral reformer Laura Ormiston Chant made a series of five visits to the Empire, determined to investigate the "character & want of clothing in the ballet" (31) and the presence of women soliciting in the theatre. Just after 9 P.M. each evening, Chant was distressed to see numerous unescorted young women filling the Empire's promenades, "very much painted" and all "more or less gaudily dressed" (58). Hence, when the Empire Theatre of Varieties' license came up for its normally routine renewal in October 1894, Chant and members of the National Vigilance Society successfully lobbied for the London County Council to either deny the license or insist upon changes in the Empire's business practices. While the council opted for changes, a slightly altered business-as-usual approach was soon restored. Predictably, the popular press vilified Chant and her supporters throughout the controversy as "Prudes on the Prowl." Or, as the *Music Hall and Theatre Review* opined, Chant and the National Vigilance Society represented the "unsworn babblings of neurotic females" (129).

Across a prologue and five chapters, Donohue tells an immensely compelling story. Besides having scoured the period's newspapers and periodicals, he relies upon the records of the London County Council for much of his narrative. Rather than composing a dry, verbatim rendering of the council's deliberations, Donohue masterfully interweaves testimony before the council with his own sharp analysis. What emerges is a fascinatingly complex portrait of Victorian England—its theatricals, performance venues' architecture, social reformers, and attitudes toward gender and sexuality. Lavishly illustrated with photographs, caricatures, and architectural renderings, Joseph Donohue's *Fantasies of Empire: The Empire Theatre of Varieties and the Licensing Controversy of 1894* is a brilliantly researched, sharp, and eminently readable case history.

—**MARK COSDON**
Allegheny College

A Companion to Twentieth-Century American Drama. Edited by David Krasner. Malden, Mass.: Blackwell, 2005. xx + 576 pp. $167.95 cloth.

The dramatic history of the United States is, in many respects, even briefer than the history of the youthful nation itself. With appropriate respect for the few significant plays produced between the late eighteenth and early twentieth centuries, American drama can accurately be said to have originated with the emergence of Eugene O'Neill less than ninety years ago. This short life span may well be one explanation for the neglect of American dramatic literature within the academy, a situation that famously led Susan Harris Smith, in 1997, to label it, arrestingly but hardly too hyperbolically, "American literature's unwanted bastard child, the offspring of the whore that is American theatre" (1).

David Krasner, in his introduction to this important new collection, is of the opinion that "perceptions are beginning to change" (1). If that is so, this volume will provide considerable additional impetus. He has assembled an impressive group of contributors (chosen, as he points out, "from various branches of American intellectual traditions, including theatre, drama, and performance studies; literary and American studies departments; and comparative literature" [2]) and has covered, in thirty-three concise, informative essays, an astonishing range of playwrights and texts. The emphasis throughout is on significantly broadening our conception of what constitutes American dramatic literature of the twentieth century, with attention paid, as Krasner makes clear, to "the institutions in which the dramas have been performed (the theatres, venues, and directors who assisted the playwrights), dramaturgical analysis of the plays, background to the playwrights, and the relationship between dramatic literature and broader historical continuities and social transformations" (2).

One of the significant aspects of this volume is that it manages, for the most part, to achieve both breadth and depth. One of the ways it does this is by interspersing broad-based essays—on historical periods, on drama from various ethnic groups, or on genres of drama—with more narrowly focused chapters on individual playwrights or on two, three, or four figures grouped together. The most straightforwardly historical essays are those devoted to the successive decades of the century: "American Drama, 1900–1915" (Mark Evans Bryan), "Many-Faceted Mirror: Drama as Reflection of Uneasy Modernity" (Felicia Hardison Londré), "Reading across the 1930s" (Anne Fletcher), "Fissures beneath the Surface: Drama in the 1940s and 1950s" (Thomas P. Adler), "Drama of the 1960s" (Christopher Olsen), "1970–1990: Disillusionment, Identity, and Discovery" (Mark Fearnow), and "American Drama of the 1990s On and Off-Broadway" (June Schlueter). Occasionally, these necessarily discursive essays deteriorate into little more than brief plot summaries or lists of primary texts; but a remarkable number of them manage to cover a wide range of plays while at the same time organizing them into patterns that make genuine contributions to critical discourse.

This balance is also present in the essays dealing with the drama produced by various ethnic groups. Because these sections often include numerous plays and playwrights unfamiliar even to specialists, the emphasis on broad coverage at the expense of depth of analysis is both understandable and welcome. Rachel Shtier's "Ethnic Theatre in America" reaches back into the nineteenth century to provide detailed and informed background for subsequent essays on "Playwrights and Plays of the Harlem Renaissance" (Annemarie Bean), "The Drama of the Black Arts Movement" (Mike Sell), "Staging the Binary: Asian American Theatre in the Late Twentieth Century" (Daphne Lei), "Native American Drama" (Ann Haugo), "Writing Beyond Borders: A Survey of U.S. Latina/o Drama" (Tiffany Ana Lopez), and "From Eccentricity to Endurance: Jewish Comedy and the Art of Affirmation" (Julia Listengarten). Bean's, Sell's, Haugo's, and Lopez's contributions are especially skillful in organizing a large amount of quite obscure material into a coherent and informative essay.

The essays one can roughly categorize as concerned with movements or genres are a bit more uneven. Deanna M. Toten Beard's "American Experimentalism, American Expressionism, and Early O'Neill," while useful in showing that O'Neill's experimentalism had its antecedents, surprisingly dates that experimentalism as originating with *The Hairy Ape* (1922) rather than with *The Emperor Jones* (1920), and for some reason she omits Lawson's *Processional* and Kaufman and Connelly's *Beggar on Horseback* from her discussion of American expressionism. Beard's essay also demonstrates a perhaps inevitable pitfall a book of this kind risks—overlap between sections. While Krasner usually provides parenthetical cross-references, it is nonetheless disconcerting at times to find a play discussed at length in two separate essays.

Overlap also occurs, sometimes without a cross-reference, in Peter Civetta's otherwise extremely useful and original "Expressing and Exploring Faith: Religious Drama in America." Predictably, Jill Dolan's essay on "Lesbian and Gay Drama" is as accomplished an introduction to the topic as one is likely to find; and Stephen J. Bottoms's "Solo Performance Drama: The Self as Other?" and Ehren Fordyce's "Experimental Drama at the End of the Century" make clear through their encyclopedic coverage that any definition of American drama at the end of the twentieth century must be a broad and inclusive one.

As noted earlier, books like Krasner's inevitably confront the question of whether one should try to cover lots of primary texts in order to broaden a reader's knowledge of the field (this is especially relevant in a field as critically neglected as American drama), thereby risking superficiality as well as the accusation that quality has not been a sufficient criterion of selection, or deal in depth with texts one considers seminal and thus ignore broader patterns. A corollary problem, most apparent in the essays devoted either to one playwright or to a small group of playwrights, is whether to organize such more focused discussions on a particular theme or aspect of the subject's work or to provide a more eclectic survey. Beyond this, of course, is the always controversial question of which individuals deserve to be singled (or, in this volume, doubled, tripled, or quadrupled) out in this way. With respect to this latter issue, devoting individual chapters to Susan Glaspell and Sophie Treadwell (J. Ellen Gainor and Jerry Dickey), Djuna Barnes and Gertrude Stein (Sarah Bay-Cheng), and Beth Henley, Marsha Norman, Rebecca Gilman, and Jane Martin (Linda Rohrer Paige) when Lillian Hellman, Thornton Wilder, Clifford Odets, and Robert E. Sherwood, among other deserving figures, get at most two pages (and often less) is certainly questionable.

Similarly, while one can hardly argue with devoting full chapters to O'Neill (Krasner), Williams (Brenda A. Murphy), Miller (Murray Biggs), Albee (Steven Price), Shepard (Leslie A. Wade), August Wilson (Harry J. Elam Jr.), and Mamet (Janet V. Haedicke) and can applaud the somewhat more unpredictable decision to treat Maria Irene Fornes (Andrew Sofer) individually, full essays on John Guare (Gene A. Plunka) and on Paula Vogel (Ann Pellegrini) will, irrespective of the quality of the essays themselves, raise questions for some. But more important than whether or not to isolate these particular playwrights for extended consideration is the nature of the essays devoted to them. Here again, Krasner's contributors generally choose either to impose a pattern or prevalent theme or to deal chronologically and eclectically with the full range of the writer's work. The results are mixed. Biggs's focus on Miller's Jewishness, Wade's emphasis on Shepard's concern with "the history and mythology of the American West" (285), and, most problematically, Paige's concentration on Henley's "characters' attachment to animals" (389), to varying degrees, limit the plausibility and usefulness of their essays.

On the other hand, Plunka's contention that Guare's plays dwell on "the existentialist dilemma of how individuals in contemporary American society can maintain a sense of dignity and humanism despite a ubiquitous fraudulence that characterizes American culture" (352) enables him to provide illuminating and convincing readings. Among the more eclectic essays on individual writers,

Murphy on Williams, Elam on Wilson, and Haedicke on Mamet are models of comprehensiveness and insight, while Price on Albee, while a bit more opaque, is nonetheless intelligent and informed. All of these essays are characterized by one further noteworthy aspect of the volume as a whole. In an era when literary criticism is too often characterized by theoretical jargon at the expense of engagement with a primary text, Krasner's group focuses firmly on extensive quotations from the texts of the plays, on statements by the playwrights about their work, and, much less, but effectively, on criticism.

For a book of this size and scope it is probably ungrateful and churlish to point out inconsistencies, errors, and questionable judgments; and Krasner's volume has an astonishingly small number. Besides the already mentioned occasional absence of cross-references, a handful of essays include birth and death dates for authors mentioned, while none of the others do so. The character played by Sam Shepard in the film *The Right Stuff* is Chuck Yeager, not "Sam Yeager" (295); Meg is not the "oldest [Magrath] sister" (389) in Henley's *Crimes of the Heart;* and it is certainly an oversimplification to say that Eben and Abbie in O'Neill's *Desire Under the Elms* end up "mad" (148), that O'Neill's *More Stately Mansions* is "fully formed" to the same extent as *A Touch of the Poet,* and that *Long Day's Journey* was not "enthusiastically received when it first appeared" (149).

But these are very minor quibbles about a landmark achievement in the scholarship and criticism on twentieth-century American drama, a book whose many uses one can only venture to predict. We have many reasons to thank Blackwell's for including a book on American drama in their Companions to Literature and Culture series, to praise Krasner for organizing the project and shepherding it through to such a successful completion, and to applaud his judiciously selected group of contributors for carrying out with such skill his intentions for the volume—"to examine the vitality and broad scope of American dramatic literature" (2).

—**JACKSON R. BRYER**
University of Maryland

Theatre Histories: An Introduction. By Phillip B. Zarrilli, Bruce McConachie, Gary Jay Williams, and Carol Fisher Sorgenfrei. New York: Routledge, 2006. 544 pp. $44.95 paper.

Theatre Histories: An Introduction was conceived and written to counter the Western-centric focus of theatre history texts of the last four decades. It was developed over a decade of collaboration by a quartet of scholars who recognized the need to examine multiple histories of theatre, drama, and performance in a more fluid way and to "provide a global perspective that allows the performances of many cultures to be considered, not in the margins of Western theatre but in and of themselves, and as they illuminate each other and our understanding of human expressiveness at large" (xvii). The result is an ambitious, wide-ranging work that is largely successful but exhibits some problems.

The book is organized topically as well as chronologically. There are four parts, each with an introduction, three chapters, and a set of case studies. Part 1 covers "Performance and Theatre in Oral and Written Cultures before 1600," part 2 "Theatre and Print Cultures, 1500–1900," part 3 "Theatre in Modern Media Cultures, 1850–1970," and part 4 "Theatre and Performance in the Age of Global Communications, 1950–Present." Threaded throughout the text are three distinct themes (what the authors call "mappings"): an emphasis on "cultural performance" instead of the more common but limited focus on only "theatre and drama"; an investigation of the interpretive processes of historiography; and a highlighting of the influences of sociological and technological change on "modes of human communication." The case studies go deeper into and expand each of these areas by discussing a wide range of "interpretive approaches," including not only literary-based theory and criticism but also an assortment of other political, cognitive, and cultural analyses. Taken as a whole, the book represents a move toward broader cultural inclusiveness in the subject of "theatre history" and is a praiseworthy attempt to challenge the common approach to teaching the past through coverage-based "survey" courses by introducing critical-thinking skills and information about the way that history is written along with the "facts."

The text displays fewer biases than most historical surveys, but there are some. The performance examples in the text reflect the scholarly strengths of the four authors, so an emphasis on Asian theatre is used as the main counterbalance to the traditional Western focus. Although Latin America and Africa receive coverage, it is primarily only in terms of their ritual and cultural performance traditions rather than "theatre" practice. For instance, although there is some very good work on religious rituals and civic festivals in indigenous cultures of South America, Australia, and Africa, there is little on the conventional theatre of those continents.

Similarly, the usefulness of relating performance to print and visual cultures is somewhat lessened by a lack of attention to the larger economic frameworks underpinning the development of these new aesthetics and technologies. For instance, the story of the mythic origins of the Natyásastra is emphasized without any reference to the underlying political and economic reasons lower-caste actors may have wanted to position that text as divine.

In a work of this size there will be an occasional typographic error; however, there are more than a handful of mistakes, among them the misspellings of names such as Ariane Mnouchkine, Maria Irene Fornes, Suzan-Lori Parks, and Amiri Baraka; no notation that Joseph Chaikin died in 2003; the full title of *Marat/Sade* is incorrect. Bibliographies are redundant in some spots; one list of sources/citations at the end of each chapter is preferable to having the same works cited twice within five pages. Finally, the weakest component of the printed text is the visual material—black and white—with multiple photos of the same productions, and poor quality. Presumably the companion Web site was intended to alleviate this, but for now that site remains underdeveloped.

As of this writing, the book's Web site (www.routledge.com/textbooks/ 0415227283) includes links to additional bibliographies, suggestions for teaching strategies, additional discussion questions, and an expanded collection of visual aids. However, the majority of the site is devoted to advertisement and sales rather than pedagogical support (four of the six primary links are devoted to advertising *Theatre Histories* and related Routledge titles). There are only twenty pictures in the "image bank," including many that are only "generally relevant" to the text itself, and at present several of the links to case studies no longer access the relevant citations. Likewise, many of the suggestions for teaching strategies (on the "Conversations about Teaching Theatre History" link) may be difficult to implement in programs that do not offer multiple theatre history courses (as the undergraduate multi-semester sequence has been reduced to a one-term survey in many programs) or that require the enrollment of large numbers of students.

One of the main challenges of the text is imagining how best to use it in a classroom. It is unlikely that every teacher will be fully versed in all of the performance forms covered, and the organization of the book suggests—demands, even—a revision of the way theatre history is taught. The text's unique narrative format requires the reader to navigate the comparison of ritualistic practices, time shifts, and theoretical applications, and so ideally the student reader should have some comprehension of standard narratives of history and at least a rudimentary understanding of a range of cultures. It is therefore probably best suited for upper-division undergraduates and for beginning graduate students.

We are adopting *Theatre Histories* as our primary graduate theatre history text for two distinct courses. Our solution to the challenges posed by the book is to use it mainly as a framework upon which we will construct unique classes in accordance with our own interests, expertise, and access to supplementary materials. Although our individual classes will therefore cover some different material, we believe the design of the book will allow us to engage the students in similar explorations of questions about the nature of cultural history itself (in fact, teaching strategies on the Routledge Web site suggest that flexibility of approach is one of the main goals of the book's design).

We are excited about the possibilities this text represents and hope it will encourage our students to think about performance across both time and cultures and draw their attention to the various ways theatre history is written. The authors articulate that the text is not intended to be completely inclusive or exhaustive and are aware that a revision is called for. A slightly retooled version would be a welcome addition to the texts on performance and the histories of theatre.

——NOREEN C. BARNES

——AARON D. ANDERSON
Virginia Commonwealth University

Susan Glaspell: New Directions in Critical Inquiry. Edited and with an introduction by Martha C. Carpentier. Newcastle, U.K.: Cambridge Scholars Press, 2006. 117 pp. $59.99 cloth.

Disclosing Intertextualities: The Stories, Plays, and Novels of Susan Glaspell. Edited by Martha C. Carpentier and Barbara Ozieblo. Amsterdam: Rodopi, 2006. 307 pp. $90.00 cloth, $35.00 paper.

These two anthologies are welcome additions to the rapidly growing body of Susan Glaspell criticism. Drawing on contributors from around the world, the books testify to the interest in Glaspell at home and abroad as well as her appeal to a new generation of scholars just emerging from graduate schools. *Susan Glaspell: New Directions in Critical Inquiry* is a slim volume (seven essays) devoted to mapping out a range of strategies that can be fruitfully applied to Glaspell's canon, while *Disclosing Intertextualities* includes fifteen essays that endeavor to place Glaspell in a diverse range of intellectual, cultural, dramatic, literary, social, and political contexts.

The majority of pieces in *Susan Glaspell: New Directions* address Glaspell's plays, the most familiar segment of her canon. Barbara Ozieblo discusses the un-published *Chains of Dew,* a witty spoof of male hypocrisy and dependency that suffered a disastrous production by the Provincetown Players. Ozieblo sees this comedy about birth control as a successor to Shaw's more didactic *Mrs. War-ren's Profession,* arguing that Glaspell employs an unusually light touch here be-cause she was aiming at a Broadway audience rather than more liberal Province-town patrons. Lucia V. Sander adds to the ongoing project of placing Glaspell in the context of her Players colleagues with a comparison of *Trifles* and Eugene O'Neill's monologue *Before Breakfast,* while Marie Molnar goes farther afield in her search for progenitors, making a convincing claim that Glaspell "uses Sophocles' *Antigone* as a subtext and a basis for the structure of her play" *Inheri-tors* (38). Madeline Morton, she argues, is a modern-day Antigone who opposes not only the state but also "the phallogocentric discourse" that supports it (44).

Thanks to scholar Linda Ben-Zvi, Glaspell students know that *Trifles* and "A Jury of Her Peers" (the short story derived from the play) are based on the murder trial of Margaret Hossack, which Glaspell covered in her days as a re-porter. Patricia L. Bryan and J. Ellen Gainor suggest two more possible judicial influences on the dramatist. Bryan argues that both *Trifles* and Glaspell's short story "The Plea" have their roots in the 1889 case of an Iowa boy who murdered his parents. The boy's fate is reflected in "The Plea," which Bryan believes "fore-shadows 'A Jury of Her Peers' in portraying the importance of empathic un-derstanding in legal decision-making" (58). Gainor makes a particularly crucial point in her essay, which addresses the concept of "slander per se": "involving accusations of sexual impropriety by women" (74), this legal category reflected the cultural belief that a woman's purity was her most precious possession—a view that is propounded, debated, dissected, and mocked by various characters in Glaspell's comedy *Woman's Honor.*

In the final pieces in *Susan Glaspell: New Directions,* Mary E. Papke and Kristina Hinz-Bode turn to Glaspell's novels. Papke focuses on the writer's "crucial call for action and hope" (88) in a career that spanned two world wars, while Hinz-Bode situates Glaspell's canon in the context of the "epis-temological crisis of modernity" (90). As Hinz-Bode observes, Glaspell came of age at a time when the writings of Darwin, Nietzsche, Freud, and others were undermining accepted views of the world and the individual's place in it. Glaspell's work inevitably reflects this upheaval.

According to Martha C. Carpentier's introduction to *Susan Glaspell: New Directions,* each of the essays in this anthology "*begins* from an awareness of the supremely self-conscious artistry that characterizes" all Glaspell's work (4). In other words, the case for Glaspell's stature as a significant artist has already been made. For *Disclosing Intertextualities,* editors Carpentier and Barbara Ozieblo have selected articles that "explore in different ways how Glaspell's allusive semi-otic exceeds 'codified discourse' to express a social, political and philosophical protest" (10). Despite these differing objectives, however, most of the essays in either volume would comfortably fit in the other, a point emphasized by some overlap in contributors. The opening discussion in *Disclosing Intertextualities,* Mary E. Papke's "Susan Glaspell's Naturalist Scenarios of Determinism and Blind Faith," for example, neatly complements Papke's essay in *Susan Glaspell: New Directions.* This is not necessarily a problem, of course, but rather indi-cates how difficult it is to categorize literary criticism.

Disclosing Intertextualities does give more attention to Glaspell's nondra-matic writings. Linking Glaspell's plays and fiction, Martha C. Carpentier ob-serves that Glaspell "often stretched generic boundaries by transposing and ex-perimenting with the same narrative in two genres" (35). Colette Lindroth finds "challenge[s] to America's political and economic sacred cows" in Glaspell's short fiction, while Cynthia Stretch argues that Glaspell's 1911 novel *The Vision-ing* echoes "early twentieth-century feminist and socialist concerns about the potential for cross-class solidarity and anticipates present-day theories of the social construction of identity and subjectivity," (227) even though Glaspell's novel is not as militant as those published by the radical press. Linda Ben-Zvi reaches still further back to Glaspell's early newspaper columns to discover the first of "the variety of ways in which she [Glaspell] refigures the political as the personal in writing that is committed to changing society" (294).

Several of the essays in *Disclosing Intertextualities* reveal how Glaspell ap-parently challenged, rewrote, or at least was inspired by a range of literary works. Even if we may not always be certain what the well-educated Glaspell read or viewed onstage, such comparisons can prove enlightening. Thus Susan Koprince delineates the similarities and differences between *Trifles* and Edith Wharton's *Ethan Frome,* and Drew Eisenhauer astutely pairs Glaspell with her contemporary Rachel Crothers, the most successful female Broadway play-wright of the early twentieth century. Both conclude that Glaspell's work is more perceptive and more overtly feminist than her counterpart's in its analysis of the ways society circumscribes women's choices. Turning to European writ-ers, Monica Stufft reads Glaspell's *The Verge* through the lens of Strindberg's *A Dream Play* (and vice versa), while Rytch Barber places the same drama—a fa-vorite with Glaspell scholars—in the context of European expressionism.

The pieces in *Disclosing Intertextualities* range widely and reveal the com-plexity of Glaspell's vision. Marcia Noe and Robert Marlowe's compelling dis-cussion of *Suppressed Desires* and *Tickless Time* stresses that these plays go "beyond warning against fads and fashions . . . [to] focus on the nature and limits of representation" (60). In one of the few essays to rely extensively on biography, Barbara Ozieblo argues that Glaspell's writings, particularly the later novels, reflect the author's need to understand her "undoubtedly tense relationship with her mother" (156)—a tension likely exacerbated by Glaspell's own failed attempts to become a biological parent. Drawing on the theories of Michel Foucault, Kecia Driver McBride explores the fragmented language in Glaspell's drama and fiction as well as her penchant for keeping her female protagonists offstage. McBride finds "throughout her works the continual breaking through of silence when meaning exceeds language" (163). Karen H. Gardiner discovers in Glaspell's oeuvre "metaphors of enclosure and entrapment, walls and chains" (184)—tropes long favored by women writers for countless reasons—while Kristina Hinz-Bode begins a necessary consideration of Glaspell's often overlooked male characters.

The most potentially controversial essay in either volume is Caroline Violet Fletcher's "'The Rules of the Institution': Susan Glaspell and Sisterhood," which draws on Glaspell's life and work to argue that Glaspell was dubious about the possibility—even the value—of feminist sisterhood. Glaspell's reluctance to join wholeheartedly with any group, including the feminist Heterodoxy, scarcely makes her unique: creative artists are almost by definition individualists wary of total allegiance to causes or organizations. Still, Fletcher's argument is a useful corrective to those who would see Glaspell as an unambiguously committed feminist, however one defines this tricky term. Like every good writer, Glaspell interrogated her own beliefs as well as the received wisdom of her society. Happily, all of the contributors to *Susan Glaspell: New Directions in Critical Inquiry* and *Disclosing Intertextualities: The Stories, Plays, and Novels of Susan Glaspell* are aware of the complexities, ambivalences, and contradictions that inflect this singular and important literary voice.

——JUDITH E. BARLOW
University at Albany, State University of New York

Strange Duets: Impresarios and Actresses in the American Theatre, 1865–1914.
By Kim Marra. Iowa City: University of Iowa Press, 2006. 378 pp. $47.95 paper.

Kim Marra's *Strange Duets* participates in the determined campaign by cultural historians of nineteenth-century U.S. theatre to demonstrate the joining of history and theory. In Marra's case, the history is that of three impresarios and three star actresses—Augustin Daly and Ada Rehan, Charles Frohman and Maude Adams, and David Belasco and Mrs. Leslie Carter—and the theory is a historicized analysis of gender that ties the three "strange duets" to patriarchal control and bourgeois respectability, closeted homosexuality and its metaphoric performance, and sexual transgression and its cultural exploitation/exculpation. In the hands of a competent, theatre-trained historian such as Marra, the reader enjoys carefully researched cultural history and the benefits of Marra's expertise in gender theory, past and present, and case studies that stand (appropriately) subordinate to the cultural norms and values they exemplify. To be sure, the latter can be pushed to the point where (to use one of the book's favored expressions) they "vibrate," like an apparatus run up to the breaking point, but the evidence of the former, the history itself, will allow all but the most uninformed reader to determine when the "two hearts beat as one."

A brief framing introduction establishes the outsider status of the Catholic Daly and Rehan, the queer and Jewish Frohman and queer and Morman Adams, and the Jewish Belasco and fallen WASP Carter. Theatre proved an enabling tool for each to simultaneously suppress and release social disadvantage through the effacing Progressive Era valorization of fame and fortune. Marra devotes two chapters each to the first two pairs and three chapters to Belasco and Carter. Of the six, Daly and Rehan were personally as well as professionally joined (curiously, Marra does not explore the former possibility in the case of Belasco and Carter), though the private aspects of the twenty-year Daly-Rehan relationship were carefully screened from public knowledge, as was the married Daly's frequent betrayals of Rehan (and his wife) with other women. Faithful to the double standard, Daly carefully orchestrated his company and repertory as respectable and disciplined, a vision, as Marra puts it, "of desirable gender and class relations creditable to bourgeois patrons" (53). As the emblematic virtuous and smart middle-class Americans, Daly's actors followed the legal and social model of paternal control for which Daly and the era have since become infamous. Marra traces how Daly fashioned, publicized, and enforced his role and how U.S. courts supported attempts by male managers to control (especially female) actors in ways similar to how courts ruled in divorce cases.

The most interesting of her three case studies, the Daly-Rehan "duet" also allows Marra to challenge received notions about theatre, for example, that of Richard Butsch recently (and, earlier, of male reporters in the later nineteenth century) that the female-dominated audience of the Progressive Era represented power ceded to theatre managers, as opposed to the pre–Civil War dominance of managers by male working-class audiences (58). Marra establishes, to the contrary, that, like Ada Rehan, who forced Daly (despite his opposition to any actor in his company rising above the line) to give her star billing, gentrification was a female agenda that forced managers to suit the theatrical event to women. Just as women transgressed received male notions of theatre reception, Marra's second "strange duet," Frohman and Adams, found ways to liberate themselves from Victorian constraints. Although a member of the vilified Syndicate, the-atrical producer Charles Frohman could not enable an actor's career as could a company manager like Daly, but the commercial producer model of theatrical production, as Marra makes clear, offered considerably more freedom to those who knew how (and were able) to use it to their own ends.

Maude Adams starred in twenty-seven productions managed by Frohman between 1890 and the latter's death (in the sinking of the *Lusitania*) in 1915. To a degree unimaginable in the fiercely controlled theatre of Augustin Daly, Adams was free not only to act but also to direct and, to an extent, produce the work she did with Frohman. Noting that Adams and Frohman were ru-mored to be romantically linked, even married to each other, Marra locates them in long-term, same-sex domestic partnerships that were carefully con-cealed behind equally carefully managed public images. Marra uses those im-ages to launch a discussion of broader race, gender, and class issues, particu-larly the formation of the categories heterosexual and homosexual, under way at the turn of the last century. Adams's work—which included playing the Duke of Reichstadt in Rostand's *l'Aiglon* and his Chantecler (the cock of the walk), Barrie's Peter Pan, and Schiller's Joan of Arc, carefully interspersed with more conventional roles (Viola, Rosalind, Lady Babbie in *The Little Minister*)—offers Marra lush opportunity to dissect "fairy plays," "a queer ascent to sainthood," a "cock fantasia," and "queer star making" as ways of being "out" while being very much "in" vogue with Adams's carefully crafted, public, "nunlike, virginal reputation" (103), a reputation Frohman enabled throughout their professional association.

The Belasco-Carter "duet" offers a third, still more modern, take on the Svengali-Trilby, impresario-actress relationship, one inflected with the full weight of turn-of-the-century psychiatry, gyno-therapy, and modernist act-ing theory. Whereas Daly and Adams claim focus in their sections of the book, sharing the spotlight with class, religion, and gender texts involving their part-ners, Belasco and Carter accumulate these texts and put their own "strange" spin on the results. As adept as Belasco at self-publicizing, Carter sought re-habilitation after a scandalous divorce had reduced her upper-class WASP sta-tus to that of a published adulteress—or worse. David Belasco, who claimed "a strange strain of woman in my nature" as key to his uncommon understanding of female actors, characters, and audience members (143), did so from a heterosexist base in which his belief that "the actor must experience the character's sensations and reactions" (173) gave him license as a stage director to arbitrate whether the actor really did so. Marra likens this attitude to that of a sex therapist administering vaginal stimulation to a female patient, a not uncommon treatment in the 1880s and 1890s for a host of gynecological complaints, an analogy Marra extends to Belasco's incorporation (as a teacher at the New York School for Acting) of the theories and techniques of George Henry Lewes and François Delsarte. To be sure, Belasco's youthful experience performing female roles, his extensive collection of pornography, the physicalized training of the New York School for Acting, and the survival of a one-act satire of its methods focusing on the exploitation of female acting students with an ability to pay the school's hefty tuition serve as grist for Marra's milling of Belasco's production of the highly sexualized actress that Mrs. Carter came to be. At the same time, experiencing sensations and reactions in acting is a far cry from the claim that "Belasco's female pupils . . . also sought weekly massages at the gynecologic clinic" (175), for which no evidence is offered that a single acting student did so.

Lapses of this sort are rare in Marra's normally impeccable scholarship, and Belasco's production of Carter's highly sexualized stage persona and his publicly reverential attitude toward her accomplishments are, surely, a sore temptation to it. Other lapses are similarly rare—strange word forms ("nightly strenuosity" [212], "Napoleonic collecting" [241], "predatious" [259]) and word orders ("Identifying as a business manager as well as a theatre manager, Daly seized this power" [33] or the sentence beginning "With the publication of DuMaurier's novel *Trilby*" [178])—and caveats are few (tying monetary value to the commodity price index, indeed, "does not take into account all the variables that can determine cost in a given historical moment" [see 272–73 n. 78 concerning Marra's translation of turn-of-the-last-century costs into twenty-first-century equivalents]). Similarly, while Iowa has (at last) provided books in its Studies in Theatre History and Culture series with bibliographies, Marra's is fragmented into "General Sources," then "Archival Sources," "Other Primary Sources," and "Secondary Sources," or variations on this scheme, for each of the impresario-actress pairs, an arrangement that is less than transparent and useful.

Kim Marra's study—simultaneously funny, insightful, revealing, and thought-provoking—offers readers a universe of cultural riches, hardly hinted at here, from jaw-dropping gender history to vicious anti-Semitism to the successful manipulation and inversion of these and other cultural premises that, once again, make clear the mythology of "controlling hegemonies." It is hoped that scholarly readers of these "strange duets" will follow Marra's lead toward a richer, more diversified view of the American theatre between 1865 and 1914.

——**ROSEMARIE K. BANK**
Kent State University

BOOKS RECEIVED

Benedetti, Jean. *The Art of the Actor: The Essential History of Acting, from Classical Times to the Present Day.* New York: Routledge, 2007.

Bloom, Ken. *The Routledge Guide to Broadway.* New York: Routledge, 2007.

Brandesky, Joe. *Czech Theatre Design in the Twentieth Century.* Iowa City: University of Iowa Press, 2007.

Brater, Enoch, ed. *Arthur Miller's Global Theatre.* Ann Arbor: University of Michigan Press, 2007.

Broadhurst, Susan, and Josephine Machon, eds. *Performance and Technology: Practices of Virtual Embodiment and Interactivity.* New York: Palgrave Macmillan, 2007.

Conner, Lynn. *Pittsburgh in Stages: Two Hundred Years of Theatre.* Pittsburgh: University of Pittsburgh Press, 2007.

Cullen, Frank, with Florence Hackman and Donald McNeilly. *Vaudeville Old and New: An Encyclopedia of Variety Performers in America.* Vol. 2. New York: Routledge, 2007.

Cummings, Scott T. *Remaking American Theatre: Charles Mee, Anne Bogart, and the SITI Company.* New York: Cambridge University Press, 2006.

Daileader, Celia R., and Gary Taylor, eds. *The Tamer Tamed, or The Woman's Prize* by John Fletcher. Manchester: Manchester University Press, 2006.

David, Deirdre. *Fanny Kemble: A Performed Life.* Philadelphia: University of Pennsylvania Press, 2007.

Demastes, William W., and Iris Smith Fischer, eds. *Interrogating America through Theatre and Performance.* Palgrave Studies in Theatre and Performance History. New York: Palgrave, 2007.

Dickinson, Peter. *Screening Gender, Framing Genre: Canadian Literature into Film.* Toronto: University of Toronto Press, 2007.

Dillon, Janette. *The Cambridge Introduction to Early English Theatre.* New York: Cambridge University Press, 2006.

Frame, Murray. *School for Citizens: Theatre and Civil Society in Imperial Russia.* New Haven: Yale University Press, 2006.

Hampton-Reeves, Stuart, and Carol Chillington Rutter. *The Henry VI Plays.* New York: Palgrave, 2007.

Hillman, David. *Shakespeare's Entrails: Belief, Skepticism, and the Interior of the Body.* Hampshire, U.K.: Palgrave Shakespeare Studies, 2007.

Jestrovic, Silvija. *Theatre of Estrangement: Theatre, Practice, Ideology.* Toronto: University of Toronto Press, 2006.

Johnson, Katie N. *Sisters in Sin: Brothel Drama in America, 1900–1920.* New York: Cambridge University Press, 2006.

Kaput, Anuradha. *Actors, Pilgrims, Kings, and Gods: The Ramlila of Ramnagar.* New York: Palgrave Macmillan, 2006.

Knapp, Raymond. *The American Musical and the Performance of Personal Identity.* Princeton: Princeton University Press, 2006.

Lee, Esther Kim. *A History of Asian American Theatre.* New York: Cambridge University Press, 2007.

Lei, Daphne P. *Operatic China: Staging Chinese Identity across the Pacific.* New York: Palgrave Macmillan, 2007.

Londré, Felicia Hardison. *The Enchanted Years of the Stage: Kansas City at the Crossroads of American Theater, 1870–1930.* Columbia: University of Missouri Press, 2007.

Magelssen, Scott. *Living History Museums: Undoing History through Performance.* Lanham, Md.: Scarecrow Press, 2007.

Mayer, Jean-Christophe. *Shakespeare's Hybrid Faith: History, Religion, and the Stage.* New York: Palgrave Macmillan, 2006.

McDonald, Ronan. *The Cambridge Introduction to Samuel Beckett.* New York: Cambridge University Press, 2007.

Miller, Scott. *Strike Up the Band: A New History of Musical Theatre.* Portsmouth, N.H.: Heinemann, 2007.

Prest, Julia. *Theatre under Louis XIV: Cross-casting and the Performance of Gender in Drama, Ballet, and Opera.* New York: Palgrave Macmillan, 2006.

Reason, Matthew. *Documentation, Disappearance, and the Representation of Live Performance.* New York: Palgrave Macmillan, 2006.

Ridout, Nicholas. *Stage Fright, Animals, and Other Theatrical Problems.* New York: Cambridge University Press, 2007.

Roche, Anthony, ed. *The Cambridge Companion to Brian Friel.* New York: Cambridge University Press, 2007.

Rokem, Freddie. *Performing History: Theatrical Representations of the Past in Contemporary Theatre.* Iowa City: University of Iowa Press, 2000.

Rozik, Eli. *The Roots of Theatre: Rethinking Ritual and Other Theories of Origin.* Iowa City: University of Iowa Press, 2007.

Schanke, Robert A., ed. *Angels in the American Theater: Patrons, Patronage, and Philanthropy.* Carbondale: Southern Illinois University Press, 2007.

Sihra, Melissa, ed. *Women in Irish Drama: A Century of Authorship and Representation.* New York: Palgrave, 2007.

Sokalski, J. A. *Pictorial Illusionism: The Theatre of Steele MacKaye.* Ithaca: Cornell University Press, 2007.

Thompson, Michael. *Performing Spanishness: History, Cultural Identity, and Censorship in the Theatre of José María Rodríguez Méndez.* Chicago: University of Chicago Press, 2007.

Thomson, Peter. *The Cambridge Introduction to English Theatre, 1660–1900.* New York: Cambridge University Press, 2007.

Thomson, Peter, and Glandyr Sacks, eds. *The Cambridge Companion to Brecht.* New York: Cambridge, 2007.

Tomlinson, Sophie. *Women on Stage in Stuart Drama.* New York: Cambridge University Press, 2006.

Walton, J. Michael. *Found in Translation: Greek Drama in English.* New York: Cambridge University Press, 2006.

CONTRIBUTORS

LOU BELLAMY is an OBIE Award–winning director and an Associate Professor in the Theatre and Dance Department at the University of Minnesota. He is the founding artistic director of Penumbra Theatre Company in St. Paul, Minnesota.

ELIN DIAMOND is Professor of English at Rutgers University. She is the author of *Unmaking Mimesis: Essays on Feminism and Theatre* (1997) and *Pinter's Comic Play* (1985) and the editor of *Performance and Cultural Politics* (1996). Currently at work on a book on modernism and performance, she is also co-editor of the forthcoming *Cambridge Companion to Caryl Churchill*.

ANTONIS GLYTZOURIS is Assistant Professor of Theatre Studies at the University of Crete (Greece) and Director of the research project "History of Modern Greek Theatre" at the Institute for Mediterranean Studies (Greece). His current research centers on the reception of European and American theatre and drama in modern Greece. He has published essays in *Journal of Modern Greek Studies* and Greek historical and theatre journals and is the author of *Stage Direction in Greece: The Rise and Consolidation of the Stage Director in Modern Greek Theatre* (in Greek, 2001).

SCOTT R. IRELAN is Assistant Professor of Theatre History and Dramaturgy at Augustana College. He is Co-Chair of the Mid-America Theatre Conference Pedagogy Symposium and Chair of Dramaturgy for The Kennedy Center American College Theater Festival Region III. His recent writings have appeared in *Cercles* and *Theatre Journal*.

REBECCA KASTLEMAN graduated from Harvard with a degree in Cultural Aesthetics and Performance Studies. She is currently living and writing in Serbia.

MARGARET M. KNAPP is a Professor in the School of Theatre and Film at Arizona State University. She has published on the Elizabethan stage and early-twentieth-century American theatre in *Theatre Journal, Theatre History Studies, Journal of American Drama and Theatre, Journal of American Culture,* and *Journal of Popular Culture.* She is coauthor of *"The Aunchant and Famous Cittie": David Rogers and the Chester Mystery Plays* (1988).

LANDIS K. MAGNUSON is the former Chair of the English department and continues to serve as Director of the Anselmian Abbey Players at Saint Anselm College in Manchester, New Hampshire. His book *Circle Stock Theater: Touring American Small Towns, 1900–1960* was designated by *Choice* as an Outstanding Academic Book in 1996. Personal scholarship has centered on the late-nineteenth- and early-twentieth-century American theatre, including such popular forms as repertoire theatre, vaudeville, and the Chautauqua movement.

FRANCESCA MARINI is Assistant Professor of Archival Studies at the School of Library, Archival and Information Studies of the University of British Columbia, Canada. She has a B.A. in Theatre and Performance Studies and a Ph.D. in Information Studies from the University of California, Los Angeles. Her research interests focus on performing arts archives and digital preservation; she publishes internationally in archival and theatre journals.

TAVIA NYONG'O is Assistant Professor of Performance Studies at New York University. He has published articles and reviews in *Social Text, Women and Performance, Yale Journal of Criticism, Radical History Review, TDR,* and *GLQ.* His book in progress investigates cultural performances in the first half of the nineteenth century that staged fears and anticipations of a racially hybrid nation to come.

KENNETH SCHLESINGER is Chief Librarian of Lehman College/CUNY. He is a Vice President of Theatre Library Association and Board President of Independent Media Arts Preservation.

MARGARET BRADHAM THORNTON is the editor of Tennessee Williams's *Notebooks,* published by Yale University Press in 2007. Her work has appeared in *Paris Review, Ploughshares, Seattle Review, Times Literary Supplement,* and *World Literature Today.*